Mediterranean *Summer*
Jane MacKenzie

I_AM SELF-PUBLISHING

@iamselfpub
www.iamselfpublishing.com

To Michel, with endless thanks for his help with medical details, his memories of 1968, and for guiding me around the Latin Quarter of Paris!

CHAPTER 1

Laure leaned back into her seat, trying to get comfortable. She'd been travelling all night in an overheated carriage, sleeping awkwardly and doing her injured back no good at all. But as she looked out of the window, the sweep of vineyards and a glimpse of the sea reassured her that she was nearing journey's end, and in spite of her fatigue, the thought set excited little butterflies fluttering in her stomach.

So much had happened since she had last been home. Too much. The last time Laure had been on this train, she'd been on her way back to Paris after Christmas, blithely planning the rest of her year at University. Since then there had been a near revolution in France, with the student uprising in Paris and the general strike, which so nearly brought down the government. It had finished badly for Laure, but it had mattered so much, and never had she felt such camaraderie as during those astonishing weeks.

And then, of course, there had been Lolo. Laure leaned her head against the carriage window and closed her eyes, allowing herself for a moment to drift back to those heady days with Lolo, the talented, beguiling Jean-Louis Lavignière. She could see it all so clearly, like a dream from a more innocent time.

Lolo's room in Montparnasse was foggy with the smoke from endless Gauloises cigarettes, lit one after the other. It stung the eyes, but Laure was so used to it she hardly noticed.

It was early May 1968 and at this moment none of the students in this room knew that they were about to carve a space for themselves in history. They only knew that some inexplicable things were happening, and France's creaking education system had turned against them. On Friday at the Sorbonne, hundreds of riot police had swarmed into the courtyard of the University and arrested six hundred students who had grouped there in peaceful protest. Laure could picture the riot police now, horribly menacing in their combat helmets, dark goggles and long black trench coats and carrying their large shields and huge batons, looking like so many extra-terrestrial beings. And it was the Rector of the University who had invited them in.

Come out peacefully, the students had been told, and we'll listen to why you're here. So they'd done so and were kicked to the ground and dragged off for their pains. Paris had never known anything like this. Our students are so well behaved, thought Laure, so timid and respectful compared to other countries. We don't march, or defend black rights, or protest about Vietnam like they do in America. But Paris was now alight with anger. Tomorrow, the student who'd led the protests was being hauled before the University's disciplinary committee and thousands of his fellow students would be outside to support him.

Laure would be there, and Lolo, and all of their friends, and the excitement of their new-found defiance was intoxicating. There was a new spirit among the students; you could feel it in the streets and outside the doors of the Sorbonne, which had been summarily closed against them. You could feel it in this room too. It was electric.

In one corner of the room, handsome Saeed from Tunisia was brewing his speciality mint tea and Lolo was beside Laure, brandishing a cheap plastic bottle of red wine. Laure accepted the wine bottle and poured a little into her glass. As Lolo's finger traced a line down the nape of her neck, she leaned back towards him and caught the flash of his blue eyes as he shot her a grin.

'We're going to have fun tomorrow, ma chérie,' he said to her, before turning to the rest of the room. 'Our journalists say we're only protesting because we're bored!' he cried out, ironically. 'Well, we won't be bored this week! We're going to take them on!'

He waved a hand in a grandiose gesture and Laure giggled. Lolo was a little drunk and more oratorical than ever.

'We're going to show the overstuffed, pompous ancients who govern us that students have the right to think and to live! You know, all over Europe people are debating the future of the world, new science, new technologies. While here in France, we get stuffed into overcrowded classrooms and told to listen without ever questioning. No wonder three-quarters of our students fail! We have the worst

7

education system in the world. Damn it, we're supposed to be intelligent people with ideas, and free to express them! Do you know that a man was fined 500 francs last month just for shouting "retire" at de Gaulle's car? French people have no free speech, no free thought, and this in the country of Voltaire and Rousseau!'

A clamour of agreement erupted in the room and everyone started talking at once. Laure took another sip of her wine and Lolo reached over to refill her glass. He smiled again and pulled her to lean against him.

'What would I be without you who came to my apartment?' he murmured, in a parody of the Aragon poem, speaking softly into her hair as his arm came round her and his hand caressed her stomach, and then higher. 'Will you stay with me this night, sweet Laure, after I kick out all this lot?'

Laure felt both mellow and excited at once, and could feel herself responding, drawn into an embrace that ignored all the others and left her wanting more. They had never done this, she and Lolo, but she had wanted it, wanted him, for a long time, and had only resisted because she didn't want to be one of his conquests.

They were the two top students on their art course this year, different in style, but equally serious and with a mutual respect for each other's work. Since the beginning of the course that respect had been growing, and recently a chord had been struck between them which was taking things to a new level. And now was the moment when the euphoria of rebellion had gripped them both with the same ardour,

8

and tonight she felt completely abandoned and knew she wouldn't leave.

She woke the next morning feeling like death, with her head splitting and her hair hurting at the roots. Next to her lay Lolo, propped up on his pillow, smoking the inevitable Gauloises, idly watching the smoke curl towards the ceiling. As she stirred, he turned and gave her his most charming smile, and she remembered how wonderful he had been, how amazing she had felt.

'Awake at last, my sweet? I was beginning to think I'd have to go and battle the police on my own!'

She looked at him through slightly blurred eyes, taking care how she moved her head. In contrast, Lolo looked impossibly composed, serene and awake, and she gave him a rather diffident smile in response to his.

'What on earth did we drink last night?' she asked him.

'The cheapest wine, unfortunately,' he answered. 'My father would disown me if he knew. But it did the job and in times of revolution, we must make sacrifices!' He leaned over and stroked her hair from her face. 'I think we need coffee, don't you? Especially if we're going to show our support for Dany at his hearing. Do you like croissants? There's an excellent bakery just next door.'

Laure had to smile at his easy nonchalance. This was the Lolo she had known for months, charming but impenetrable, and she pulled her head together, and accepted the offer of croissants in the same light manner. She sat at his table and drank strong coffee, and marvelled at how normal, how pedestrian, their relationship seemed this morning, compared to the passion of last night.

9

But as they left the building an hour later, he put his hands on Laure's shoulders and drew her towards him. She put her arms up to circle his neck and as she opened her mouth to speak, he placed his own gently on it.

'You were lovely last night, my sweet, and we must do this again. You're a very special person. Beautiful artist, beautiful woman, and beautiful lover.'

She felt her pulse racing slightly and kissed him back, trailing her hand down his back. Say something yourself, she thought, berating herself for playing the passive woman.

'You were lovely too, Lolo,' was what she said. 'And the croissants made up for the wine! Do invite me again, and I'll bring my own bottle next time.'

Laure held the memory for just a moment, and then deliberately let it go and opened her eyes to the Mediterranean sky above. Around her people were moving, collecting their belongings as the train drew into Perpignan. It was the ninth of July and there was a holiday weekend approaching, but for today it was just a Tuesday, a working day like any other, and the train was full of ordinary people coming to Perpignan to shop, or on business. A mother grabbed a complaining child, and a young man in workman's clothes reached over Laure to take his bag from the shelf above her head. He smiled at her rather self-consciously, and she gave him a smile back.

She had a couple more stops to go herself and then she would be home. It was an amazing thought and helped to banish Lolo from her mind. She was going home and just for today that mattered far more than Paris.

CHAPTER 2

With Perpignan left behind, it was mainly holidaymakers who remained on the train with Laure, and many of them left the train with her at Vermeilla. It was only at this time of year that Vermeilla got so many visitors, drawn to the sun and the sea, and housed either by family and friends, or *en pension* at the two hotels. Mass tourism hadn't yet hit the sleepy village but it was threatened, and the new campsites had crept to just a few kilometres away. For now though, Vermeilla was just home and the place of refuge in Laure's life that never seemed to change.

As she stepped out onto the platform, the July heat hit Laure full on her face, and she tilted her head to let the sun stream over her, an unbidden smile holding her there until she was jostled impatiently from behind, which made her move.

Then, emerging from the station, she saw with a smile that Papa had come to meet her. The main baking work would be finished for the day and he would normally be resting now, having started work at two in the morning. But he would never let her carry her case the short distance to the village, and he would have fretted that the train might be late or she had missed it, or that something else might go wrong on her journey from Paris.

She moved towards him with a mixture of pleasure and trepidation. It had been nearly a year since she left the village, with just one quick visit back home at Christmas, and she had changed. She saw the surprise in his eyes as he registered her cropped hair, tapered *gamine* style into her neck, and then took in her clothing. She was only wearing trousers and a shirt, but women still didn't usually wear trousers down here and he would think these trousers, in particular, too tight and the gingham print shirt too manly. She would have done better to wear a miniskirt, she thought. Exposing flesh was only mildly shocking, but what she was wearing was just too offbeat for Vermeilla. She would have to unearth some of her old clothes.

She gave him a wistful grin. 'Papa?' she said tentatively and to her relief he smiled back. He had never been a demonstrative man, Jacques Forestier, but as she reached for him, he took her in his arms and gave her a hug.

'What have you been doing to yourself, girl?' was all he said, but though it was gruff it wasn't aggressive, so she was content for now. Thank goodness she had thought better than to wear makeup!

She climbed into the passenger seat of the old van and they drove down into the village, past the deserted village square with its shaded corner, which was waiting for the old men to come to play their evening game of *pétanque*, and then on along the short avenue of plane trees, down towards the shore. Laure had been waiting to see the sea – counting as nothing the views she'd had of it from the train, further along the coast. The Mediterranean was never as blue as in Vermeilla, and today it was a deeper blue than she remembered, with not a fleck of white from here to the purple horizon. The little throb of expectation that had been building up inside her since early morning found its way to her chest, and seemed to burst physically inside her.

Papa parked the van in its usual place, on the corner of the little pedestrian side street where their apartment sat above the bakery, a stone's throw from the quayside. He got out of the van to retrieve her bag from the back, but Laure sat still for a moment, unwilling to take her eyes off the sea. She let it sink in that she was here, at home, where all was peace and routine, moved only by its own rhythms.

Papa opened her door and grinned at her. 'Going to sit there all day?'

She smiled. 'I was wool gathering,' she admitted, gesturing to the quayside and the bay. 'I've missed this view.'

'You look all in,' was all he replied, but he reached out a hand to her, to help her out of the van. He was a man of few words, used to working with his hands and driven to silence, he would sometimes say, by living with a wife and two daughters. When he wanted to lay down the law, he was loud enough, an authoritarian in command in his own house. But the rest of the time, he was content to live in his silent space with his ovens and his dough machines, and let his women talk.

He picked up the suitcase and went to the door that stood to the left of the bakery, opening it onto the narrow corridor and the stairs which led up to their apartment. Laure followed him up the stairs, hardly registering the familiar whitewashed walls, grubbied by the years, or the little statue of Saint Elizabeth, patron saint of bakers, which an aunt had bought but Papa wouldn't have in the shop downstairs. They arrived at the first floor and turned right into the kitchen, where they could hear noises indicating they would find *Maman*.

As they came through the open door, she surged forward immediately to meet them and took hold of Laure's shoulders, kissing her firmly on both cheeks and speaking the whole time.

'What an age you've been! Was the train late? How was your journey? You must be starving – and, oh my God, how thin you are! Don't you eat in Paris? Or were all the shops closed in all those riots? Come in here, *chérie*, and sit you down at the table – I'll give you some of the sausage left over from lunchtime. There's a courgette gratin to go with it.'

Laure shook her head. 'No, no *Maman*, I had a huge sandwich on the train and I'm not hungry, I promise you.'

'Well, you'll have coffee and a choux bun.'

This brought Laure's broadest grin. 'Mmm! Well, yes, if it's a choux bun you're offering, how can I refuse? There are no pastries anywhere in Paris to match Papa's.' She threw herself contentedly into a chair and let her mother fuss over her as they sat around the kitchen table altogether, drinking their coffee from the same little floral cups that Laure had loved as a child.

She studied her parents as carefully as they were studying her and was struck, not for the first time in her life, by how solid they both looked, how resilient. They never seemed to age, although her father's hair was receding, and both of them had some new grey hairs. But they were still as fit as ever, with no thickening waistlines, despite the endless quantities of free pastries available to them, and they bore testament to a hard working but measured lifestyle.

Maman had a particular briskness about her, with her long, lean face and sharp eyes. She ran their shop, serving the same village neighbours twice a day, nearly every day of the year, with the same efficiency and composure. She knew every plan there was for village events and every bit of village gossip, but while *Maman* always helped with the former, she kept the gossip to herself. Papa certainly wouldn't want to hear it, Laure thought with a private smile, picturing him hiding behind his bread ovens to avoid all the talk over the shop counter.

She continued watching them over her coffee, with these new Paris eyes, and kept herself quiet, wondering when the conversation would turn to everything that had happened in Paris. She'd lived in a world where no one had talked about anything else for the last two months, and surely it must have touched them here too – the whole of France had been touched. It had caused a general election, for goodness sake!

But her mother talked about everything else – about Laure's sister Sylvie, who was expecting her second child, and about Sylvie's husband's new job. She took several long, appraising looks at Laure's hair, but said nothing about that either. There would be plenty said later, Laure was sure, but not, it seemed, over her first coffee at home.

And Papa had more domestic matters on his mind. It was after his fourth restless glance at the kitchen clock, that *Maman* turned on him.

'You stop looking at that clock, Jacques! I'm fully aware that it's four o'clock and I'll open the shop when I'm good and ready, and if anyone wants anything they know they can knock on the door downstairs! And what's more, everyone knows that Laure is coming home this afternoon. They will find it only normal that I should spend some time with her. And as for you, shouldn't you be taking a nap right now, if you want to be able to spend any time with us this evening?'

He looked as though he was going to reply, so Laure quickly stepped in before he could bite, since her parents' occasional wrangling was a pet hate of hers.

'It's okay, *Maman*. Why don't you go and open the shop? I'll unpack my suitcase and then I'll probably take a stroll round to see Sylvie, if she's at home. I'll call into the shop and see you before I go.'

Papa harrumphed and looked cross at being blocked from having his say. 'You'll change out of those damned trousers before you walk around the village,' he challenged Laure, as though to vent his spleen.

Maman leapt to her defence. 'Jacques, don't be silly! Girls all over France are wearing trousers these days.'

'Not in this village,' Papa insisted, and Laure raised her hand.

'Don't worry, I'll change,' she said, with an apologetic smile at *Maman*, who actually hated trousers, she knew, except when worn for manual labour.

She rose from her seat and passed by her father, giving him a kiss on the head as she went by. 'Thank you for coming to meet me Papa when you would normally be sleeping. Do go and take your siesta now, so that you can be with us this evening. I brought you a nice Chablis from Paris and some *brie de Meaux*, which I know you love, and some of those hand-made chocolates I brought down at Christmas time.'

'Then you'd better tell your sister to come and eat with us,' Papa muttered, but his voice had softened and he yawned as he rose from his chair and turned towards her. He reached out a hand to touch her cropped hair and shook his head with a frown, but then squeezed her shoulder before he stepped purposefully out of the kitchen and up the stairs.

Laure rooted the foodstuffs out from her case while her mother cleared the coffee cups and then she stood ready with a tea towel to dry them as her mother washed them. It took just a few minutes and the women worked in comfortable silence.

'You go off and sort yourself out now, Laure,' *Maman* said once they'd finished. 'I'd better open that shop before your father comes back down to remind me! You'll have a lot to tell us, what with all those riots in Paris and all, and I'm assuming that's why you're home now and not staying for that summer exhibition of yours, with all the Universities being closed up.' She shot a look at her daughter as she spoke and Laure felt she was being very thoroughly appraised.

'Of course,' *Maman* continued, 'It's been over two months now since the strikes started and all the Universities closed, and your father has been fretting, wondering if you were safe and what you might be up to. He didn't want his daughter getting involved in all of those demonstrations and riots, but I told him not to worry because you have a good head on your shoulders. You're a senior student now, after all, and not a hot-headed eighteen-year-old.'

Laure felt the twinges in her back that were left from when she'd been pushed to the ground as a wall of students fled from the police and grimaced inwardly.

'No, there was nothing to worry about,' she reassured her mother, giving her a quick hug. 'I was perfectly safe. I stayed on because we thought perhaps the University might manage to reinstate the exhibition, that's all. But it didn't, so here I am.'

'Well, well, it's all over now. It was a shocking thing!'

It was a mild way to describe events that had brought the French government to its knees, brought two-thirds of the French workforce out on strike and rocked the whole of Europe. Even here in sleepy Roussillon, there had been no trains or buses, and even no petrol for a while. But such a moderate view of the world was typical of *Maman*, who focused on the pragmatic and her own life, and Laure was grateful for it – she didn't want too many questions. She breathed a rather guilty sigh of relief and slipped away to her room.

CHAPTER 3

She took the long way to Sylvie's house, walking around by the quayside, where she sat for a while on the wall and watched the waves lapping very casually at the pebble beach. There were a few visitors on the beach, but no one else. The fishermen had all gone now and there was just one old barque tied up to the quayside, alongside a modern powerboat that looked strangely incongruous against the old stone wall. The fishing had all moved to Port-Vendres now, where modern trawlers had been brought in that needed a proper port to operate from.

Laure remembered as a child watching the fishermen cleaning their nets and drying them on this same wall, and the fishwives gutting sardines in summer. The boats had littered the beach and the smell of fish always hung in the air. Now the beach was clean, and the noise and bustle of the women calling to each other and the men pushing the boats out to sea had gone. Behind her, in the row of old painted stone houses, the Hotel Bon Port had added a covered terrace and was now doing a brisk summer trade in lunches and dinners for the tourists.

But the bay itself was as magical and timeless as ever, and the movement of the water had a hypnotic, almost soporific effect in the heat of the sun. Laure sat for longer than she had intended, feeling the tiredness of the journey. Here, Laure felt she could forget all the tensions of the last few weeks, but just bringing the thought to mind was enough to wake her out of her somnolence. With a last, lingering look at the bay, she got to her feet and headed for Sylvie's apartment, tucked into one of the back streets behind the quayside.

In this little village nothing was far and within two minutes she was climbing the stairs that led to her sister's first-floor apartment. At the bottom of the stairs, just inside the door of the building, was little Julien's empty pushchair with a toy dog abandoned inside, so it was safe to assume that Sylvie would be at home.

She gave a knock at the door and then walked right in, onto a scene of messy domesticity, as a newly awakened Julien was having his nappy changed. Sylvie had laid his changing mat on the floor and had a bucket next to her into which the old nappy had been placed for washing. When Sylvie saw Laure, she gave her a muffled '*Bonjour*' from between her teeth, which were holding two nappy pins. But she still managed to grin and waved her sister to a chair beside her.

Laure sat down and leaned over, so that her face was above little Julien's. She smiled at him and sympathised.

'Oh, *mon petit chou,* what is she doing to you?'

Julien gave her a thoughtful look, as though assessing whether he was supposed to know her. He protested as his mother turned him to put in the last of the nappy pins, but he didn't stop watching Laure, even as Sylvie fastened his shorts and pulled him upright.

'There you go, you rascal, stand up and show *Tata* Laure how big you've grown.' She turned to Laure. 'He doesn't often soil his nappy now,' she told her proudly. 'But he's just woken up and it's excusable when he's asleep, isn't it, young man?'

'Of course it is!' Laure agreed enthusiastically as Sylvie pulled herself off the floor and onto the sofa beside her. With less than two months to go, her bump seemed huge – bigger than the last time she was pregnant. But she looked well and happy, and she hugged Laure with her normal high spirits.

'It's so good to see you. Look at me properly, so that I can see what you've been doing to yourself. Oh my Lord, Laure – how trendy are you! Look at your hair!' She stroked Julien's curly hair. 'You won't recognise your aunt, little man, with that cropped hair. She's been gone away too long for you to remember her anyway, hasn't she? But I must say, Laure, that hair suits you. It goes with that spiky face of yours!'

'Tell Papa that!' Laure retorted. 'He has already shown his disapproval. And I was stupid enough to turn up today in trousers! It's a good job I still have some sensible skirts in my wardrobe here. All I wear in Paris is trousers and some miniskirts, but I don't suppose he'd think much of them either.'

'What nonsense! There are lots of girls in the village wearing miniskirts now, and although not so many wear trousers, we see lots of tourists who do and no one blinks an eyelid. Papa just spends too much time with his bread machines, but he'll get over it.'

She pulled her own full maternity dress around her knees and stroked her hand through the long curls that had always framed her very feminine face. 'You make me feel dowdy.'

'Rubbish, Sylvie, I just dress practically for life as an art student. You look fine – it's not your fault if you're shaped like an elephant!'

Sylvie reached out and punched her. 'Take that little sister!' She pulled herself to her feet and smiled at Laure. 'You'll have tea with me, won't you? I find I can't drink coffee at the moment, and it never seems worth making tea just for me. I have some lovely jasmine tea that *Maman* gave me, too.'

They stood together in the kitchen as Sylvie heated water for the tea, and Laure lifted Julien up so that he could reach the biscuits down from the top cupboard.

'Will you come to dinner tonight?' she asked Sylvie. 'Papa told me to ask you, so that we can all be together. I brought him some cheese and stuff from Paris.'

'Of course! We'd love to, but it won't be until Daniel gets back from Paulilles. You heard that he has a new job? It's very exciting – a much better wage than he ever earned at the fishing or working in the port, and they rate him very highly – he's got great technical skills! But he finishes later than before and, of course, he has to get all the way home from Paulilles, although mostly he can get a lift. There are a few of them now from the village working at Paulilles, and it's not much further than the fishing at Port-Vendres anyway.'

Laure put Julien back down on the floor and gave him a biscuit, which he disappeared to eat in private. Paulilles – the name was famous around here. Or should she say infamous? Paulilles was a secluded bay along the coast where Alfred Nobel had built one of the first ever dynamite factories, a hundred years ago, and they still made dynamite there today. They'd had some pretty spectacular explosions there in the early years and paid high wages as danger money – that's what the local people said. The last explosion had been ten years ago. Laure remembered everyone talking about it because the blast had killed someone and stopped production, and they'd brought in all kinds of experts afterwards to stop it happening again. Since then, all had gone quiet and she'd heard nothing about Paulilles. Until now!

It seemed a strange thing to have someone in the family working there. It felt unnatural and alien, but Laure had enough sense to keep quiet. She knew so little about it, ten times less than Sylvie. Daniel wasn't working making explosives, Papa had told her, but in maintenance, so presumably out of harm's way. He no longer wanted to go away to sea, now that he had a family, and he couldn't afford his own modern fishing boat, so Paulilles would offer him a different future.

Sylvie's little apartment looked out over a miniature square created by the junction of three village streets, alleyways barely big enough to get a car through – not that

23

there were too many cars in Vermeilla. But the junction created a little social hub, with an old well in one corner, against a wall overgrown with Virginia creeper, and women would come to sit around it and share stories at this time of day. The sisters took their teacups onto Sylvie's tiny balcony and sat on the narrow bench set against the wrought iron railing. Julien followed them and lay on his tummy at their feet, making quite realistic sounds with a couple of toy cows and a farm truck.

Here, between the buildings, the sun rarely got through and the shade was blissful in summer, but it was warm, nevertheless. The air hardly moved today, and the heat of the day was fading only slowly to early evening. Laure leaned back against the railing and closed her eyes. She raised the cup to her lips, still with her eyes closed.

'My, that tea tastes good!' she exhaled.

'*Bonsoir*, Sylvie,' an old lady's voice came to them from the street below. 'Is that Laure you have with you there? Well, how nice. Your mother will be pleased to have her home. You know that Céline Albert is in labour? She started this morning and the midwife has been there for four hours now.'

Laure grinned and opened her eyes, and found Sylvie smiling too. Trust old Francine to have all the news – and to spot the newcomer too, even though Laure was hidden behind the railings. Laure stood up and leaned over the balcony to greet Francine.

'*Bonsoir*, Francine. Yes, that's me back home for the summer from University. I just got in today. And Céline's baby is on the way, you say? Well, it won't be long till it's my

24

own sister we'll be calling the midwife for! I can't believe the size of her.'

Francine gave a cackle. 'Yes, she's carrying it good and high too – it'll be a girl, that one, you mark my words.'

She passed on to join the other women by the well, drawing their attention to Laure's arrival, very content to be the first with the news.

Laure settled down again on the little bench, leaning her head against Sylvie's shoulder.

'I'm tired, dear sister,' she murmured.

'I'm not surprised. How long is that train journey from Paris? Twelve hours at least, surely? Were you on the night train?'

Laure nodded, 'Yes, but my modest budget doesn't stretch to a sleeper, so I grabbed what sleep I could sitting up. It wasn't too bad, but I admit to feeling pretty sleepy now and my back hurts.'

'You should have had a sleep at home, when you arrived.'

'But I wanted to see my big sister! And anyway, I don't want *Maman* and Papa to get in a fuss because they think I'm tired. They think the journey from Paris is a world marathon, and I want to let them think I had a bed on the train.'

Sylvie sighed. 'It's true that they find it difficult to cope with you being in Paris. Papa still thinks you're going to come back here when you finish, you know, and take a teaching job or something.'

'Well, I am going to take a teaching job! But my goal is to teach at the École des Beaux-Arts in Paris, I'm afraid.' Laure stretched and grimaced. 'That is if I am still accepted back onto the course after the summer.'

'Why shouldn't you be?' Sylvie was startled. 'Don't tell me you've failed your exams?'

'No, we haven't even had any exams this summer. The whole University shut down in complete chaos before the end of term, and our department says they're going to assess students when they come back in September.'

'But that doesn't matter, surely? If none of the students have taken any exams yet, then you're all in the same boat. You'll pass them fine in September, when you go back. You're the top student in your year, after all!'

Laure nestled her head further into Sylvie's shoulder. It felt so good lying here, with the evening warmth lulling her half to sleep. And Sylvie was so supportive, so partisan. Don't give her anything to worry about, she thought. And give yourself a day or two off from worrying too.

'Did you get involved?' Sylvie was asking, rather tentatively. 'I mean, did you go on any of the demonstrations?'

'Hmm,' Laure replied, sleepily. 'I'm afraid your little sister marched and occupied buildings and got chased by the police with the best of them. I'll tell you all about it, Sylvie, I promise you, but could you lend me a bed for half an hour first? I'll love you forever!'

'Okay, but only if you really do love me forever.' Sylvie pushed Laure off her shoulder and stood up awkwardly. 'Come on, young Julien, let's show *Tata* Laure where she can have a little sleep. And when she wakes up, she can read you a story – she has promised, haven't you, Laure?'

Laure brought her eyes to focus on her nephew, who was regarding her speculatively. She winked at him. 'I tell the best stories,' she assured him, and as she leaned over to give him a kiss, Julien gave her his first proper smile.

'Story,' he said, and held out one of his cows to her as an offering.

'You want a cow in your story? Well, you shall have one, little man, a fat cow and her twin calves, just down from the mountains. But first, Auntie Laure needs just half an hour to sleep and forget all about that silly Paris and the journey and everything.'

Julien nodded sagely, as if he understood everything she was saying. Sylvie led the way into the house and Laure and Julien followed, hand in hand.

CHAPTER 4

Daniel never changed, Laure thought. He was the brother-in-law her sister had brought into the family, but he had always been like a real big brother to her, from when she was a child. She and his younger brother Martin were in the same class at school, and she'd spent so much of her early childhood running around the tables of their mother's café with Martin, before getting chased out by the waiters to play in the street outside. Daniel was older by nearly ten years – already working as a fisherman when they were still mere scrubs, and had been glamorously away at sea for much of their teenage years.

Typically, when Martin had discovered football, he'd stopped playing with Laure, a mere girl. But she had tagged along anyway and clung on to the boys when they played around Daniel's fishing boat or the other boats after he'd left, helping with the nets and more often than not getting in the way. She'd longed to be a boy, Laure remembered; unlike Sylvie, who by the age of seventeen had already attracted the attention of the exotic Daniel on his visits home, before he came back home to marry her.

Seeing Daniel in her parents' home this evening, carrying his son in his arms, Laure was struck by how complete he seemed and how mature. He was in his thirties now, of course, and had spent seventeen years of his life working long, outdoor hours, which had toughened his tall frame and turned his skin a leathery brown. But it wasn't that which was so striking. There was an assurance about him that sat well alongside his natural deference. He was an able man, a man people could lean on, and with his new job, he had rediscovered his vision.

'I'm working on the conveyor systems, for now,' he told Laure. 'It's good, steady work and I can develop my mechanical skills, and it keeps me away from the factory – it's pretty toxic work up there. But what I really want to do is to work on the new project they're starting up. They've brought in some top engineers and are developing techniques for using explosives to put special coatings on metals for signs and hoardings, and for lots of other applications. They're American techniques, but they say Paulilles will take the technology even further.'

'It sounds glamorous but dangerous! Surely you're safer in maintenance?'

'Not with the levels of security they have in place! The people there know what they're doing and no one plays around with those materials. It's not about glamour, but being part of something new.'

They were at the table. Laure placed one of her mother's home-cured anchovies on her fork and added a little crumbled boiled egg.

'Mmn,' she murmured, through a mouthful of salty heaven. 'So, where do you get these anchovies from, *Maman*, now that you don't have a fisherman son-in-law to bring them home for you?'

'Oh, I still have my contacts,' Daniel assured her.

'Not always!' *Maman* said ruefully. 'We've been reduced to buying them. And as for sardines, don't ask. We never see any!'

Daniel grimaced. 'Don't you start! My mother never stops complaining that she doesn't get her old supplies and her old prices.'

'Yes, and she has a whole café to supply – no wonder we poor bakers get nothing!'

'It's good bread, though!' Daniel grinned at his mother-in-law.

Laure finished her last anchovy with a sigh. 'How is your mother, Daniel? I must go and visit tomorrow. Is Martin home?'

'Yes, for now, though I don't know how much of the summer he'll have off. He's at home and being spoiled to death for the moment. I swear he's getting fat, too,' Daniel said, waving his fork at her.

Laure smiled. Martin was a sportsman and in no danger of getting fat, but he would never have the hard muscle of his brother. Where was he now in his medical studies? He must just have finished his fifth year at Montpellier, and now things would be getting serious. She would go and see him tomorrow.

They decided not to open Laure's Chablis with their fricassee of chicken that evening, and instead drank local red wine, fruity and strong and hard on the throat, which made Laure feel that she had really arrived back on home soil.

It was over the cheese that the subject of the Paris riots finally came up, but even then there weren't many questions thrown at Laure. Instead, she listened while Papa gave his opinion of the students as deranged utopians, and of the workers' strikes as disorganised and unforgivably disruptive. Laure realised that he had been frightened, believing his beloved country was going to descend into chaos. He was a traditional working-class man, was Papa, but no revolutionary!

'I'm no apologist for that man de Gaulle,' he was saying, 'But I ended up voting for him in the elections they called. He was the only one who could restore order. Otherwise, we were going to end up being governed by a bunch of mad intellectuals and their Communist sympathisers.'

That's me, thought Laure, a mad intellectual! They had all been mad for a few weeks in Paris. Never again would she feel that intense sense of freedom, empowerment and fellowship. What were they fighting for? Sometimes, they had all wondered themselves, but they knew they were fighting against something – against the suffocating old University and its lack of freedoms, against the brutality of the police and the authorities, against the old regime that was leaving France a century behind the world.

Her favourite poster that she and her fellow art students had produced showed the shadow of de Gaulle gagging a young man, with the caption: *'Sois jeune et tais toi'* – 'Be young and shut up.' The students had simply refused to shut up any longer and the more brutal the police became, the more the students had chanted and fought back with their torn up cobblestones against tear gas and makeshift barricades, until ten million people rose up with them.

When you were caught up in the heat of it all, it seemed as though everyone who was against you was the enemy; but here, in Vermeilla, she could see that it must have looked different. Papa was continuing his diatribe, silencing his wife and the young people around him with a lecture on what represented sensible unionisation, and he seemed far away from her right now; but she could imagine that eighty percent of people in Vermeilla would agree with him.

On 13th May, when one million people had marched through Paris, she had felt almost overwhelmed herself by what they had unleashed, with all its unpredictability, but she had at least been sure that nothing would ever be quite the same again. She still felt that but here in Vermeilla, it was harder to believe!

'They even closed the high schools around here,' Papa was continuing. 'Imagine a bunch of school kids going on strike! And their teachers, of course – they just wanted an excuse to look intellectual and never mind the kids' education. Our youngsters here in Vermeilla just hung around the square or took their fishing rods down to the rocks. They didn't have any idea what the strike was all about – it was just a holiday for them.'

'Calm down, Jacques!' It was *Maman* who answered him, with an edge of exasperation. 'It's over now and you said yourself, if de Gaulle and his cronies learned a lesson it would be a good thing. And when he made that broadcast sounding all pompous after the election, you almost threw your coffee at the radio!' She smiled. 'Talking of which, who would like some coffee?'

Papa looked as though he might say something more, but at that moment Julien toddled over to the table, wearing his grandfather's cap over one ear. There was a burst of laughter that made Julien grin delightedly. The toddler looked around the room, and as his grandfather lifted him onto his knee, he made an important announcement.

'*Pépé*'s hat is too big,' he said, before taking hold of the cap and placing it back to front on Papa's head, squashing it down over his ears. He looked around the table speculatively in case there was something good to eat and Sylvie held out half of an apricot she had just prepared. Julien took it, squeezing it in his little hand, and then stuffed it into his mouth.

Jacques Forestier took the cap off his head and automatically picked up his napkin to wipe his grandson's face. He gave him a kiss and then looked over at Sylvie with a smile.

'He's grown again, *ce petit.*'

'*J'suis pas petit, j'suis grand,*' Julien protested. His grandfather laughed and then passed the boy over to his mother.

'Indeed you are, very big! How could I call you little? *Pépé* made a mistake – it's the baby in your mummy's tummy

33

that's little, and you're the big brother.' He got up from his chair and gave a yawn. 'You'll forgive me everyone, if I go off to my bed now.'

He passed behind Sylvie, pausing to kiss the top of her head, and tweaked Julien's cheek. When he came to Laure's seat, he took hold of her shoulders and she turned around to face him.

'It's good to have you home, *ma puce*. You came out of all of that all right, whatever happened, and you can forget the Sorbonne for a while and live among ordinary people.' He almost smiled at her as he spoke, and she stood up and hugged him.

'There are only ordinary people, Papa,' she said.

'Not with that hair, there aren't!' he said with wry humour.

She grinned at him. 'It'll grow in the sun.'

'You think? You'll need to hang around here for a good while then. You'll be around for your sister's new baby coming, at least, won't you?'

Laure nodded. 'Provided it comes on time!'

'Good,' he continued and kissed her on the forehead. 'You look drained. Go to bed, my pretty, and put it all behind you, and tomorrow maybe we'll see you without those tired lines on your face.'

He didn't miss that much, she thought to herself, as she watched him lumber out of the room and off for his few hours' sleep before his night's work. He was naturally weary at the end of a long working day, but her tiredness was different and alien to his ordered existence. I am going to sleep though, she swore to herself. I'm home in Vermeilla and there's nothing I can do about anything for a few weeks anyway. I'm going to clear my mind.

Chapter 5

And she did sleep; a deep, dreamless sleep, tucked in the high wooden bed she'd had such trouble climbing into as a child. The wooden shutters kept out the morning sun and she slept on and on, so that it was well past the normal rising time in the Forestier household when she finally woke up, feeling almost groggy as she pulled herself into consciousness in the darkened room. For a moment, she didn't know where she was, and then she thought, I'm in Vermeilla, no one can touch me here. No one could touch her, but one day she would want to go back out to the other world. Would they let her in? The little frisson of fear that went through her had to be quickly suppressed.

She took breakfast alone. *Maman* was in the shop below and Papa would be working hard in the bakery behind. The bread for the first half of the day would all have been baked by now, and the croissants would all have been sold, and he would be making cakes and tarts for lunchtime sale.

Maman had left out fresh bread for her and newly made cherry jam, and Laure made a cup of milky coffee, strong enough to wake her up and big enough to dunk in. The local Perpignan newspaper talked rugby, tourism and local commerce, and Laure immersed herself in it, letting the local news lap gently over her, until she realised she'd let her coffee go cold and had to make another.

By halfway through the morning, she had showered and dressed in one of her more acceptable miniskirts (it was hot out there, dammit!), and she called into the shop to say hello to *Maman*.

Maman was beaming. 'We have a new baby in the village,' she told Laure, as happily as if it had been her own. 'Young Céline Albert had a bouncing little girl last night. She had a long labour, poor soul, but all is well and the baby weighed in at a strapping three and a half kilos.'

She looked at Laure almost triumphantly. 'All we need now is for your sister to have a little girl as well, and then there will be two ready-made playmates in the village.'

Laure smiled and protested. 'She could play with Sylvie's baby if he's a boy as well! Look how I was with Martin.'

Maman waved a dismissive hand. 'You and Martin! Pair of silly intellectuals, that's what you are! No, Sylvie will have a girl this time, mark my words, and Julien can play big brother.'

She paused in the act of filling a beautiful little box of pastries. 'You can drop these into the Albert house when you're in the village.'

Laure nodded and moved around the counter to take a closer look at the delicacies being placed in the box. There was a little round chocolate tart and another almond one, and a triangle of apple slice, caramelised and gooey, and a deep filled custard tart, all made with the thinnest, homemade, buttery pastry. Her mother was scanning the remaining selection of pastries in the glass counter, trying to decide what to choose to complete the box, and Laure held out a finger towards the choux buns, bursting with coffee cream, which nestled on a tray beside her. *Maman* nodded and selected two of the buns, placing them delicately in the box, and then closing it with infinite care before tying it with coloured ribbon.

Laure moved along the counter, registering all her old favourites. If there had been anyone in the shop she would never have been allowed to do this, but they were alone, so she leaned forward to drink in the smells, from tangy lemon tarts to rich chocolate and the sugary candied fruits from the *pains aux raisins*. On the glass top, there were little cellophane packets of *bonbons* and flavoured croutons, and a tray of the sugar doughnuts the labourers came in for to eat with their morning coffee. This had been Laure's world throughout her childhood and she and Sylvie had worked here when not in school, helping Papa at first, and then working at the counter when they were old enough to be trusted to handle the money.

Old mother Pujol came in just now and Laure took her nose out of the patisseries to say hello. The old lady wanted the smallest of baguettes for herself and her husband, and Laure took pleasure in serving her, taking the bread from the wooden racks behind her and wrapping a twist of paper around it, so that *Mère* Pujol could carry it easily. All the time *Maman* chatted, asking after the husband's chest and the old lady's rheumatism, and passing on the news that

Vermeilla had another baby, another member of the village family.

Two other women came in and the talk turned to Laure. How happy she must be to be here again, they all told her, away from busy, dusty, unfriendly Paris, and Laure could only agree with a smile and an impulsive hug for her mother. Today, she was ecstatic to be home.

Of course, to these ladies in the shop, it was incomprehensible why anyone would ever want to be elsewhere. Parisians were not popular here, with their condescension and arrogant airs, and lots of other parts of France were viewed with almost equal suspicion. Laure remembered with amusement similar, dismissive comments that were made when she'd been a student in Toulouse. The Catalans were a self-sufficient bunch who loved their own culture and their sunshine. Visitors were received here on Catalan terms!

It was over half an hour before Laure finally slipped away from the shop and made her way to the Albert house to deliver the gift of pastries. Céline's mother was in attendance and Laure had to refuse invitations to come inside, saying she would come back when Céline was more rested. She'd known these people all her life, and Céline had been several years behind her in school. In this village, I'm an old maid at twenty-four, she thought with wry amusement, and made her way to the Café de Catalogne to seek the solace of Martin.

The café sat in a shaded back street running down to the shore. It was doing a brisk trade and the little row of outside tables was full. The glass doors to the bar area had been pushed wide open and the windows opened, so that the tables inside could benefit from the little breeze wafting up the street from the shore. Laure greeted a group of old men playing cards at a secluded table, but the majority of the customers were tourists. She could never remember seeing so many.

The Café de Catalogne was yet another home from home, its interior so familiar to Laure, with its dark wood brightened by colourful Spanish tiles and two rather lovely old chandeliers. And behind the long wooden bar, the barman was yet another old school friend, just a couple of years younger than Laure. He gave her a big welcome and told her she would find Martin up in the apartment, so she stuck her head around the little wooden door at the back of the café and called up the stairs. An answering voice told her to come up, so Laure made her way up, as she had so many times before. Martin and Daniel's mother Colette met her at the top.

'Laure! So you're home!' Colette took hold of her and gave her a resounding kiss on both cheeks. 'Come on through, my dear, and see Martin. He's been complaining that there's no one around this summer and threatening to go back early to Montpellier. Maybe now you're here, he'll stay around for a while.'

They went down the corridor, which opened up into a large living room, with a dining table on one side and a set of comfortable old chairs on the other. Light streamed into the room from double glass doors, which were open, onto a large balcony that was much larger than Sylvie's. This had some of the most intricate railings in the village and yet more patterned tiles. The Café de Catalogne was one of the oldest buildings in the village and its style reflected its age.

On the old sofa in the corner of the room sat Colette's husband Philippe, with his long legs thrust out before him. He'd had his head buried in the newspaper, but on seeing Laure he rose to his feet and held a big hand out to welcome her. Before he retired, he'd been Laure's teacher at the local primary school and she'd been a favourite of his, she knew, especially when he discovered her artistic talents. He'd nurtured them and encouraged her parents to recognise them, and had cheered her through her studies in Toulouse, and then on to the Sorbonne. She loved him.

'It's our artist!' he exclaimed jubilantly and folded her into a hug. He was tall and gangly with hands and feet that were too big for his bony frame. He always said it took an ungainly oaf like him to appreciate the lightness of touch of an artist, but Laure knew that he sketched in private. She had even persuaded him to show her his drawings once and found them surprisingly delicate.

'*Tonton* Philippe!' she said from within his endless arms. He was her *Tonton*, her uncle by adoption, just as he was Martin and Daniel's. When he'd married their mother, he'd only cemented a relationship with the boys that had existed since their birth.

'Hey, Martin,' he was calling, from over her shoulder. 'Come out here and see who's come to see you!'

And then Martin was with them, emerging from the corridor leading to the kitchen and bedrooms on the other side of the living room.

'Just out of bed, pal?' Laure asked and got a grin in reply.

'It's my duty to rest!' he answered. 'We doctors need to be on form when we're on duty.'

'So, now he's a doctor!' Laure shook her head in wonderment.

'Well, maybe not quite, but I'm already an essential member of any medical team I work with, I'll tell you!' was the retort. 'Hey Laure, will you go swimming with me this afternoon? Do you realise that we're the only twenty-four-year-olds in this village who are still students? Every other student who's back here on holiday is a mere babe in arms, and all our own classmates are married, and either plumbers or bank clerks.'

'Tell me about it! Have you heard that Céline Albert had a baby girl last night? She's just nineteen, Martin, and she's already been married for a year. It makes me feel so old!'

Laure sat down next to Philippe; while Martin dropped into the chair opposite. He waved to his mother to sit beside him, but she shook her head.

'I won't join you people – I was just on my way down to check things in the bar when Laure arrived.'

'They don't need your help,' protested Philippe.

'Maybe not, but it's busy down there today.'

'It sure is,' Laure agreed. 'I can't remember ever seeing so many people before.'

Colette nodded. 'It goes up every summer. We're becoming a real tourist destination and lots of people come in for the day from the campsites around. It's good business! I won't be long, and I'll bring you up some coffee from the bar.'

As she disappeared, Philippe shook his head in vexation, sending an errant strand of grey hair flying over his broad, lined forehead. 'She has no reason to keep working, you know. I could keep us both, and she could let the café go, but she has the idea that one day Daniel and Sylvie will take it over, and so she won't hear of giving up the lease.'

'Take over the café? Daniel and Sylvie?' Laure was startled. 'I've never heard either of them mention it!'

'No,' Martin agreed. 'Daniel has worked here a lot, helping our mother over the years, and knows the hard work involved. He doesn't want Sylvie to live the way *Maman* has.'

'It doesn't have to be done the way Colette does it,' Philippe put in. 'She just makes work for herself. Daniel and Sylvie could have a nice living here, and a nice home.' He waved at the comfortable space around them, which was three times the size of Sylvie's sitting room.

'Should he, do you think?' Laure asked anxiously. 'He seems so keen to have an engineering career now at Paulilles.'

'And before that, he was as keen to stay working with boats.' Martin frowned. 'He was better with the boats.'

'Why so?' Laure watched his face. 'I asked him if the job at Paulilles could be dangerous and he said no. Was he wrong?'

'Wrong? Why no... not really. Not if by dangerous you mean the threat of explosions, but there are some strange illnesses out at Paulilles. I was speaking to a doctor in Port-Vendres the other day, and he's sure there are some people getting sick because of the chemicals out there.' He hesitated. 'Daniel doesn't work among the chemicals, but who knows?'

Help! Laure felt all her old prejudices against Paulilles returning. Martin was such a positive soul and so measured; he wouldn't speak up unless he had some reason. Was he letting himself be swayed by the fact that this was his brother they were talking about? The factory offered so much opportunity, more than anywhere else in this forgotten outpost of France, and Daniel worked on the conveyor systems outside, not in the production area itself.

She spoke at last, rather pensively. 'Well, he and Sylvie can't take on the café right now, not in the high season, with Sylvie just two months away from giving birth. Daniel said last night that the work in the factory can be pretty toxic, so he knows it himself, but like you say, he isn't personally exposed to it. Not from what he was saying. If he changes jobs there then things could change but surely, for now, he's all right, and earning good money? And he's so inspired!'

Philippe reached an arm around her again. 'You're right, of course. Don't worry, *ma petite*, Colette isn't going to give up this café any day soon, whatever I say, and even if Daniel decided to come in with her she wouldn't stop working – I know her too well! We'll just carry on as we are for now. As long as she doesn't try to get me working downstairs, I'm too old for all that!'

He gave Laure a squeeze, and as he did so, her shoulder twisted and Laure let out an involuntary grunt of pain, drawing her breath in hard.

'What's the matter?' It was Martin who spoke, leaning forward in his chair with immediate concern.

Laure adjusted her position more comfortably. 'Calm down, Doctor, it's nothing serious. It's the fault of the riots, that's all. I got caught up and I got injured, but nowhere near as badly as a lot of others. My back is sore, but it gets better every day.'

She had their full attention now. 'Why yes!' It was Philippe who spoke. 'Here we are, talking about everything else but you, and yet we've been waiting for you! We didn't doubt that you would have played a full part in something so exciting. But you got hurt? Tell us, Laure.'

She looked at them. Here were two people who would listen sympathetically, who could understand the hope and enthusiasm that had infected Paris. My closest friends, she thought, and it didn't seem strange to include Philippe. He would find the students young and over hopeful, perhaps, but he was a man who had never lost his passion and ideals. How to start, though? '

'You heard about the Night of the Barricades?' she said at last. 'How first of all the authorities closed Nanterre University, and then when the Nanterre students came to the Sorbonne for support, the police shut the Sorbonne and arrested all of the students who had grouped there? They'd promised that if the students left peacefully, they could all go home, but then they picked them off as they came out and arrested the lot. There were several nights of demonstrations after that, but it culminated in the Night of the Barricades.'

CHAPTER 6

They'd been there for hours now, in the middle of the night, nervous and yet determined, waiting to see what the riot squads were going to do to them. Laure looked around at their hastily erected barricade, made up of an old car, some publicity panels, fencing torn from around nearby trees, and piled up paving stones. Anything, in fact, they could pull up or scavenge to give them some shelter against the expected police attack. Further along the street, there was a similar barricade. The word was that there were more than fifty now in place on all the strategic corners of the Latin Quarter, where they might expect to be attacked. On top of the barricades, students stood chanting and waving flags, their voices jubilantly defiant.

It had all started as a peaceful demonstration in the sunshine of early evening at the Place Denfert-Rochereau, monitored by the students' own highly disciplined marshals. There had been ten thousand at first, swelling to twenty thousand students, as well as their teachers and lecturers. They'd all shouted, "Free our students," and demanded the release of the demonstrators the authorities had jailed so ridiculously earlier in the week. They wanted their University back too. They wanted the Sorbonne reopened. They were quite simply sick of being controlled, set upon, told what to think and excluded from learning, simply because they had dared to meet and to talk.

This evening's demonstration had circled the Latin Quarter on the grand boulevards, defiantly passing before the helmeted, armed CRS detachments. The police had not reacted, standing foursquare and doggedly silent behind their shields. Perhaps the public outrage at their excessive force had finally made the authorities think, or perhaps the student numbers made them wary. But the riot squads, nevertheless, blocked all roads leading across the river and were massed all around them, closing the demonstration into the Latin Quarter, a stone's throw from the University.

Three days ago, the students had marched across the river and thirty thousand of them had massed at the tomb of the Unknown Warrior, singing La Marseillaise. The Unknown Warrior belongs to us all, they had been saying. He belongs to the young as much as to de Gaulle, and so does our national anthem. We are ordinary, intelligent young people, Laure thought, but we live under an archaic regime which gives us no rights and treats us with contempt.

De Gaulle had said they'd desecrated the tomb of the Unknown Warrior by their very presence, and tonight it was clear that the police had orders to stop them crossing the river. Well, so be it. The Latin Quarter had seen the first battles with the police, exactly a week ago, and tonight it would belong to the students.

But what a waiting game it was. A nervous waiting game of negotiations and alarms. They followed it all over their radios as several student leaders and lecturers were received by the University Rector, who was in phone contact with the Minister of Education. Laure held her breath, but no one would leave here now unless there was at least an amnesty for the students locked up last week and the University reopened. Meanwhile, the students heard that the security forces had received reinforcements and closed down the whole area.

A flurry of activity two hundred metres away on the main boulevard had many running to see. Two police buses, caught under a hail of stones thrown from the mining school, had driven straight into the crowd to get away, mowing people down, and then taken refuge behind a police cordon. The police fired tear gas at the students, but the incident was quickly handled by the students' own demonstration marshals, who returned to form a chain in front of the policemen with a sangfroid which calmed everyone, keeping the other students behind them and stopping them from overreacting. Everyone returned to their ranks and the word went around that the student marshals had everything under control. Laure breathed again.

The night was cool and Laure wished she had a thicker jacket with her. Above her, on the barricade, Pierre and Lolo were sitting, casually swinging their legs. She climbed up to join them and Lolo put his arm around her. From up high, the view was amazing, but what struck her most was how much laughter and singing there was, and how much energy she could feel from the mass of students around them. And they were so ordinary – young men with neat haircuts and ties, and young girls in sensible skirts. Laure, Lolo and Pierre, and their group of art students, provided the only splash of offbeat colour among them all. How could the young of France be so far behind the youth of the world? And how dare de Gaulle label them as an unruly rabble?

Laure waved at a man who was looking out of a window above them. They'd built their barricade just below his apartment, but he didn't seem to mind. He waved back and smiled, and the next thing they knew he was holding out a package, which he threw towards them. Lolo caught it, and as he opened it, a big pack of sandwiches was revealed. A whistle of thanks went up and a cheer, and Lolo divided them out among those around him.

'Hungry, ma chérie?' he asked Laure, who shook her head. She couldn't imagine eating anything, but she accepted water from a flask.

The singing started up again and the chant of 'de Gaulle, Assassin!' and then it broke off as the radio news came through – the negotiations had failed.

'That's it, then,' Lolo said. 'They'll be coming for us!' They jumped down to help as the students pitched in to dig up more cobblestones and build ever higher defence piles.

Soon after two o'clock in the morning, many hundreds of CRS, with shields in one hand and truncheons in the other, moved out onto the Boulevard St. Michel, pushing students physically before them. Half an hour later, the first barricade fell and the students fell back towards Laure's barricade. The noise was incredible and the searing stench of tear gas had reached them already. Any student who fell to the ground

49

was truncheoned viciously by the CRS. A huge fire could be seen on the Boulevard St Michel, where the students had set fire to the fallen barricade. A shot was heard and someone shouted, 'My God, they're firing at us!'

Students ran towards them from St Michel to reach the safety of their barricade and then turned to join them. The CRS advanced towards them up the narrow street and Laure found herself hurling stones and screaming, 'de Gaulle, Assassin,' again and again. It was strange how slow the police advance seemed, and yet how inexorable. Tear gas grenades rained down on them, and Laure wondered how long they could stand against them. Her eyes were streaming and she could hardly breathe, but then their friend from the apartment above stuck out his head and threw a bucket of water down. This helped to clear the gas, so they could breathe again. He withdrew quickly when a policeman fired a tear gas grenade directly at his window.

'We'll have to withdraw!' one student yelled and Lolo answered, 'Not yet!'

Suddenly, a tear gas grenade exploded right next to Laure. As the acrid smoke scorched her eyes and throat, she gagged and cried out in pain. She couldn't see. All around her students were pushing, trying to get away, until she found herself lying on the ground, their feet trampling her, and all she could do was bring her arms up to protect her head.

It was Pierre who saved her, grabbing Laure's arm and pulling her to her feet. 'Come on, Laure, run. I'll hold you.'

He half dragged her and they stumbled along the street, turning left and then right, away from the biggest crowds. Laure was bleeding and had lost one of her shoes.

'I can't see, Pierre!' she gasped in panic. 'I can't see anything! I've gone blind!'

'I know. I saw – that tear gas grenade hit the wall right beside you, inches from your face. I couldn't get to you in time to stop you falling. You'll be all right though. Trust me, it'll go away. But we need to get you somewhere safe. Just hold on to me. Just hold on, do you hear? You'll be all right, Laure. You'll be all right!'

Pierre's voice faded gradually, as Laure brought herself back to Colette's living room in Vermeilla. Philippe and Martin were watching her intently, perhaps also lost in the fear of that moment.

'I've never been so scared!' she told them. 'Pierre looked after me and took me to a local church, where we heard there were some medical students offering first aid. They bathed my eyes with water and gradually I could see again, although my eyes stayed swollen for hours, and my throat was sore for days. But the worst injury afterwards was my back.' She rubbed gently across her shoulders and then down the line of her spine.

'I didn't go to a doctor. It didn't seem worth it when there were other students who actually needed serious medical help. All I had was bruising, but my back was black and blue, and horribly stiff! It's easing off, and I only get pain from time to time, but I still don't seem to have full use of my left arm.'

Martin was frowning. 'You need physiotherapy,' he said.

Laure shook her head. 'Not if it means telling my parents I got injured.'

Martin considered. 'We'll have to see what we can manage,' he said after a moment. 'You can come to Perpignan with me one day. I've got a friend there who's studying physiotherapy – just finished his final year, in fact, so he's pretty near qualified.'

Philippe was wagging a finger in agreement. 'You'll go with Martin, Laure,' he instructed, just as he might have done all those years ago at the primary school.

Laure felt uncomfortable as always at being the centre of concern. She was relieved to see Michel the barman arrive from downstairs with the coffee Colette had promised them, so she didn't actually have to answer them. She took her cup and sipped it appreciatively – there was never any coffee as good as this, even in Paris.

'You'll know what happened next,' she said, once the barman had left. 'There was such general outrage at how brutally the police behaved that night, and somehow we seemed to ignite people, so that the next thing we knew the workers had joined us. It was on the Friday night that I got trampled on, and by the Monday there were a million people marching through Paris!'

'Don't tell me you were on that march too? With your injuries!'

'No, *Tonton*, don't worry. I couldn't have stood for so long. But by Tuesday morning we were in the University! They gave in and let us in, and in the art school we took over the lithographs, borrowed some silk screen printers and created the *Atelier Populaire*. You've never seen anything like it, Philippe, with artists from outside the University joining us, and workers who were on strike coming in to help and paste our posters all over Paris. We produced thousands of posters for the campaign.'

'We saw them in the newspapers. Very creative! And now they're already collectors' items.'

Laure sighed. 'Yes, I know. Some American gallery wants to put on an exhibition of them, and they got stolen right, left and centre. But what worries me is that, after all that struggle, the only things left are a few posters to titillate the world and another de Gaulle government bent on punishing the students for their effrontery. All the same, people who'd cheered us in May turned on us in June and started calling us scum.'

Philippe nodded. 'Yes, I heard one commentator say that in May the people were slightly drunk and generous. They wanted to give everyone a chance and start a new world, and then in June they sobered up and had a hangover, and were as cantankerous as hell about getting everyone back to work and to the old order of things.'

Laure agreed – that was exactly how it felt. She remembered one of those same local factory workers who'd helped them, coming back to see them towards the end, in June. He told them he'd never been so happy as in May, when he'd thought his and other lives might actually change. What they'd got, their twenty percent pay rise, felt nothing like a victory.

'I'll be in that factory now until I retire in forty years' time,' he said miserably.

'But you don't have to!' was the resounding response of the students in their *Atelier*. 'You could study, move, do anything!'

And he had shaken his head. 'Nay, those were just dreams,' he'd said. 'I don't have the money or the schooling to study, but I have loved learning about your work.'

He'd taken away with him some new posters, fresh from the drying lines, and as he left Laure had asked for his address, so that she could send him a sketch she'd made of him weeks ago, while he was helping with the inks. He'd sent her back a jokey little cartoon he'd made of the students at their *Atelier* desks, and for a while she'd been exultant, thinking that maybe they had changed someone's life even just a fraction.

She told Martin and Philippe about him. 'It's what the *Atelier Populaire* stood for,' she said. 'Opening up art to the whole world. But at the end of the day, you can't change the fact that he is stuck where he is. Did we just make a young guy even more dissatisfied with his life, do you think?' she asked.

Philippe shook his head. 'Not at all. You didn't destroy the class structure, but the workers who occupied the factories of France will never feel as voiceless as they once did, and that young man will probably go on to become a leader because he's not scared now to think and do something different. And maybe he'll come to your next exhibition at the *École des Beaux-Arts*, you never know! No, I think it's easy just now, in the backlash, to underestimate how much you have achieved. Even at the political level. You scared people just that bit too much and they voted for safety in the elections, but I'd say you have holed de Gaulle below the waterline and exposed his real lack of public support. There'll be some continuing backlash, but de Gaulle will soon be history, you mark my words.'

'I for one believe you have forced people to listen to new ideas,' Martin added. 'We had a series of student marches in Montpellier too, and it's been interesting that the University Council have changed their membership to allow students a say.'

Laure was pleased. She relaxed back into the chair and thought positive thoughts. Maybe everything would be okay after all.

'We did do some impressive work,' she said, as much to reassure herself as the others. 'I was on the organising committee at the *École des Beaux-Arts*, and at the very least we ran the school effectively – much more efficiently than it normally is, I can assure you! And we did produce some amazing posters. I've got some in my luggage which I must show you!'

'Did you design them yourself?'

'It was a team effort. Everything was a team effort. But it was natural that we senior students should be looked to for some of the design ideas. In artistic terms, they were basic, but that was part of the fun – you had to find original ways to express ideas on a budget that were easy to print mono-colour.'

She looked at Martin's broad, tanned face – healthy and honest and familiar – and gave him a big smile. 'I'll tell you more later if you really want to know. Meanwhile, it is summer and we can't let the tourists have Vermeilla all to themselves. So what time do you want to go to the beach? The water must be at twenty-one degrees already this summer, and I want to swim around the bay and find the old flat sunbathing rock. Who knows, it may help my injured arm. Above all, this poor city girl is in need of some sun.'

CHAPTER 7

They met up immediately after lunch, when the rest of the world might perhaps still be resting and they could have the beach more to themselves. The sea breeze was just enough to stir the water. There wasn't a swell in sight and it would be a great afternoon for swimming around the rocks, which were so often impossible to approach from the sea.

You could see a lot of small fish and little shrimp if you snorkelled under the fishing rocks and once Laure had spied a tiny seahorse, nosing brilliant blue among the seaweed. A little further out, where the fishing lines were cast, were sea bream, grey mullet and the occasional sea bass, and near the bottom you could sometimes see cuttlefish, or even squid.

You had to come at a time of day when there weren't too many hopeful fishermen lining the rocks above, so you didn't annoy them by getting in their way. To see the most fish you had to lie flat on the surface of the water, moving as little as possible, with your face just under the surface, and just watch. Among the village boys, Martin had always been the best at seeing things because he was the most patient. And as the years had gone by, he had accepted Laure's company.

They swam from the beach together and the water bit cold and hard to start with, despite the summer temperatures, but within a couple of minutes, Laure was swimming easily out into the bay, until she stopped and lay half upright in the water, twisting her shoulders so that she revolved slowly around and around to give herself a 360-degree view of the bay.

Martin was far away already, swimming fast out to sea. He could go for miles, Laure knew, so she turned and headed at her own, slower pace along the shore towards the fishing rocks. She pulled up her snorkel from around her neck and spent a short time snorkelling close into the rocks, where some weed lay under the water line and attracted the fish. The sun was on her back and she floated on for a while feeling it on her shoulder blades, but what she really wanted was to lose herself in the heat. So she clambered out of the water and over the rocks to reach the flattest rock of them all, the one that had always been her sunbathing rock.

In the heat of the middle of the day there were no fishermen, so Laure had her space to herself. She spread herself out on the bare rock, which was almost uncomfortably hot to lie on, and gave herself up to the sun.

Martin found her there some twenty minutes later. He flung himself down on the flat space beside her and yelped.

'Ouch, that's hot!'

'It soon becomes cooler, don't worry. Oh Martin, this is heaven!'

'Better than the excitement of Paris?'

'Different! You can't compare the two. But I can't imagine living in Paris and never having this to come back to.'

'You couldn't live here all the time, though, not anymore.' He said it as a statement, not as a question.

'And could you?'

He didn't reply for a moment and then nodded. 'Yes, I think I could, but then I don't need a world of academics or specialists around me to work in general practice. I want to be a community doctor, and this is a better community than most.'

'You wouldn't be interested in specialising and becoming a surgeon or consultant?'

Martin shook his head, but she had already known he wouldn't go in that direction. Martin was clever, a very bright product of whom this modest community was immensely proud, but he was just that – modest. He would leave it to his fellow medical students, those from higher flying families, to pursue the lucrative consultancy positions.

Laure often felt the same at the Sorbonne – out of place and above her station, and it did nothing for her confidence. There was no reason why her work should seem less worthwhile than anyone else's, but for some reason, Laure always felt that she had to produce the top work to justify her place there. It was stupid because she was an award winner on a privileged programme, but in many ways that just made it worse.

And thinking about her award suddenly made her want to cry. She shifted on the rock and felt a shaft of pain in her shoulder which made her wince out loud. Martin raised himself on an elbow and looked across at her.

'Are you all right? Is your back sore?'

She turned her head towards him and she felt her eyes prick at the look of concern on his face. All right? No, if the truth be told, she was far from all right. She suddenly felt the need to tell Martin – to let someone else into the little, isolated place of worry which she could never quite escape at the moment.

'Not really,' she said to him. 'Or at least, it is, but no worse than usual. But Martin...' She stopped, reluctant suddenly to bring the complications of Paris into this tranquil scene.

'Yes?'

'There's much worse than my back,' she continued with a sigh. 'Something else happened during the last couple of months. Something so serious that the University are threatening to withdraw me from the course.'

She'd succeeded in startling Martin. He sat bolt upright and the frown on his face was almost comical.

'Threatening to throw you out? Why on earth should they? If they withdrew students from study just because they'd been involved in the occupation, then they'd have no students left! And they'd have the unions on their back too! Wasn't there a general amnesty?'

Laure nodded. 'Yes, but they're accusing me of plotting to deface or even set fire to the art school buildings.' She said it as baldly as she could and was relieved to hear Martin's snort of derision. It gave her the courage to explain.

'You see, it was towards the end of June, and the students occupying the Sorbonne's main buildings had been cleared out by the police a couple of weeks before. It was all over as far as people in France were concerned, and it was really.

Loads of students had gone home and we'd already had the first stage of the elections, but there were a lot of University buildings still occupied. We were still there at the *Beaux-Arts* in reduced numbers, producing some posters, but were expecting to be evicted at any time. And then on the Tuesday, the word went around that the police were coming. It didn't actually happen that day, but people were sure it was going to. I hate to say it but a part of me would have been happy to see it all over. The main part of the Sorbonne was closed, we'd lost the factory guys, who were back at work, and all of the architects had left their building as well. So we were left with just a few moderates from the organising committee, and rather too many of the wildest thinkers and those looking for a fight.'

She settled back on to her smooth bit of rock and closed her eyes to remember better. It all came back to her how tense they'd been.

The sun was shining as she came into the building that morning. It seemed ironic that throughout May, when life had been so alight and free, the weather had been dismal. Now, in June, the sun shone; de Gaulle's sun, they were calling it. It would bring people out to vote for him on Sunday, for sure.

Through the door to the atelier, she could see that work was ongoing on reprinting a poster they'd first produced last week. 'The Elections – a Trap for Fools' read the words, which came from Jean-Paul Sartre, but Laure wondered who would read them now. She could understand those who were determined to keep working until the end, but since

61

the Sorbonne had been emptied and closed, she felt their work was increasingly futile.

They'd been three hundred occupying artists at the height of the protests, with thousands more helpers. Major trade unions had sent delegates each day to ask for specific posters and they'd brought in screen printers to produce them two thousand at a time. They'd been organised, efficient, dynamic, and they'd revolutionised the way the world looked at the École des Beaux-Arts, which had been known as stuffy and privileged for so long.

Now, the main concern of most of those who were still there was to finish their protest with dignity and hand the buildings back in good order, while harnessing the support of many of their teachers to work towards constructive change and the future reform of the École des Beaux-Arts. To stay proud, challenging and focused, and to look towards the future with a positive eye, that was the key. And all the auspices were good that they would win some important reforms.

If only they could control the anarchists. Too many had found their way into the school and now that the main body of students had gone, the extremists were too dominant, too menacing. They hung around, occasionally lending a hand, but mostly just argued politics with everyone else and gearing themselves up for a battle with the flics when they arrived, as they would now at any time. At the Sorbonne, the moderates had been able to stop the extremists from doing any harm to buildings or people. Here, at the Beaux-Arts, they now had to do the same.

There was a group of them in the main atelier, which the students were still using. They were clustered around the printer, watching the work going on, lending a hand when asked. In the corners, behind the printers, Laure spied little piles of iron bars and Molotov cocktails. *Oh no,* she thought, *they've brought their weapons right inside! What are we going to do? There aren't enough of us left,* she thought in dismay.

She stood in the corridor and watched them working for a moment. *Where were all the committee members in the atelier this morning? Instinct told her that they must be in the room they now used for their meetings, no doubt discussing this crisis,* so she turned left and headed down the corridor.

She found them as expected, heads down in serious conversation. The moderates at the Sorbonne had actually come to blows with the extremists in order to control them, and the discussion was about how to avoid the same thing happening. The weapons downstairs could burn out the historic buildings, destroy valuable artwork and smash equipment. They could also be turned on them if they got into a confrontation with their owners.

'If we can get the guys outside, then we can remove all those weapons,' said Pierre.

'How? They're making a show of working just like the others.'

'They'll have lunch outside, like everyone else. They won't take the weapons then – they would expect to barricade themselves inside if the police come. That's why they've brought them inside. They'll keep the stash where it is.'

'Yes, and what are you going to do about them? We won't be able to touch the stash over lunch. They'll be watching us like hawks.'

It was Laure who had the idea. 'They don't know I'm here,' she said, as though that should be fully understood. 'I didn't stay over last night, and I didn't go through into the atelier when I came in just now.'

'And so?'

'Get everyone outside for a meeting, altogether, in the main courtyard. There's enough reason, with the police imminently descending on us. You can discuss what to do with the current batch of posters and have an argument over how to react when the police arrive. Group together all the others too, from all over the building. That'll take time! Keep everyone talking and I'll remove the weapons while you're out there.'

The idea was so simple, it was brilliant. Laure was impressed by herself! They had to think where to put the weapons because the anarchists would ransack the buildings looking for them. The idea that dawned on Laure was to take the stuff out by the side door and along the path behind to the main exhibition gallery. If she put the stash into the ladies' toilet, would they think to look for it there? She didn't think so. They'd stopped using the Perret building now there were fewer people, and she might even be able to lock the toilets, if she could find a key. It would take several journeys and they would need to keep the meeting going, but knowing how the students could talk once roused, she didn't doubt that she could get all the stuff away and out of sight.

It was tricky work though, stuffing the unwieldy bars into the cloth bag she used for her art material and stopping them from jangling against each other. There was even a mini machete. The journeys took even longer than she'd thought and she began to sweat, worrying that at any moment the meeting outside might break up, or some of the anarchists might decide to come back inside. But finally, she was on the last run, carrying with infinite care the Molotov cocktails.

She breathed a sigh of relief as she went through the door of the Perret building for the last time and eased it shut behind her, closing out the outside world. She put the heavy bag down for a moment and leaned against the wall, fishing out a handkerchief to wipe her face. Then she headed down the hall towards the toilets. She was halfway there when there emerged from a side corridor three figures. She froze.

'Mademoiselle Forestier!' called out one of them and her heart lurched. It was Professor Duchamp, the Senior Professor in charge of the Student Awards Committee.

She couldn't have been more surprised. What was a senior member of staff doing in the art school buildings? The students had secured all the entrances, surely? Everyone coming in and out had to pass by the main gate on the rue Bonaparte, and no one would have admitted old Professor Duchamp. He was one of the old guard, who made General de Gaulle look like a left-wing reformer. What was he doing here?

She halted in the middle of the hall, watching as the three besuited figures approached her.

'Well, Mademoiselle Forestier!' said Professor Duchamp, in mock astonished tones. 'What on earth could you be doing here?'

He must know that any student here was part of the occupation. What he wanted her to understand was that the holder of one of the University's most prestigious awards should not be one of them. He was looking at her as though she was a rather surprising feral animal who had crept under his garden fence.

She found herself stammering and then stopped herself. There was nothing this man could do to her.

'I was just passing through the building, Professor,' she answered him.

'Indeed? Well, I must say, Mademoiselle, I hadn't expected you, of all our students, to be in this vicinity at this moment. You are our representative to America later this year, are you not, and one of our exhibitors at the summer exhibition, if ever that happens this year? I am disappointed.'

He looked down at her both physically and morally. Duchamp was a tall, thin, very distinguished looking man. He was not casual like many of the art tutors, but always dressed to a nicety, and very conscious of his own importance. He had always borne in upon Laure that she was very privileged to have won the Beaux Arts prize, and she had heard he'd been strongly against awarding it to anyone who had found their way to Paris from a provincial University like Toulouse. She didn't know what to say to him now.

'I'm just passing through, Professor,' she repeated. She was terrified. There was nothing to apologise for in being part of the student events, but she had a bag full of Molotov cocktails strung on her back and needed to get away.

She hitched the bag further behind her, but a clink attracted the attention of one of his companions.

'What on earth are these?' he asked, pointing to the tips of two bottles sticking out of the bag. The professor's head peered around Laure, and his eyes widened, and then a satisfied smile lit his weasel's face.

'Mademoiselle,' he said, in a voice whose softness was its own threat, 'I think it is a very good thing that my colleagues and I decided to visit this building today. You have some explaining to do, young lady.'

CHAPTER 8

The image of the professor was so strong in her head that Laure felt almost sick. She opened her eyes deliberately to banish him and blinked in the blinding light of the sun. She pulled herself up so that she was sitting upright and grimaced at Martin.

'There you have it,' she said. 'God knows what made that bunch of pompous bastards come to the *Beaux-Arts* that day. I'd have expected them to wait out the occupation, and let the police clear the building before they tried to come back in. I gathered, from listening to them, that they'd come into the Perret Building from the Quai Malaquais sideusing a private key, suspecting we would no longer be occupying that part. Perhaps they were checking for damage, looking for stuff to report to the police or just being nosey. I don't know, but I did know that I'd been caught red-handed near the door they'd opened from the street outside, and by the one person in the University with the keenest desire to see me brought to book. He hauled me outside and called both the police and the Rector from a building a few doors along.'

'Phew!' Martin exhaled. 'And once you were outside, you no longer had any of the students to help you.'

'You've got it in one. I was completely on my own, carrying a load of Molotov cocktails with my fingerprints all over them, facing three serious witnesses, and none of the students had any idea where I'd disappeared to. The flics came and arrested me. I was charged with being in possession of the Molotov cocktails, with intention to harm. It wasn't until later that day that I was able to contact the Students' Union, who brought in Lolo and Pierre and Jérôme to argue for me.'

'So you ended up in a police cell?'

'Oh yes, in a kind of holding pen, and I didn't even have any company! At least in the thick of the riots, when the other students were arrested, they had others with them, but by this time everything was over and I was entirely on my own. And the flics were glad to make me squirm too, since it had been a few weeks since they'd seen any actual weapons, but memories of the riots were still sharp in their minds. They weren't exactly gentle.'

'Oh, my God!' Martin was appalled. 'What happened?'

'Well, thanks to the Students' Union and the arguments put forward in my defence, I was bailed and given a warning, but the charges are still on file against me, which has been very useful for the *École des Beaux-Arts*.'

'What have they done to you? Have you been thrown out of the University?'

'To date, no, but I'm expecting it. There was a general amnesty for students after the riots, but as I was found actually on University property with the weapons, Professor

Duchamp is arguing that makes me unfit to be a student at the revered *École des Beaux-Arts*. And at the very least he wants them to do is to take my award from me.'

'You mean the award your mother told me about? The one you won in the spring?'

'Yes, it was a competition set up by a new lecturer from the USA. It allows a student to go to New York for an internship in his or her final year, and it would have been the key for me to be able to get into research at the University after I finish my course.'

Tears pricked at her eyes in the ensuing silence. It was out now, but she wondered what she had achieved by pulling Martin into her sphere of trouble. He didn't look as worried as her as he sat there, leaning backwards on his hands, but he kept his eyes steady on her face. Eventually, he spoke.

'You only have one year to go, to finish your diploma. Could you transfer closer to home, back to Toulouse, perhaps? You would still have your grant, even if you don't have your special award.'

'No, I don't think so. You know yourself how all end of year assessment was suspended. They're all trying to decide right now how we will get assessed on last year's work, and the plan is for the exams to be run in September, instead. Well, if they won't let me back into the school, I'll leave without any results for this whole year of study, and how on earth could I transfer elsewhere? I wouldn't even get any references and what hope do you think I'd have of a decent artistic career without them?'

Martin whistled. 'But you have no final decision from the University?'

'As good as! I received a letter from the Rector's office telling me they will be recommending the withdrawal of my award to the next committee meeting, and if that goes through I'm sure they will recommend barring me from continuing.'

She wrapped her arms around her legs and squeezed hard. The position made her back twinge, but she was glad of the distraction. Martin appeared to be thinking hard and she left him to it. She'd given up thinking herself.

'I think you need Robert,' Martin said eventually.

'Robert?'

'Yes, my relative Robert Garriga. You know who I mean, Laure! He's a lawyer in Paris, but he's here right now on holiday, visiting his sister in Céret.'

Laure pulled her thoughts together. Yes, she knew who he was talking about – or she kind of did. The Garrigas were old village people, weren't they? The family had left the village, but the sister and brother still visited from time to time, and they were great friends with *Tonton* Philippe and Martin. Weren't they half English? There had been some whispering among the young people in the village that they were illegitimate members of Martin and Daniel's family, but when Laure had mentioned the gossip to Sylvie she'd got a very frosty 'no' in reply.

Laure's family wasn't an old village family. They weren't even Catalan. Her father had come here after the war to work with his uncle. Laure herself had been born near Carcassonne, which village kids had always delighted in reminding her when she got too uppity. She didn't speak Catalan, or only snippets she'd picked up, and had accepted long ago there would be things in the village's history that she would never understand. She'd never cared – this coast was full of incomers and it was the village of today that she loved.

So Martin's family history hadn't been something she'd probe into. She remembered he'd been a couple of times to England when they were teenagers, and they'd all been incredibly jealous. And he'd introduced some Spanish relatives who'd made a visit to the village a couple of summers ago. Spanish relatives were pretty common around here, with them being so close to the border, but London connections were seriously posh!

'I think I remember Robert,' she answered Martin. 'He's your relative, you say? Isn't he the one who lived in London, whom you went to visit?'

'To Oxford,' Martin corrected. 'He was a law student there, before going to Brussels to specialise in European law, and now he works for some big British company which has established its European headquarters in Paris.'

Laure's first reaction was profound surprise. She'd had no idea that Martin or Daniel had any such high-flying relatives. Was he born into that privileged world, this Robert, or had he, like Martin and her, pulled himself through the education system, holding his breath along the way? She was intrigued.

But she couldn't see how some fat cat English corporate lawyer was going to be able to help her in this present dilemma. She hadn't been prosecuted, after all, just charged and warned. Did Martin mean that Robert could use his influence for her? Well, that wouldn't work either. Laure could imagine the raised eyebrows at the Sorbonne at the very idea that the sordid, moneyed classes – no matter how well educated or well connected they were – could influence any decision they might take about an internal faculty matter.

Martin seemed to sense that Laure was less than enthused by his suggestion. He leaned forward on his elbow. 'I'm not saying that Robert can definitely do anything for you, Laure, but he could give you some advice.'

'Advice? What advice?'

'Well, there must be some loopholes in the case against you that could be exploited with the University authorities. They haven't taken a final, official decision yet, you said so.'

'Well, the only thing stopping them is that they're all on holiday,' she replied glumly. 'I was told the Committee will meet again at the end of August, not before. But the Rector and the Professor are both members, and the evidence against me is so strong that no one can deny I'm no longer a fit person to represent the University abroad, or indeed anywhere. Barring a miracle, I haven't a chance – although I have to admit I've tried to believe in miracles, this last while.'

'Aren't there some student voices on the Committee?'

'No chance! We're talking about a professional, academic group here! They make all their decisions in private.'

'But you would have the chance to make additional representations before the meeting?'

'In writing, yes, if I thought it would help in any way. But it won't, Martin! You don't understand, it just won't!'

Martin shook his head as though to clear it. 'Well, I don't know enough about these things to help you, Laure, but won't you please speak to Robert? He'll be here tomorrow for lunch. We could meet afterwards, for a coffee or something. Please, Laure! You have nothing to lose and he's the most discreet person I know – he won't betray you or anything. But he can look at the whole thing from a lawyer's point of view, and if anyone can find any way out of this it'll be him. Really, it will!'

Laure was hot and tired now and could feel the back of her neck burning. Good, she thought, relishing the idea of some trivial soreness to focus on, other than her stupid back injury or the nagging in her head.

'All right, if you insist,' she answered, getting to her feet. 'Come on, let's get out of this sun and see if there are any fish to be seen in the shade under the overhang.'

As they got up to leave, a fisherman appeared, carrying a parasol, a rod, a bucket and what looked like a full bottle of red wine. It made Laure laugh to think what he might be hoping to catch, if he was planning to drink the full bottle, but Martin went over to him and came back a couple of minutes later with a satisfied look on his face.

'It's old Pierre. He comes down every summer on holiday for the fishing. He's only bringing his stuff down just now, ready to fish later. He caught three fine sea bass last night, he tells me, and he's going to give me a couple for *Maman*.'

'Nice gift!' Laure commented.

'Indeed! But we'll pay him with a couple of drinks this evening. That's the advantage of having a café – there's a lot that people will trade with you for a couple of beers and a *plat du jour*!'

'Shame on you, doctor!'

'Yes, indeed, but fish is fish, you know. It'll be brain food for Robert tomorrow and get his lawyer's mind working.'

Laure was putting on her snorkel, preparing to dive into the pool under the overhang, where it was deepest. At Martin's words, she turned again and all her disquiet returned. He held out a hand in contrition.

'Sorry, Laure. Let's not talk about it anymore today. You're on holiday, and I'm sure there are seahorses down there waiting for us. Remember, for now, you're still a student at the Sorbonne! Don't go worrying all night, will you?'

'I don't worry all the time,' she admitted. 'It isn't worth it. I don't think there's anything I can do anyway, and I might well end up making my father a very happy man.'

Martin looked puzzled. Laure raised a comic eye.

'By coming home and becoming a village teacher!' she grinned and dived gracefully into the sea.

CHAPTER 9

When Laure turned up at the café after lunch the next day there was no sign of Martin. A young waitress she hadn't seen before told her that the family were still at lunch upstairs, and Laure considered coming back later, but then her old school friend the barman appeared and told her to go on up.

'Martin told me they were running late but you were to join them upstairs.'

'Are you sure?' Laure hesitated to intrude when she didn't even know the family's lunch guest. But she reluctantly complied when the barman insisted and made her way up the steep stairs, calling out as she went to let them know she was coming.

She found the four of them sitting around the lunch table, with newly filled coffee cups in front of them. A place had been set for her, with a coffee cup and a plate for dessert.

'I'd have told you to come for lunch if Martin had only said earlier that you were coming round!' Colette was indignant. 'What on earth was he doing not inviting you himself, I'd like to know?'

Laure shook her head and smiled. 'There wouldn't have been enough fish,' she said. 'Martin would have had to negotiate for the other one as well.'

She turned to where Martin was waiting to introduce her to their guest. She'd seen Robert Garriga before without ever being introduced, and she'd been aware of him as a rather debonair city dweller in expensive clothes, who was formal and conventional beyond his years, as would befit a lawyer, of course. He had surprisingly southern features for someone half English, and she remembered that his family had lived here in Vermeilla before. Looking at him now, close up, she was struck by his dark eyes, broad cheekbones and olive skin tone, which weren't that far from Martin's own, archetypal Catalan looks. They were both good-looking men and they could well be related, but if so, the link must be through Colette, since Martin's late father had been from the north of France. He had been lean and much fairer, more in the style of Daniel.

Robert held out his hand to her and she held out her own more diffidently than she liked, aware that nerves had dampened her palms. She might not believe this man could help her, but she couldn't help hoping he would, even if only a little. It was Martin's fault – he shouldn't be so damned positive. Had he spoken to this Robert yet, she wondered? If so, the man was giving nothing away.

'You're studying art at the Sorbonne, I hear,' he said to her and she nodded.

'Yes, I've just finished the fourth year of the five-year diploma at the *École des Beaux-Arts*,' she confirmed.

'Don't go expecting Laure to blow her own trumpet,' Philippe interjected, gesturing at her with the pipe he'd just lit. 'But she finished her first three years at Toulouse with the highest grades they'd had in many years, and was advised to take her studies forward to the Sorbonne, and this year she has won a very prestigious prize there. She just won't tell you, that's all.'

'And what movement are you involved in? Pop Art or Fluxus, or one of these trends? Or do you prefer to do your own thing?' Robert asked.

Of course, a member of the Parisian bourgeoisie would know the trends in art. He would attend all the exhibitions and follow the right artists' careers; it would go in hand with attending the opera and seeing the latest plays. It put Laure on the defensive – her Paris was so different from his. She answered noncommittally.

'Well, we can't ignore any one of the current movements, but in all honesty, I am a figurative painter, not an abstract artist.'

'No major influences?'

Laure felt her rebellious hackles rising. This felt like an inquisition and she suspected him of patronising her, but she decided to treat the question seriously.

'Everyone has influences,' she said crisply. 'A lot of mine are dead, but among contemporary painters, there are some working in your own country whom I follow.'

He looked a question.

'In England,' she specified. 'People like Francis Bacon and Frank Auerbach are doing work I find interesting.'

'Ah! I understand. The London School! And what about Lucian Freud? Do you like his work too?'

'I think you misunderstand, *Monsieur*. It's a bit different from just *liking* it.'

Why am I being obnoxious, she asked herself, and looked across at *Tonton* Philippe, who was sitting watching them. I am being aggressive to your guest, and I'm sorry. Philippe smiled at her as though she'd actually spoken out loud and she reached out a hand to him.

'It's Philippe who loves Freud, even more than me, I think,' she said, much more mildly this time. She grinned at Philippe. 'I swear it's all that flesh that grabs him!'

She took a sip of the excellent coffee. Colette had brought out the best coffee cups, she noticed, and her embroidered tablecloth, and was sitting back in her chair, a little withdrawn from the family which she normally managed with consummate matriarchal care. She looked composed, but not one hundred percent relaxed. All this for a man who was younger than Daniel.

Philippe was drawing Robert's attention to a portrait of Colette which hung on the wall behind him. It was one of Laure's, but done some years ago, when her work was still conventional enough to win even her own father's approval. She'd moved on since then and had more things to explore, but she still liked the picture she'd painted of Colette standing next to the downstairs bar, with a lovely old mirror behind her. It reflected the shape of her back and the neat, grey-brown bob of her hair, and some of the tables

79

of customers around her. But Colette stood very much on her own, and in charge, with her arm resting on the dark wood of the bar. Her face, worn but still handsome after a life that was often not easy, had been softened in the café's dimmed lights, and she looked, if not confident, at least serene.

Philippe always said that Laure had captured Colette's essential gravity and stillness, which seemed strange to say of a woman who moved all the time, but Laure knew what he meant and was proud of his evaluation.

Robert seemed to agree. 'Why, that is yours?' he asked, with new respect in his voice. 'I've studied and admired it for the last few years, without ever knowing who had painted it. *Félicitations, mademoiselle*, that's a really good portrait.'

Laure squirmed as always when faced with flattery. 'It's an old piece,' she muttered, 'And Colette made a very good subject. I'm not sure you'd like the stuff I'm doing now.'

'And were you part of the *Atelier Populaire*?' Robert asked, sounding genuinely curious. So Martin hadn't yet told him anything about her problem. She was relieved. She hated the idea of them talking through her situation behind her back.

It was Martin who answered. 'She was on the organising committee,' he said, with almost brotherly pride. It made Laure laugh.

'So, between the events in Paris and my portrait of Colette,' she put in, 'we have established my credentials as an art student, and talked about it for far too long! Shall we talk about Martin's brilliant exam results now, or your own illustrious career, *Monsieur* Garriga? Or about this excellent coffee, perhaps, since seriously the coffee in this establishment gets better and better each year! Do you have a new supplier, Colette?'

She'd found the right tone to take the heat off herself, but it wouldn't be for long if she was really going to confide her problems to this rather daunting young man. After her offer to help clear the table had been rejected by an indignant Colette, the young people were dismissed. Philippe was in the little kitchen, pottering around amongst the dishes, but Laure knew he would soon retire to the sofa for his afternoon siesta in front of one of Vermeilla's few televisions, bought for his indulgence. His pipe already sat on the little coffee table, with his tobacco pouch and lighter placed neatly next to it by Colette in readiness. Colette would do anything to take care of Philippe. She'd told Laure once that when he'd finally moved out of friendship and into her home, well past their middle years, he had completed her life and made growing older seem like a blessing, rather than a loss.

It was funny to see Robert being dismissed with herself and Martin. He must only be a few years older than them, but he was a different creature from Martin in his old, comfortable trousers and loose shirt. In contrast, Robert was dressed in slim-fitting trousers and a tailored shirt that had come straight from London or Paris, and he was wearing a discreet tie.

He had an appropriate effect on the young waitress downstairs, who was making her way to the kitchen when they emerged from the stairs. She waved briefly to Martin when she saw him, but when Robert appeared she stepped back hurriedly with an apology, and effaced herself against the wall to let him go by. Martin put a hand on her arm to stop her, and turned to introduce her to Laure and Robert.

'Hey Isabelle,' he said, in his usual cheerful way. 'Have you met Laure, from the village here? You won't know Robert Garriga, our grand visitor from Paris, but he doesn't matter anyway because he'll soon be leaving! But you should know Laure! Laure, this is Isabelle Bariol, who lives out at Paulilles, and her father works with Daniel – or rather he's Daniel's supervisor, I should say. So he's an important man in our lives now! Isabelle has just finished school and she is going to trek all the way here every day by train to help us out for the summer, or for as long as she can cope with us anyway.'

Isabelle smiled shyly at Laure, her eyes flickering over Laure's cropped hair and then to the sleeveless minidress that Laure had put on defiantly when she saw the baking sun this morning. *Touché*, thought Laure – I've been assessing our young lawyer's Paris clothes and yet I don't exactly look the village part here either. She reached out a hand to Isabelle.

'Great to meet you, Isabelle. Have you just done your Baccalaureat?'

'Yes, we just got the results.'

'She got top marks, didn't you Isabelle?' Martin interjected.

Isabelle blushed. 'I did well, yes, thank you! But I was lucky. They say the marking was made lenient this year because the schools had been closed for so long during the strikes.'

'And what do you want to do now? Have you plans or are you happy just taking some time out and running around after this lot?' Laure gave Isabelle a smile and gestured to the café around them.

'Oh, I don't know.' Isabelle raised helpless hands. 'My father wants me to work at Paulilles, and says I could get a well-paid job in the administration, but I'm not sure – I'd kind of like to carry on studying, if I can. I've always wanted to study Law. But that's a big step for my family. We'll have to see.'

'And you actually live at Paulilles?' It was Robert who asked the question, and Isabelle looked nervously up at him before answering.

'Yes, there's a worker's village there. I've lived there all my life.'

'I've heard of it,' Robert sounded really interested. 'Isn't it some kind of model village, created for the employees of the factory, with free electricity, medical care and a school and things?'

Isabelle nodded. 'Yes, *Monsieur*, that's right. We're very lucky.'

At that moment a customer called her and she looked relieved. No one likes an inquisition, Laure thought, whether from Robert or from me!'

'Do excuse me, won't you?' Isabelle said, picking up the tray she had been carrying. But before she left, she turned and smiled at Laure. 'I think you're Daniel's sister-in-law, aren't you?'

Laure nodded. 'Yes, and I'm around for the rest of the summer. So we must talk properly sometime and you must come and visit my sister and the baby.'

'I'd like that,' Isabelle said, and then she was gone, whisking herself off to the customer's table.

Chapter 10

'What a great addition that girl is to the café!' Laure remarked, as they made their way out into the afternoon sun. 'She seems really nice, and bright too.' She was amused to see Martin blush slightly. She's really pretty too, Laure thought, with those golden curls, but she kept that to herself.

'I'm interested in that place Paulilles,' Robert said to Martin. 'A factory built to make explosives for war, paying danger wages. But it poses as the model employer too, with social benefits that most people in France couldn't hope for, even extending to the families.'

Martin nodded. 'Daniel would love a house out at their village, but I gather there's a huge waiting list. You have to prove you're a key worker, needed at night and such. But families like Isabelle's have been there forever and are sitting pretty.'

'It would be interesting to see it,' Robert said thoughtfully. 'It's good though that you've been able to give work to Daniel's boss's daughter. It may help him as he starts out there.' He pulled off his tie as he spoke. 'Now, shall we who don't have to work today go for a walk?'

They headed off by one accord to walk along the coastal path. Out in the open, with his tie off and his sleeves rolled up, Robert looked less daunting and younger. The path bordered the beach at first, heading south-west into the sun, and then started to climb up to the rougher cliff walk. Laure was grateful for the flat pumps she'd put on that morning, knowing where they would probably end up going. They passed the steep path that led down to the fishing rocks from, which she and Martin had snorkelled yesterday, and continued towards Collioure.

The only break in the blue sky was the white trace of a plane, heading down the coast towards Spain, taking tourists to the Costa Brava, perhaps. That was where the foreign sunseekers all went on holiday, to Franco's new beach complexes. Here, in this little corner of France, only their own compatriots ventured – those who couldn't afford the Riviera for their holidays!

The breeze was stronger today, flecking the sea white below them. It saved them from expiring with the heat, for they'd chosen a walk with no shade. Laure picked a stem of wild fennel and rolled it between her fingers, holding it up to her nose to breathe in the aniseed scent. She was happy to walk and listen to the guys talking about football, and forget what she was here to do – talk to Robert about her troubles.

After half an hour of solid walking, they were very hot and glad to stop where the cliff path wove down to a small bay with its own beach. There was one family at the other end of the beach but no one else in sight, and Robert and Martin immediately rolled up their trousers and waded as far out as they could into the waves. Laure was at an advantage in her miniskirt. She threw off her pumps and stepped out into the water until she found the sand beyond the shingle. It was shallow, and she walked quite a long way out, splashing her arms in the water and bending to rinse the sweat from her face. Back on the beach, in her little shoulder bag, she had nothing but a handkerchief with which to dry herself, but the sun would dry her fast enough.

When she came ashore Martin offered her water from his flask and she drank thirstily. The two men had thrown themselves down onto the pebbles but Laure stood for a moment, watching a huge yacht passing by under full sail, taking advantage of what looked like a lovely fresh breeze. The yacht seemed too big for most of the harbours around here, and far too adventurous.

'Look at that,' she said, waving towards the yacht. 'What an amazing boat! Where do you think she's heading?'

'Sètes, perhaps?' Robert ventured, naming a port along the coast.

'No, no!' Laure retorted, 'Not Sètes. A yacht like that can't be heading for somewhere as boring as Sètes! I believe it's got Brigitte Bardot on board, and it's heading at least for Corsica, or even Italy!'

'Dreamer!' Martin said. 'I happen to know that she's been tied up in Port-Vendres for the last few weeks, having some work done on her. The word is she belongs to some industrialist from Paris.'

Laure sat down with a bump on the shingle and exhaled sadly. 'Damn Paris,' she said, handing Martin back his flask. He grinned sympathetically at her as he took it from her hand.

'Well, that's what we came here to talk about, after all. Paris.'

'Yes.' Laure looked over at Robert. He didn't look too scary, sitting in his shirt sleeves, without his shoes and socks. Right now, he just looked puzzled.

'Laure needs some help,' Martin explained to him. 'She told me a story yesterday, which I think she should tell you too. I think she needs a lawyer.'

Robert looked at Laure and said nothing, but he seemed to be inviting her to speak. Her throat felt tight. Forget that he's a lawyer, she thought, but then if he wasn't a lawyer, she wouldn't be about to tell him her story.

In the end, Laure just told him exactly what she'd told Martin yesterday, word for word. Martin sat back and let her talk, and Robert gave her his full attention, not speaking until she reached the end.

And then he asked just two questions. Did the police take her fingerprints? And did they take formal statements from all of the students who had come to back-up her story? The answer to both questions was yes.

'They told me they'd found my fingerprints on every bottle,' she said. 'And as for the students' testimonies, from what Pierre and Lolo told me afterwards, the police gave the impression that they would have expected nothing less than that we would all back each other up.'

'But their statements were presumably made before you saw them, while you were still in custody? Could they have known what your story was before they told their own versions?'

'You mean, if I was inventing something?'

Robert nodded.

'Well, I didn't see anyone I knew the whole time I was being held by the police but when I was allowed to notify the Students' Union, I got to speak briefly to a legal adviser there, and I told him what I'd actually been doing.'

'In full detail? I mean did you tell him everything, starting from that morning's meeting to how you went about removing the weapons?'

He was at it again with his inquisitions, but this time Laure thought his questions made sense.

'No, I just told the guy that the committee had agreed we needed to get the weapons out of the building, and I was the one who did it while the others had a group meeting outside.' She looked long at Robert. 'I know what you are suggesting, and it's something I hadn't thought of. You mean that if the others' statements were fuller than what I told the Union's legal adviser, then they are their own accounts, not some primed story, and must be genuine.'

'Not one hundred percent, no. You could all have concocted a story together ahead of time, but it does add weight to your version of events. A lot depends on how much detail your friends gave in their statements. Do you know?' Laure shook her head.

'Then, I think we need to ask them.'

Laure rolled a pebble from one hand to another. Could she contact the guys and find out exactly what they'd said? Everyone had left Paris now for the summer and she didn't have anyone's home address apart from Lolo, at his wine chateau near Saint-Emilion, and she was shy of using that one, for many reasons. But she would write to him if she needed to – he would want to help her, after all. And there was Jérôme still in Paris – he was one of the outside artists who'd joined the students in the *Atelier*. She didn't have any address for him, but he had told her that he had some paintings exhibited in a gallery in Belleville, and she knew the name of the gallery. That was a start, surely?

And the last of her witnesses was Pierre – she knew that his family lived near Lyon and his father was a doctor, a heart specialist at some big hospital. Between them maybe they could track him down – there couldn't be too many Dr Roussets in Lyon.

She told Robert and Martin, and saw Martin's eyes light up. He'd sat quietly throughout her retelling of the story and Robert's questioning, but now he became quite animated.

'Hey, this calls for detective work! Robert can find the gallery in Paris and I'll find the doctor – I can consult our records at the hospital in Perpignan!'

Robert smiled. 'Martin is his usual enthusiastic self, but he's not actually wrong in this case. We'll do both of those things, but I'd also like to take a more legal, boring approach to the problem as well, with your permission. Please bear in mind that I don't have any authority to act for you here in France, and all I am bringing to this is perhaps a bit of legal thinking. I would like to appoint a solicitor friend of mine who does have the authority to act and can ask for access to police files. There are three lines I think we should be following. One, we should ask to see the full statements both of yourself and of the other witnesses, of course, and two, we should ask for details about what fingerprints were found on the weapons you touched. Three, I would like you to write down as many names as you can of the troublemakers you suspect brought the weapons into the *atelier* in the first place.'

'But there is no evidence against them! The police didn't actually come to close the *atelier* that day, it was finally closed on the 29th, four days later. I have no idea whether those same anarchists were still there by then, as I wasn't there myself at the end. I didn't dare go back near the place – but I still saw the other students a couple of times.'

Robert nodded. 'Understood, but what I'd like to take up with the police is that they didn't pursue any enquiries regarding anyone else in the *atelier*, and just took the least line of resistance and assumed your guilt. If there wasn't anyone in authority giving orders to empty the *atelier* that day, then the donkeys who arrested you wouldn't have thought to suggest it. Had they done so, they could have fingerprinted everyone else. It's just a point to make to them, but any point we can contest, we will.'

Laure looked at him with respect. He was intelligent and had bothered to listen and take her problem seriously, and his slight formality had actually made things easier and helped her to think objectively.

'What do you hope to achieve?' she asked him. 'We can't prove my innocence.'

'We don't have to, *Mademoiselle* Forestier. What I want is just for the case to be sufficiently undermined, so that the charges are dropped and expunged from the records, and then we can address the issue of the University's decision against you.'

Laure thought of Professor Duchamp and grimaced. 'That professor has it in for me, so much so he's unlikely to back down,' she sighed.

'Yes, but he can't maintain a case against you if the police find you have no case to answer.'

'I was one of the occupying student body there, in the *atelier*. Nobody else got picked out and the University kept their distance deliberately, but now that I've been thrust under their noses, the committee might well decide that even without police charges, I'm enough of a troublemaker to be unfit for the prize and for further study in their august institution. Don't you think so?'

'Not if we present your actions in the favourable light they should be seen in.' Robert smiled again, and this time seemed to be really amused. 'I've heard that even the *Prefet de Police* in Paris spoke warmly of how the student organisers at the main Sorbonne building tried to keep control of the extremists and protect property, and I'm sure we can get someone like him to say something similar about your actions at the art school.'

'You think so? How?' Laure couldn't imagine anything of the sort.

'Well, *Mademoiselle*, you'll already have gathered that I'm a member of the nasty Paris bourgeoisie! Thankfully, I have here to run to when I want to remember the other sides of my personality,' he said, gesturing to the sea and the beach, 'but when in Paris I do know quite a lot of people you would no doubt seriously dislike! I'm sure we can find someone of influence among them to praise your actions on paper, and then let's see what your committee make of it!'

Phew! It was a lot to take in. Would the committee consider such representations, given how inward-looking they were? It wasn't at all sure, but suddenly it didn't seem as though her case was quite so desperate after all. Martin was grinning like a Cheshire cat and whooped at Robert.

'I knew you'd do it!'

'I haven't done anything yet, Martin,' was all Robert answered. Laure pulled herself together and asked the question which was burning in her mind.

'Why should you go to so much trouble?' she said. 'I don't mean I won't be grateful, but all I was hoping for was some advice.'

'Let's just say it's so that I can stay in touch with the better side of my personality!' he smiled. 'Now, let's make some immediate plans. Can you write down for me as much of that day as you can remember, leaving out no details, however trivial they may seem, and also list all the names you can remember of everyone who was there? And would you object to me taking your fingerprints?'

Laure shook her head. 'Not at all!'

'Right,' he continued, 'Then I'll need to find the necessary equipment, and we'll need to meet somewhere where we won't have the whole of Vermeilla village wondering what on earth we're up to. Can you come to Céret?'

Laure nodded. 'I'm sure I can borrow the van.'

'Good, well tomorrow's Friday and the beginning of the holiday weekend, and my sister has all kinds of things planned for me, I think. Why don't you take the weekend to think about this and make your notes, and then we'll meet on Monday at my sister's house. Come in the afternoon because the children are going off to some summer camp, and we'll have the house to ourselves. Can you be there by around two thirty?'

Laure nodded and they both rose to their feet. Robert wiped the sand from his hand and reached out to shake hers.

'*Mademoiselle* Forestier,' he said very seriously. 'I wouldn't say you've got yourself a lawyer because I'm not a proper French solicitor, but I promise I will help you if I can. Let's just call me your legal adviser. The big people in this world always have one, and I don't see why you shouldn't have one too!'

CHAPTER 11

The national Bastille Day holiday on 14th July would be an opportunity for the French establishment to reassert its authority over France. The usual military parades would be held with an extra flourish this year and de Gaulle would hold himself even firmer, even straighter, as he stood to inspect them on the Champs Elysées in Paris. The fourth of July had seen fresh demonstrations in America against the war in Vietnam, but here in France all popular protest was over, and Laure was glad that they had no television at home, for there would be nothing happening that she wanted to watch.

This year, 14th July fell on a Sunday – a disappointment to many because it meant they wouldn't get an extra day off, but for the workers at Paulilles, Laure learned it was good news. It was difficult to close down the factory for a day during the week, but with it being a Sunday, the management had agreed to fund a beach party.

Isabelle was ecstatic. 'Colette has agreed to give me Sunday off,' she told Laure, 'even though it's such a busy weekend. I think she realises that we don't have such big parties at Paulilles every day. And families are invited too, of course. Daniel will be bringing his family and I wondered whether you and Martin would like to come too? You're both part of Daniel's family, after all.'

It came as no surprise to learn that Martin had already accepted the invitation, braving his mother's potential disappointment at him not being home for the Bastille Day lunch. But already Daniel wouldn't be there, and anyway Sunday would be really busy in the café, so it was just as well – that was his argument!

Colette took it with good humour. 'You'll all just come and eat on Saturday evening, instead,' she decided. 'Both families, since Sylvie and Laure won't be at home on Sunday either. Laure, you'll invite your parents for me? We'll eat downstairs in the restaurant, so we have enough space for everyone, and come early, since your Papa still has to be up early to bake his bread on Sunday, holiday or no holiday.'

It always amused Laure when she came home how much life revolved around food. As a student, she often forgot to eat, but she would finish this summer a good deal less skinny than she had started it! It would set her up nicely for University again, if Robert was successful in getting her back in. The whole problem still caused a tight constriction in her chest when she thought about it, but she focused her mind on action and spent Friday making her notes and trying to compose a letter to Lolo.

Why should it be so difficult? Lolo had not been her regular boyfriend, but there had been a complicity between them that quickened her pulse whenever she remembered it, and this had grown during May, fired by the excitement and intensity of events. They'd had one or two special nights and she'd always assumed they would be properly together once the occupation was over. During the occupation, Lolo was always busy. He was their leader, among the senior students; the endless ball of energy who drove their designs and could always think of some new twist or challenge to keep the momentum of the *atelier populaire*. No one was more provocative or more original, but it was rarely he who actually produced their work. He would set his bees busy working and then find his place outside, sitting on the wall, waving his endless little roll ups and expounding the philosophy of revolution to the groups of students who surrounded him. Jean-Louis Lavignière, otherwise known as Lolo.

There were all sorts who followed him, from the most conventional students to the hippies, but Lolo wasn't a hippy, in spite of his mophead of hair. And nor did he seem in any way pretentious. He was puck-like, mobile and deft in all he did, with keen blue eyes and a goatee beard. He would curl his long thin legs underneath him on the wall and call people in towards him with a little tantalising, self-deprecating grin, while shrugging off the green velvet jacket that accentuated his elfin look.

Males and females alike enjoyed his company, but it was the girls of the *École des Beaux-Arts* who formed his most loyal coterie. He smiled and caressed, blowing hot and then cold, for he loved to be loved. But it was with Laure he spent those private moments they could steal from the struggle.

Laure pulled herself out of her reverie, and decided to leave writing to Lolo until Robert told her it was time. She had to stop thinking about Lolo. His family of vineyard owners had many centuries of old money behind them, and as much as Lolo was playing with proletariat ideals at the moment, it was obvious that one day he would return to the fold and put his brains to marketing his family's endless cellars. Even his studies were just a game to him – one he excelled at, but a game, nevertheless.

Well, they're not a game to me, thought Laure, and focused on making her list of names. By Saturday morning she had finished writing her notes, as complete as Robert had asked for. And now, let's live in Vermeilla, she told herself, looking out of her bedroom window at the blue sky above. Enough of these solitary activities that make you think too hard. She put the notes into her briefcase and shoved it firmly under her bed, and spent the rest of the day helping her mother in the bakery, gossiping with the customers and laying out the most tempting pastries to attract the weekend's tourists into the shop.

And in the evening they ate at the Café de Catalogne, which was busy with families looking for good, simple *brasserie* food, while their children ran loose around the tables. Papa and Philippe had spent the hour before dinner playing *pétanque*, and Papa was on great form. On the one or two occasions each week Papa managed to play, he was acknowledged as the village champion, a master of quiet finesse. Today, he had trounced Philippe and two of their friends in a battle that had left him sweetly magnanimous, underscoring his victory more by what he didn't say, than what he did.

He drank little as a rule, but on this rare evening out he was in festive mood and allowed Daniel to refill his glass several times. Daniel winked at Laure after the fourth refill and she grinned, filling her own glass at the same time. Papa might regret this at two o'clock in the morning!

Isabelle was there at the beginning of the evening but went off duty at seven o'clock, running for her train. She paused to say goodbye as she was leaving the restaurant. 'It'll be good to see you tomorrow,' she said to Sylvie. 'We're all looking forward to getting to know Daniel's family.' She smiled at little Julien, wide-eyed and on his best manners in the bustle of the café. 'We should even have some little ones for this young man to play with,' she said. 'There are always lots of children around when we have a picnic.'

'We can take your bucket and spade along, eh Julien?' Sylvie said, taking the fifth piece of bread out of his hands. 'And meanwhile, we'll keep some space for the *blanquette de veau*, shall we?'

'And for Colette's famous custard flan, remember!' Laure grinned at him. 'Hey, Sylvie, we'll need to think about what food we're taking along with us tomorrow.'

'Do we ever think about anything else?' Sylvie asked. 'And I'm ahead of you on this one, remember? Daniel was invited earlier this week, and I've already got a terrine pressing at home.'

'You don't need to bring anything,' Isabelle assured them. 'The factory has given us funds to cover the food.'

'Yes, but we'd like to contribute, and anyway, the funds are meant for the employees' food, not for remote family members like me. And I have Papa's bakery at my disposal. Don't say you don't want one of his prized tarts – he'll take grave offence!'

Papa didn't look as though he would take offence at anything at the moment, but Isabelle grinned.

'I'm sure we'd love to have something from your bakery,' she said. 'See you all tomorrow then – I must dash or I'll miss my train.' She turned to leave, and as she did so, bumped into Martin.

'You're running late,' he said to her. 'I've got my moped outside. If you're happy to hop on, I'll give you a ride to the station.'

Isabelle looked a little self-conscious and grabbed her bag quickly. 'Okay, thank you,' she said, flushing very slightly, and they left the café together. Sylvie looked quizzically across at Laure, but Laure just raised one eye back at her. Speculate, dear sister, she thought, you go ahead and speculate! And as the waiter appeared bearing dishes, she turned her attention to the *blanquette de veau*.

She dreamed of the *atelier* that night in the twisted way that dreams have of starting out quite normal, before taking you and all the protagonists off at weird tangents, until it becomes just too disturbing and the extremes of unreality nag you out of sleep. She was sitting in the sun with Lolo, laughing, with all their friends around them and their latest set of posters drying on the line. Then, suddenly, the clenched fists on the posters changed shape, so that they were holding

Molotov cocktails and no one seemed to think it wrong. They were all still laughing, but she couldn't understand why, and the committee had changed into a bunch of young thugs that had her penned into a corner. She woke in a sweat, well before dawn, and Lolo's face was before her, with the eyes of the professor.

Not a breath of wind came in through her open window, and it was hot and stuffy in her room below the eaves. She threw off the tangle of sheets and lay as still as possible, blanking out the dream from her mind, and trying to feel any touch of air from outside. She didn't want to sleep again because the dream's images were too vivid in her head and could so easily return, but she eventually dozed off, and when she woke it was daytime.

It was Sunday and Vermeilla was eerily quiet. Papa would be working two floors down, but all Laure could hear from the roof were the swallows squabbling in the plane trees around the corner in the main street. She liked to think she could hear the sea as well, but on a calm day like this, it was impossible.

It was breakfast time. A day out awaited and there were things to prepare. Laure got up and dressed with the shutters open to the sky. It was cloudless again and she hoped that a breeze might pick up during the day to cool them down. For such a windy coastline, Vermeilla had been unnaturally calm these last few days.

She went downstairs to coax some tarts out of Papa. *Maman* was serving, as usual. 'I'll come and work again this week,' Laure said remorsefully. 'I feel bad that it's a holiday today and you have to work on your own. I'll definitely work tomorrow and perhaps you can take some time off.'

Then she remembered that tomorrow she was to go to Céret. 'Actually,' she asked, 'Could I help tomorrow morning, and then could I borrow the van in the afternoon? Martin wants me to meet some friends of his in Céret.'

Maman shrugged. 'I don't see why not. You've only just come home, and it's natural that you should want to see your friends. We'll be glad of your help when you're ready, but don't stress yourself. We manage fine for the rest of the year.'

'Yes, but it's busy.'

'It'll be super busy in August. We'll get you working then, don't worry!'

Maman gave her the fruit tarts. 'Don't bother going back there to see Papa,' she advised her, gesturing to the dark cavern of the bakery through the door behind them. 'He's not feeling one hundred percent himself today! But he did remember your tarts and made some extra. And there's fresh-made lemonade upstairs, too, and some goat's cheese, if you want to take it.'

Laure accepted the lemonade – the weather was hot and *Maman*'s homemade lemonade was famous – but she turned down the cheese because she could imagine the offerings that Martin and Daniel and Sylvie were likely to pitch up with. They could end up providing enough food for the whole Paulilles workforce.

As she packed the lemonade into her big cloth bag and carefully positioned the tarts on top, Laure was conscious of a feeling of well-being which made this morning's bad dream seem many light years away. She was at home among friends after all and on holiday, and the professor hadn't got her yet.

And the sun was shining and she'd never been to Paulilles, except to pass by it on the road or on the train, so today was an adventure. She picked up the bag, grabbed her sunglasses and headed out to meet Daniel, Sylvie and Martin.

Chapter 12

They had their own station at Paulilles, but the train only stopped there on request. The train journey from Vermeilla took them through Collioure and on through Port-Vendres, following the coast. For a while, they ran by the sea and then through a tunnel that had been cut through the rocks, and then out into the valley, where the vineyards clung to all the slopes around them, their vines heavy with grapes. It being Sunday, many of the *vignerons* were out working in their fields, weeding and checking for pests. Vineyards were so often small, part-time undertakings here, for men with other jobs during the week.

Daniel had his own small vineyard once, Laure remembered, but he'd given it up when he went to sea. Did he miss it? He would struggle to find any time for it now, even on a part-time scale. And this year, when others were busy grape-picking in September, Sylvie would just have had their second child. Daniel was going to be busy!

For today, though, he was on holiday and he held little Julien on his lap during the short journey, counting out for him the number of boats they saw, and then the three donkeys who were resting in a field by the vines. It was his Uncle Martin who made the little boy giggle though, every time they entered a tunnel, by putting his hands over his ears and rolling his eyes at the screech of the train's whistle. There was no holding back Martin's exuberance today. He had kept them laughing ever since they met at the café, with his own particular style of nonsense which Laure remembered so well from their childhood. He could be almost intensely serious and also be very silly, but today he was no older than Julien.

The railway journey only took a short while, not long enough for Julien. When the train came to a stop at Paulilles, he planted his foot and refused to move, his bottom lip trembling. Sylvie had to show him his bucket and spade to stop his impending tears, and it was Martin who eventually lifted him down onto the platform, swinging him in the air as he did so and making him laugh in spite of himself.

They even looked like a bunch of holidaymakers, Laure thought, as they manhandled their baskets of food, beach blankets, toys and spare child's clothing from the train. Thankfully, they weren't the only people so loaded down, as a group of people had boarded the train at Port-Vendres with bags of beach gear, and it seemed they were also here for the picnic. Daniel stood by the train to take first the wicker baskets from Sylvie and then Laure's own big cloth bag. He then helped Sylvie down with a very tender solicitude, turning afterwards to offer his hand to Laure. But Laure was catching Martin's impish mood and just grinned at Daniel as she jumped down onto the platform unaided, looking around her with frank curiosity.

It was just a bare platform where they had been set down, more a halt than a station, with sidings where a pulley system was in place, presumably to lift goods from the wagons of freight trains. All the raw materials for making explosives must be delivered here.

Directly behind them were what were known as the Paulilles 'barracks', a network of white painted buildings that housed the most privileged factory employees. They were actually good sized houses, built in terraces between the railway line and the road, strung out in an irregular line. Away to the right were some other buildings that might perhaps include the school. All around the houses were little gardens, with fig trees and olive trees providing shade, and what looked like well-ordered vegetable patches in every corner. The houses were simple, but there was something gentle about this little hamlet, something that was sympathetic with nature and the vineyards, which stretched up into the hills behind them.

Across the road though, was the factory. Laure had seen it throughout her life, but now she looked at it with new eyes. Two huge chimneys grazed the sky and around them were long, hangar-like structures. Nearest to the road there stood what looked like administration buildings and a number of rough looking sheds, possibly storerooms. Further away to the right was another network of buildings set apart, on a hill overlooking the sea. Laure had heard tell of that area, known rather extravagantly as the 'mountain', and knew it was where the really dangerous, toxic production took place. That was why it had been built away from the rest.

The whole complex was walled in, surrounded by fences that kept it away from the world and hidden from public gaze. It stood as a strange background to the houses right in front of her, but it was even stranger that such a factory sat in a natural beauty spot with the piercing blue of the Mediterranean right behind it.

Just recently, during the month of May, Laure had gone to help distribute leaflets outside the occupied Renault factory in Paris. The gates there had been locked too and the whole place had a dehumanised air, intensely automated inside, graffitied brick, metal and concrete outside. It had struck Laure as incongruous that one of the largest factories in France should have been built on an island on the River Seine. It occupied the whole island and was like a town in itself, except she hadn't seen a woman or a child, or any sign of anything personal or remotely sympathetic during the whole time she'd been there.

This factory at Paulilles seemed equally incongruous. But people had to work. She knew that's what Daniel would tell her, if she were to say anything. And Paulilles didn't dehumanise, did it? It had this close community, who grew vegetables and loved being here. And if it looked so discordant to her, wasn't she guilty of a kind of aesthetic narrow-mindedness particular to artists?

One day, the Nobel factory would be gone, but the bay and the vineyards would remain. The bay was more powerful and infinite than the factory could ever be. And meanwhile, here was Isabelle coming to meet them, happy and at ease.

She took Julien from Martin in a laughing, maternal gesture, looking far beyond her nineteen years, and held him up so that he could touch the still unripened figs in a tree.

She was followed by two little boys of around eight or nine-year-old twins, identically dressed in blue shorts, who pushed each other and giggled rather shyly in the face of the strangers invading their home.

'Now be quiet you boys,' Isabelle said over her shoulder. 'Off you go and call Jean-Claude or Laurent to come and help carry the bags.'

The boys obeyed her without question and disappeared up the earth path. Isabelle moved forward to greet the visitors, handing Julien back to Martin, so that she could shake everyone's hand. Her tone was welcoming and only a touch shy.

'It's lovely to see you here! Welcome to our little community. If you hold on just a minute, one of my brothers will come and help with your bags. You seem to have brought enough food for the whole party.' And even as she spoke a young man, who was perhaps a couple of years younger than Laure, came walking towards them with the twin boys shadowing him. He was the image of Isabelle, small and compact, with the same gentle face, amber eyes and hair.

'This is Laurent, my older brother,' Isabelle explained, rather unnecessarily.

'And the little ones are also your brothers?' Sylvie asked with a smile, and Isabelle nodded.

'We're a big family – seven of us,' she said, 'and I'm the only girl, would you believe! There's Laurent, then me, and then five more, finishing with the twins. Laurent works at Paulilles too – it's a family affair!'

Laurent shook hands all round and then picked up two of the heaviest bags and led the way down the path. They stopped briefly outside one of the terraced houses to greet Isabelle's mother, who was standing in the shade of a tree waiting for them. She was a woman of around forty, pretty and rather plump, with the same golden colouring of her children, dressed in a serviceable, sensible dress, and with her curls pulled tight into a simple bun. She spoke in the same easy, pleasant way Isabelle did but was more matter of fact, with less laughter in her voice. Laure was to learn that all of Isabelle's family shared her unselfconscious, mild nature, like people whom life had cocooned, islanded in a placid place of sunshine and order, where everything was known and few things changed.

Madame Bariol greeted them with old-fashioned courtesy and had a piece of candy in her pocket for Julien. Behind her, in the yard by the house, some men and the teenage Bariol boys were man-handling half of a metal drum on legs, which was clearly going to serve as a barbecue. And by Isabelle's mother's feet was a large net of snails. So they were going to have a *cargolade*! Now there was something you didn't get in Paris! Laure just loved the Catalan method of grilling snails over wood ash, and then picking them out of their shells and dipping them in garlic mayonnaise. It was the ultimate act of sharing, a festive diving in, where people would boast of how many they could eat in a sitting.

Her own enthusiasm was nothing compared with Martin's and Daniel's though. The two were in the yard helping the men in seconds, and as other men appeared from another path carrying folded tables, and bundles of wood, men and young boys merged in procession towards the beach, jocular and ribald, turning left along the road to skirt around the factory boundary in a river of noise.

The women followed in a more leisurely fashion with the snails and baskets, Julien trotting behind them holding onto his mother's skirt. Other women appeared with more children and there were greetings and laughter, and some unflattering comments about the men in front of them.

On the beach some children were already in the water, playing with old inner tyres in which they floated like little coracles. The factory was to their right behind them and Isabelle explained that the children could swim here, where they were picnicking, but not further up the beach, where toxic spills had soiled the sands. It was a strange kind of idyll, Laure thought.

Then, she went to help prepare the snails and sat next to two young women with hands stained deep orange. It was from filling the dynamite cylinders, they told her, which they did by hand – the powder, which they called the '*matière*', stained the fingers they used to tampon it down into the cylinders, and had eaten badly away at the skin around their nails. It chilled her to see it and yet they laughed – they had jobs and decent salaries, and were better off than many, or so everyone said. Laure wondered.

'Tell me, do they really pay you danger money to work here?' she asked, hoping not to give offence.

'Not a bit of it! That was in the old days. For years now, they've frozen our wages, saying our pay is too far above the average for around here. And now that the government has given all those big pay rises all over the country, we don't look so hot down here after all.'

'You want to go back to gutting fish, Jeanne?' the other young woman was dismissive. 'We do all right!'

Isabelle had come beside them while they were talking, with a heavy-set man by her side, who the young factory woman turned to. 'Don't you agree, Monsieur Bariol? We're better off here than in most places, that's what I say.'

So, the man with Isabelle was her father. Laure studied him with interest. This was Daniel's supervisor, after all. He was compact, like his son, with massive shoulders, a very Catalan square head and unusual, very steady grey eyes. He would only be in his early forties, perhaps, but he looked older, comfortable and middle-aged. Laure thought he was someone you would respect, who would only speak of what he knew, but who had experienced enough here at Paulilles to be able to speak with authority.

He had an easy smile for the two women. 'You girls don't do badly,' he agreed. 'A fair day's wage for a fair day's work, when you're not too busy making fools of yourselves over my boys in maintenance. I've never thought you needed danger money myself – it's the rest of us they ought to be paying!'

He turned to Martin, who was hovering close to Isabelle. 'What do you think, young doctor? Do you think these girls' yellow hands should earn them danger money?"

Martin blushed. 'I'm not a doctor yet, Monsieur Bariol, and I don't know much about what happens here at your plant either. I have heard some things about the effects of the nitro-glycerine here on employees, though. Is that related?'

Bariol gave him a quizzical look. 'You've heard about that, have you? I didn't know that anyone outside of Paulilles was talking about our little issues.'

His raised eyes made Martin blush even redder, but he answered manfully. 'It was just a local doctor I was talking to, and I happened to say that Daniel is now working here. I think the doctor has been consulted by your union about some curious cases he's had and, of course, he mentioned them to me,' he half stammered.

Bariol shrugged. 'I see, well there's not much you need to worry about as far as your brother is concerned. He's unlikely to absorb much nitro-glycerine working in maintenance, after all. But if you want reassurance, I'll introduce you to Raymond Py over there.' He waved towards a group of men sitting by the barbecue. 'He's our union man, who's been looking into the whole nitro-glycerine issue. We'll see what you make of what's been researched so far.'

Isabelle stood quietly beside her father, and Laure wondered what her relationship was with this rather magisterial man. Then Monsieur Bariol looked down at Isabelle, and it was instantly clear from his softened expression that his only daughter held a very special place in his world.

'I wanted to introduce you to our guest Laure Forestier, Papa,' Isabelle prompted him. 'Laure is Daniel's sister-in-law and a student at the Sorbonne.'

The slightly awed hush in her voice as she spoke amused Laure, and didn't escape Monsieur Bariol, who drew his daughter to him and ruffled her curls as he took time to study Laure. He would have the same opinion of her dress and hair as her own father, Laure was sure, and have even more reason to be against 'modern' women, but Monsieur Bariol would never be impolite. He held out his hand to Laure.

'Welcome to Paulilles, Mademoiselle Forestier. It seems my daughter has been making some distinguished friends in Vermeilla.' He gestured to Martin to include him in his remark.

Laure made haste to demur. 'Hardly distinguished, Monsieur Bariol, or at least not me, anyway. Martin is heading for an eminent career, but I'm just an art student with few prospects. It's Isabelle who is to be congratulated, I gather, for some rather spectacular Baccalaureat results. She has a real future!'

Monsieur Bariol still had his arm around his daughter, and as Laure spoke he squeezed her against him. 'She's a good girl and has done well. We're very proud of her. The Nobel Company are even offering to train her as an accountant, aren't they, *ma puce*?'

Isabelle looked a shade uncomfortable. 'Well, it's not full accountancy training, but I could do a diploma in Finance and Administration, working and studying part-time. It's a good opportunity.' She didn't sound convinced.

'Have you thought of any other careers?' Laure prompted, thinking back to their chat in the café. 'Didn't you say you were interested in becoming a lawyer?'

Monsieur Bariol frowned. 'We're not people meant for the city, Mademoiselle. We've built a good life for ourselves here, and we value what we've been given.' He gestured at the scene in front of them. The two youngest Bariol boys were in the sea with a dozen other children, while the teenage Bariols were involved in a very competitive football match to their left on the beach. Older brother Laurent was watching them with Daniel and a large group of young men, and there was much shouting of encouragement and criticism.

'All of my family are here today,' Monsieur Bariol continued, 'And I don't want to lose any of them, especially my girl. If Isabelle doesn't want to study accounts, then she can do something else. My sister lives in Perpignan and she could possibly stay with her, but still come home at weekends.'

He looked rather fiercely at Martin, standing silently looking at Isabelle. 'Nobody could be prouder of my daughter than I am,' he said with emphasis, and Laure waited for the 'but' which would inevitably follow. But you don't want her to turn out like me perhaps, she thought.

'But she's nineteen years old, and needs her family,' was what he actually said. 'And believe me, young Martin and Mademoiselle Forestier, we also need her, far too much to let her go.'

Chapter 13

Martin spent the whole afternoon of the picnic shadowing Isabelle, carrying for her, laying out tables by her side and ignoring his own brother to spend time with hers. It wasn't very subtle, but then Martin was a creature who lived in open spaces. From Isabelle's father's reaction, he was watching this very direct opening with a mixture of interest and vigilance. Martin would be a very good match one day, if he had a local practice, but at the moment he was just a student at a University two hundred kilometres away, and it would be some years before he was qualified. And he and Isabelle were just friends – for now.

Laure was left with a strange mix of sensations at the end of the day. She had watched Daniel and Sylvie make new friends and knew that they would vote the day a success, without any qualification. For herself, she had felt the warmth of the welcome and the contentment of the people, but she couldn't help remembering the factory girls' stained, cracked fingers and the stretch of the acid-stained beach where the picnickers hadn't strayed.

How many of these people, she wondered, had safe jobs away from the production line, like Isabelle's father, and their family homes paid for in full by the Nobel Company? His certainties had rubbed at her rebel self, but she was a guest and so had held her silence.

She'd heard that Nobel had created the Nobel prizes to counteract his reputation as the merchant of death, and he'd created this strange world of patronage and high wages here in one of the poorest areas of France. But it was also one of the most beautiful. And Paulilles was a happy, simple place on this national holiday, blissfully far from Paris and the military parades, and General de Gaulle.

That night Laure slept for once without remembering her dreams, and turned up the next morning at seven o'clock to help her mother in the bakery. A lively Monday morning followed, with housewives stocking up after the holiday weekend and tourists looking for local delicacies, so that lunchtime came around before she had time to think. Within half an hour of closing, she was taking the keys to the van from their peg and heading for Céret.

It was well over an hour's drive away, through avenues of plane trees which bordered the winding road leading inland through village after village, through the plains of Roussillon, past fields of apricot and peach and cherry trees, and on towards the foothills of the Pyrenees and Canigou – French Catalonia's own little mountain standing distinct on the horizon from wherever you looked. In the heat of July, its peak was now briefly bare of snow.

It was an intensely pleasurable drive, with the windows down in the van and the hot wind sending her Parisian crop flying around her face. Laure passed the turn off that led the few kilometres south into Spain and continued instead inland. She then drove into the outskirts of Céret, a town she had always loved but hadn't visited since she came to the famous cherry festival a few years ago with *Maman*.

Robert's sister lived in a modern house about a kilometre from the centre. She and her husband ran a pottery studio and art shop in the old town, Martin had told her. They had lived for years above the shop, but as their two boys grew bigger they had opted for a house with a garden, in a new residential area where young bougainvillea bushes were beginning to cover the walls in a riot of pink and purple.

Laure drew up outside the house and studied it for a while, reluctant to get out of the car and go inside. It was a modest, cream painted house, identical to those around it, except for some very beautiful, hand-painted pots in the garden, and an almost Picasso-style ceramic number plate attached to the wall by the gate. The house wasn't frightening, but Robert was still daunting. Had she written full enough notes for him? She still didn't have an address for Pierre, but she'd written down the name of the gallery in Paris where Jérôme could hopefully be traced, and the names of everyone she could remember who'd been in the *atelier* on the day she was arrested. It was for Robert now to tell her if it was enough. She drew her papers and her courage together and walked towards the house.

Robert Garriga opened the door as soon as she knocked. 'Come in, Mademoiselle Forestier,' he said and stepped back to let her pass into the hallway before him.

She faced him and held out her hand. 'I think you should call me Laure, don't you, Monsieur Garriga?' she said and gave him what she hoped was a confident smile.

He smiled back. 'All right, but then you must call me Robert. Come through here, Laure, to the sitting room. I've made fresh coffee if you would like some?'

She agreed, thanking him, and he disappeared, returning a few moments later with two little cups on a tray and two glasses of water.

'Do you take sugar? No? That's good because I forgot to bring it!'

He put the tray down on a little coffee table and handed a cup to Laure. She was gazing around at the room, which was decorated in an eclectic mix of old and new with bold pictures covering the walls, together with a couple of Picasso prints. There were some rather beautiful cushions around the room and children's toys stuffed behind two old leather sofas.

'Whose are the paintings?' she asked Robert.

'My brother-in-law's,' was his answer. 'He works in ceramics and pottery mainly, but he has done some striking painting as well.'

'So the art shop they have is for his own work?' Laure was surprised. Robert had said nothing about this when they had discussed her own work the other day.

'A mix,' he answered. 'They sell a lot to tourists, so they have some more commercial stuff for sale as well, by other artists. Jordi's work doesn't appeal to everyone.'

Laure studied the paintings. One was of a man behind a barbed wire fence, his face bleak but challenging, and behind him, in the shadows, there was a face. It was of a child, she thought, although it was fluid. The others were more abstract montages of animals and people, including one striking painting of many images of bulls, proud, fierce and then bleeding. They had power and artistry in a minimum of brushstrokes.

It was the painting of the man and child which drew her back. 'Is this from the time of the *Retirada*?' she asked hesitantly, for looking at the picture somehow seemed intrusive.

Robert nodded. 'Yes, my brother-in-law came to France as a child with his family. He was one of the many Spaniards who fled Franco at the end of the Spanish Civil War in 1939, and of course we congratulate ourselves in France for having given them homes, but the reality was that we put them in concentration camps for a while and, of course, Jordi remembers.'

'I hadn't realised your sister's husband was Spanish,' she said, then regretted her comment for she didn't want to seem to probe into his family affairs. In truth, she hadn't ever heard anything much about Robert Garriga's sister, and had barely known she existed until a few days ago.

But Robert continued very readily. 'Yes, my sister came down to Vermeilla ten years ago and met Jordi through Philippe. Jordi's father and our father fought side by side in the resistance during the war, two Spaniards together. It made a strong bond.'

Laure would have loved to ask more, but she held her tongue. A silence grew between them in which Robert seemed to be lost in the past, while Laure straightened her papers uncertainly. Then, just before the silence became too uncomfortable, he turned to her and moved them on to business.

'So, Mademoiselle, or rather Laure, would you like to show me what you've written down about your arrest in Paris?'

She handed over her notes rather timidly and waited, again in silence, while he read them through, taking his time, referring back several times to previous pages. Finally, he spoke.

'Well done, Laure, this is a very complete account of the day. I am especially pleased that you've put in the precise times when things happened. Can I ask, were you as specific in your statement to the police?'

She thought back to the grim little interview room where she had given her statement that day. She'd been so stressed and so desperate to make them believe her account of what had happened, that she had gone to great lengths to explain.

'I probably wasn't as coherent,' she replied, finally, 'but I was certainly voluble! There was a really bored policeman taking down my statement and he made it pretty clear that he didn't believe a word I said. But I kept repeating the facts, saying why I was there, what I was doing, and how we were trying to prevent a group of troublemakers from using the weapons. He gave me the statement to read afterwards and I remember thinking it was pretty garbled, but it was long and detailed, and I think I got most of the facts across. Maybe not all the exact times, though.'

Robert nodded. 'It sounds as though you said enough, though – enough to match up with whatever your colleagues said, even if individually they each only knew part of the detail you gave. I'll get onto that gallery address you've given me to see if I can track down your friend Jérôme, and I'll speak to the solicitor I know to ask him to take the case. He can ask to see your statement, and all the others, and if he is successful we may not even need to contact the witnesses ourselves. At least by next week, say, we should know better what our starting point is.'

Laure felt guilty at how much work he seemed to be taking on. She had no claim on him, after all. She hardly knew him. But there was one positive contribution she could make.

'Martin has made an appointment for me to see his physiotherapist friend on Wednesday in Perpignan, and while I'm there he says he'll meet a friend of his at the hospital, who can check where Pierre's father works. If we find the town, then I can trace Pierre's phone number, surely? They're sure to have a telephone.'

'That would be excellent, if you can manage it, but you don't need to call him for now. We'll try the legal route first to access what he and the other witnesses each told the police. Now, if you don't mind, I'd really like to take your fingerprints, just as back up. I'm not saying the police would have lost their copy, or indeed that they would misuse them, but they haven't shown much respect for evidence in the May events, and I don't want to take any chances.'

He brought out an ink pad and a piece of blank card. 'You won't believe it, but this is actually an ink pad they use at my sister's shop, for stamping receipts. It's not the most professional way to take prints and you'll have to scrub your fingers afterwards, but it's the best I can do, and the prints should be clear enough.'

He smiled at her as he spoke, to reassure her, and she held out first her right hand, then her left, allowing him to manipulate her fingers to roll out clear prints onto the card. It had felt demeaning and coldly clinical when the police had done this a month ago, but it felt worse, and more invasive, to have her prints taken in someone's sitting room by this young relative of Martin's, and the care he took almost made it worse.

It was while she was washing her hands afterwards in the kitchen that she heard the front door open and then heard a woman's voice talking to Robert. Help! This must be Robert's sister. Did she know that Robert was using her house as a consulting room that afternoon? It felt very wrong to be in her kitchen, making ink splashes in her sink.

Laure cleaned the sink and dried her fingers, and then came out through the hallway and back into the sitting room, her face flushed. A fine looking woman of about thirty was standing chatting to Robert, very evidently his sister, although her face was finer and her eyes a clearer shade of hazel. She didn't seem to be at all surprised to find Laure there and was examining the prints with interest.

'They've come out very clearly,' she was saying, 'for prints taken using our stamp pad.'

She turned as Laure came into the room and gave her a smile which crinkled her eyes, before coming forward to shake her hand.

'You must be Laure! You're Sylvie's sister, aren't you? How nice to meet you! Robert, dear brother, I'm hot and bothered and would love a coffee, or better still a cup of tea. Won't you make some, so that I can stay here and talk to Laure?'

She watched him out of the room and then flopped down unceremoniously in a chair. 'Won't you sit down Laure? I can call you Laure, can't I? It would seem strange not to, when you're Sylvie's sister.'

Laure sat down opposite her, feeling more at ease than she had all afternoon.

'And I'm Madeleine, if Robert hasn't told you that already. I'm his poor, indigent older sister, but he's kind enough to come and visit us two or three times a year, despite that high-class life of his in Paris. Is he helping you, my dear? He told me a little about what has happened to you, and I've so hoped he'll be able to help. I would have loved to do what you did when I was younger, but I'd never have dared.'

Madeleine had a low-pitched, very relaxed voice that sat well in this informal room, and she had a style which suited its unpretentious creativity. She was a restful person, Laure thought, who would be easy to know. She also smiled more than her brother, which made Robert's rational articulacy seem even more formal.

'I'm not sure I contributed very much in Paris, apart from getting into trouble,' Laure answered her, thinking back rather ruefully, 'But Robert has been very helpful indeed, so much so that I've found it worrying. He's on holiday, after all, and there's no reason why he should take so much time over my problems. I've been worried that he feels obliged to because Martin asked him.'

Madeleine didn't reply for a moment and then she shook her head with a little frustrated laugh.

'No, no Laure, please don't feel that way. Has Robert's legal style been freezing you out? It's the most natural thing in the world for us to want to help you, you know. After all, you're part of our extended family.'

Chapter 14

Laure could feel herself staring blankly at Madeleine, and then she understood. 'You mean through my sister? You're related to Daniel, aren't you? So Sylvie is an in-law of yours?'

'Well, yes, in a way. You're the same age as Martin, aren't you? And a close friend of his? Well, then I think you should ask him for the full story of the links between the Perrens family and our Garriga family. It's not my story to tell; it has to come from Martin, but if we're going to be friends, and I hope we are, then it would be easier if you know our interesting past.'

Laure looked at Madeleine, who was watching her serenely. There was a smell of real mystery here, but it didn't seem as though the story was bad news. Remembering back to old discussions with Sylvie, she was sure that her sister knew the story too, but for some reason, Laure had not been allowed to know. Sylvie had pushed away all questions about the relationship between Daniel's family and this one.

So it was only Martin's story to tell? Goodness knew why, but if that was the way it was then she would make him tell her!

'All right,' she answered Madeleine, 'I'll ask him. Hopefully, he'll be more open than my own sister. She cut me dead once, when I asked who Robert was.'

Madeleine gave a nod. 'Yes, I can imagine. It's a tricky one for Daniel, I know. But that's enough mystery for now. Tell me how your sister is. She's having another baby, isn't she?'

'Yes, in September. She's like an elephant right now!'

'Poor Sylvie.' Madeleine looked amused. 'I have every sympathy for a woman in the last stages of pregnancy in the height of summer. I haven't seen her for ages. She's not much like you, is she?'

Laure grimaced. 'No, Sylvie is the easy one, and I'm the trouble-maker.'

Madeleine thought for a moment. 'I was actually thinking more of your physical appearance, but you're right, you're very different in character too. But I wouldn't call you a trouble-maker. Sylvie is contented with Daniel and her family, while you've had the itch to look for more in your life. And you're a creative – you can't help challenging the world.'

Laure gestured to the paintings on the wall. 'Like your husband? He's amazingly creative too.'

'Indeed, like Jordi! Though he doesn't really believe he's an artist. He runs a business, that's what he would tell you, and he feels very keenly the fact that he has never had any formal training.'

At that moment Robert came back into the room, carrying a tray on which sat three rustic terracotta cups and a rather beautiful Chinese style teapot in blue ceramic.

'Jordi may not have any formal training,' he interjected, having overheard Madeleine's last sentence, 'but he has built himself an impressive network of artist friends and I've rarely known anyone share and build so many ideas, not outside of Paris, anyway.'

He placed the tray on the coffee table and Madeleine leaned forward to pour the tea.

'Yes,' she sighed. 'But he's not free, not like you are, Laure. Make the most of it while you can.'

Laure snorted. 'While I can, indeed! I'm probably going to lose my University place next month, so I may have exhausted all my opportunities already!'

'Rubbish, Robert will get you off, won't you brother?'

'You think so, sister? Well, it's good that you have so much faith in me. Don't worry, I'll do my best to meet your expectations, and then you and Jordi and the boys can all come up to Paris and see Laure's next exhibition!'

It was astonishing to see the difference in Robert now that his sister was here. He was suddenly relaxed and affable, in a way that Laure had briefly glimpsed when he was with Martin, but here he was warmer, and somehow younger, as though his older sister enabled him to be a different self.

'And tell me,' he was now asking Laure, 'how is Martin's love life? Has he made any progress with that young waitress of his?'

'You didn't tell me that Martin had a girl!' Madeleine was indignant.

'Oh, he doesn't, or at least he didn't when I saw him last Thursday. But he didn't look as though he was going to hang around long before making a move.'

Laure sipped the excellent fruit tea and smiled as she looked back to yesterday, and Martin's attendance on Isabelle.

'We went to Paulilles yesterday,' she told them, and went on to tell them all about the picnic and Isabelle's family, stopping short of anything which might reveal how keen Martin had been. If they had a story which Martin could only tell for himself, then so had she. Friendship had its loyalties, after all.

Madeleine wasn't going to let the subject go though. She wanted to know about Isabelle.

'She's a delightful girl, very natural, very composed, very bright,' Laure told her.

'Rather young for Martin,' Robert objected.

'She's nineteen! Not so much younger, and with a bright future in front of her, if her father will let her.'

Robert looked sceptical. 'It doesn't seem likely, from what you've told us. The father sounds as controlling as Grandpapa, don't you think, Madeleine?'

Madeleine winced. 'We had a very authoritarian upbringing with our grandfather,' she explained to Laure, 'and he wouldn't let me study either, beyond the local secretarial school. But I got away in the end, and anyway, that was over ten years ago. Things have changed since then. This is 1968, and the young people of France have been standing on barricades to make themselves heard!'

Laure wasn't so sure that much had changed in Paulilles. Isabelle's father was as dogmatic as her own father, in his way, and even more old-fashioned. And he didn't have the influence of an adopted Uncle Philippe to persuade him to change his mind and let his daughter leave home to study.

As if he'd read her mind, Robert commented drily, 'I'm not sure there are many barricades in Paulilles. How did you find it, Laure? Was it the model village we've been told about?'

Well was it? Robert's analytical mind would share her sense of the ambivalence of the place, she was sure, if she could explain it properly. She took time to sketch for him the village, the cocoon of it, with the factory across the road to which everyone was tied, that linked everyone's lives, and the strange way in which people accepted the toxic waste and its physical effects on their bodies.

'And yet they're happy,' she finished, 'and all glad to be working there. Especially those who live in the factory housing. They have beautiful gardens and live surrounded by vineyards, with everything paid for, and their own school, and so count themselves very fortunate. Martin was the only one who seemed to share any of my doubts. He has a medical interest, of course, and asked about the nitro-glycerine. Monsieur Bariol arranged for him to talk to one of the union leaders about it.'

Robert said nothing when she finished and just sat, nodding his head slowly, as though digesting what she'd said. It was Madeleine who spoke.

'It must be over a year since I last saw Martin and a lot seems to be happening in his life. I must find time to come over to Vermeilla some time.' She sighed. 'There just never seems to be enough time.'

Robert scoffed at her. 'That's just rubbish, Madeleine, and you know it! You could take the boys over any Sunday, when the shop is closed, and they would love to go to the beach. It's just Jordi who doesn't like Vermeilla.'

Madeleine laughed. 'He does have a bit of a thing about seaside tourist centres, but he laid to rest most of his prejudices against Vermeilla years ago. You're right, though, we could go over one Sunday, once the boys come back home. Jordi would love to meet you, Laure. You must talk to him about the *École des Beaux-Arts*. He'd enjoy having the company of an artist, particularly one who has been exposed to what's happening in Paris. In fact, why don't you come with me to meet him now? Would you like to see our shop? I'm heading there in a few minutes, to remind my husband that I still work with him sometimes! I'll take over the sales and he can show you around, and you can talk about Paris.'

Laure doubted that her academic training could add much to someone with Jordi's depth of experience, who had fled Spain and then lived through the war, and whose art had so much to tell. She felt suddenly like someone playing with art and didn't know what to say. Madeleine and Robert talked on, making arrangements to buy eggs for the evening's meal, easy and comfortable. They seemed to assume that Laure had accepted Madeleine's invitation. Well, she was curious, if the truth be told, so why not make the detour via the shop before returning home?

Robert turned back to Laure. 'Sadly, I have to leave here on Wednesday at the latest, Laure, so I won't see you again before I go. I wanted to ask you, do you have a telephone at home, so that I can contact you when I have some news?'

Laure gulped. 'Yes, but the phone is mainly for the business, for taking customers' orders and things, and it rings in the shop and upstairs at the same time. It's not exactly private! I only use it for the simplest of social arrangements.' She felt small and apologetic yet again. She wasn't able to help much, was she?

Robert was sanguine. 'That's no problem. I'll call Martin at the café and arrange for you to call me back from there. You're going to Perpignan on Wednesday, you said? So you should have your fellow student's address by Wednesday or maybe Thursday, and if I need it, you will be able to give it to me. But don't try calling anyone just yet, will you? Let me do my work in Paris first. The key thing is not to pre-empt anything that our solicitor friend may want to do.'

He had put his legal hat on again and Laure found herself shaking his hand, stammering her thanks as Madeleine put the tray back in the kitchen.

'Don't lose sleep, Laure,' he said to her. 'If I were a betting man I'd put money on you being back at the Sorbonne after the summer.'

'And so would I,' added Madeleine, coming back into the room. 'Robert, will we see you at the shop later?'

'Yes, I'll pass by. I'm having a drink with Albert in town at six, so I'll be in the vicinity. And then, if you want, your useless lawyer brother can even cook this evening's omelette for you. I have world renowned expertise with an omelette pan! I'll even buy some truffle oil.'

His sister grinned and kissed him on the cheek. 'I'd like to know whom you ever cook an omelette for. I've always been grateful that you rented an apartment above a restaurant, to save you from starvation. Shall we go, Laure, and leave my little brother to blow his fictional trumpet in private? His delusions won't turn into dinner, believe me, truffle oil or no truffle oil!'

CHAPTER 15

Laure knew the road where Madeleine and her husband had their gallery, so she drove the van into Céret town centre and parked it just around the corner from the modern art museum. She was tempted to stop, even if only for a moment, but made herself pass by. She didn't want to keep Madeleine waiting, and she knew that if she went inside she would never make it out again in under an hour.

The shop was just a street or so away from the museum, nestled between a specialist wine shop and an expensive bootmaker. It was a classy company in a street bathed in yellow light from the old stone, and Laure thought the whole area must bring in some high-spending visitors to Céret.

Madeleine was there before her and was on her own, which was a surprise. 'Jordi had been waiting for me to come back so that he could pop out to see a supplier,' she said apologetically, 'but he'll only be gone for twenty minutes or so, so you can have a look around without him at your elbow and then grill him when he comes back.'

It was something of a relief and Laure looked around the interior of the shop with renewed interest. It was a real den of a place, with what was obviously Jordi's work filling one side and four other very good artists taking the rest of the space. Jordi's more commercial work was his pottery and ceramics, and Laure could see where the very special pots and number plate had come from in the garden of the house she'd just left. It was beautiful craftwork, with some Picasso-like hand-drawn figures and some sculptures of animals, similar in form to those she had seen in his paintings at the house. She picked up a horse, the most difficult animal to sculpt, and stroked it lovingly. It was exquisite. Jordi had captured the movement of this great working creature and she could imagine the wind in its mane. It wasn't over finished, leaving the muscles exposed, and the horse looked as though it was straining slightly, leaning into the weather.

'I want this!' she said reverentially, holding it up to admire its lines from underneath.

Madeleine smiled. 'I love Jordi's sculptures best of all he does,' she agreed. She came over to sit on the corner of a table opposite Laure. 'I'm so glad you wanted to handle it. Our best customers always do, although we do have a sign up telling tourists not to touch.'

'You can feel the tension in the muscles,' Laure said. She placed the little sculpture carefully back on its shelf and looked around at the walls to see the paintings. She was looking for more work like the *Retirada* painting, but what was on show here was more of the abstract work and montages, plus some powerful trees, hooked and gnarled and aged on the canvas.

'I loved the painting of the man and child in your sitting room,' she told Madeleine.

'Oh yes, *The Welcome*. That's what Jordi calls 'that picture'. It's not a subject which would sell to our genteel French customers, I'm afraid. People don't like to hear what was done to the Spanish refugees in 1939. Jordi painted that one for himself.'

Laure was more and more curious to meet this Jordi. Madeleine had already won her over, with her warmth and easy charm, and all the evidence was that the man she had married would match her in stature, though he might be more challenging to know.

'Robert told me that you met your husband through Philippe,' she said, rather tentatively.

'Oh yes, *Tonton* Philippe! He didn't exactly make our match, but he certainly threw us together!'

'You call him *Tonton* Philippe too!'

Madeleine nodded slowly. 'Like you and all the others. I often think it's lucky that Philippe didn't have any children of his own. It meant he could be Uncle to so many.'

'I haven't heard your brother call him Uncle though.'

Madeleine frowned. 'No. Robert and I left Vermeilla when we were children and he was too young to remember Philippe. When we came back, Philippe was immediately my *Tonton* to me, but to Robert, he was a new acquaintance.' She looked at Laure and a little shade of worry chafed at her eyes. 'Robert's quite a fragile mix underneath. He was always so carefree and gregarious when he was a child, and I was the buttoned up, awkward one, especially in the stuffy, high society our grandparents mixed with. Robert dealt

135

with it better than me, but then I got away, of course, and he didn't. Our grandfather made him study Law and Robert had to conform, and somehow over the years he's lost his spontaneity. He does love Philippe, but he has lost the knack of being close to people.'

Laure said nothing. She almost felt as though she was trespassing, and part of her didn't want Madeleine to continue, but she had the sense to see that Madeleine was fretting and needed to talk.

'I was watching how formal Robert was with you this afternoon,' Madeleine continued with a sigh. 'He's not like that with everyone, but there's always a distance, somehow. I admire him for working his way around grandfather's expectations and not accepting the role of a London barrister, or some English county solicitor. He desperately wanted to live in France and found a way to do it, through hard study. But that job of his in Paris is soul destroying. Well paid, of course, but soul destroying. It's definitely destroying his.'

Her low-toned voice robbed the words of their drama, so that she could have been telling a story about someone she loved a good deal less than she obviously loved her brother. When she stopped she gave a slightly self-deprecating laugh.

'Do forgive me,' she said. 'It's just your mention of Philippe that got to me. I need to come to Vermeilla soon, I think. I'm suddenly missing him very badly.'

Laure treated the confidence with the respect she felt it deserved. 'Robert opens up with Martin,' she commented.

'Yes. But it's not the same. Do ask Martin to tell you our story, Laure, because it will help you to understand a good deal better.' She stood up and moved towards the back of the shop. 'Would you like a coffee? We have a coffee machine back here, and it makes a reasonable brew.'

Laure said yes and then wandered over to look at the work of the other artists sold by the gallery as Madeleine made the coffee. She was just admiring a rather bland, elegant landscape painting of the Canigou when the door opened and set the shop bell ringing. She looked around and saw a large, slightly overweight man with untidy hair. He was carrying a dirty canvas bag that seemed to be heavy, and as she watched, he dumped it unceremoniously on the shop counter, letting out an 'Ooph' of relief as he did so. This was not a customer, she realised. This unlikely looking man was the beautiful Madeleine's husband.

He dusted off his fingers and looked over at her. 'You must be Laure,' he said and came forward to shake her hand. Close up he looked better, with an attractive smile, a lot of humour in his slightly crinkled eyes and little wisps of grey that lightened a shaggy brown mop. He must be around forty years old, Laure thought, maybe ten years older than Madeleine.

She took his extended hand and felt the hard skin which grained his palm and fingers. They were sculptor's hands, used to working clay, and he shook her hand firmly, but not brusquely. She could see the provocative energy and passion in him that had made his art, and as he smiled again she could also see his charm.

'You're admiring Serge Benoit's *Canigou*, I see.'

Laure studied the painting again. 'Well yes, he's a skilled draughtsman, and more than that, he uses light well and has captured the beauty of the mountain. But...'

137

'But?'

'I wish he had made me feel the Canigou's presence more... its energy and dominance, out there on its own on the skyline. After all, it isn't sacred for nothing.' She turned to gesture to the other side of the gallery, where Jordi's paintings were displayed. 'I prefer your work!'

Jordi laughed. 'Well thank you for the compliment. And I agree with you completely about Paul Benoit. He sells quite well, though, and is considered a safe investment by conservative buyers. They pay good money for his work, and I'm glad to display him.'

Madeleine had come out from the rear of the shop with coffee and biscuits. There were three cups, so she had clearly heard her husband's arrival. She agreed with him. 'Business is business, *n'est-ce pas, chéri*? We have to eat, after all.'

'Indeed,' he said, eying the biscuits, and she tapped his belly disapprovingly.

'These are for our guest,' she admonished him, but he merely grinned and took one anyway.

'And you can take that bag of clay into the back, as well!' Madeleine continued, pointing at the counter where Jordi had dumped his load. She cast a despairing gaze at Laure. 'Are you a messy artist, Laure? Is it a requirement of the vocation that you have to be incapable of keeping any order?'

There wasn't a hint of real concern in her tranquil tones and Laure grinned. 'I'm not as messy as some! Recently, I haven't been working much in oil and I don't sculpt. Sculptors are the messiest people I know.'

Jordi looked injured. 'It's not mess, it's necessary fallout,' he protested, before launching into a defence of sculpture, using his hands as he spoke to show why shaping what you see was the purest form of art. Laure listened fascinated and found herself drawn in as he wanted to know about her studies, how she gained her influences, who had stretched her, where her art was taking her and what type of recognition she craved. He was plumbing her for what she genuinely felt about art, and she responded by really trying to explain. His own work was exposed to her here, after all, and the viewer could truly read Jordi's soul through his art, whereas Laure's gifts had to be taken on trust, since her work was in Paris.

'You don't have anything down here at all?' Jordi said, disappointed.

Laure shrugged. 'I have stuff here from last summer, when I was playing with seashore scenes, but none of it was ever really finished. And I have older paintings, on various walls around Vermeilla. But I'll probably have to bring all my work back down here soon, if I'm thrown out of the *Beaux-Arts*, and if it stops being a useful portfolio, then maybe I'll give it to you to sell for me!'

'Why not? Though we hope it doesn't come to that. Do you have photographs of your work with you, at least?'

Laure nodded. 'Yes, I do. I'd be glad to show them to you.'

Madeleine interrupted. 'We'll go over to Vermeilla one Sunday, Jordi. Not this Sunday, because the boys will only just be back, but the weekend after that. Talking to Laure has made me want to see Martin again, and Philippe, and Sylvie and Daniel.'

'That would be good,' Jordi agreed. 'Now tell me, before we let you go, Laure, what really happened in Paris these last few months? I've been longing to talk to someone who was actually there, instead of reading the malignant claptrap published by the local press here. Are you sick of talking about it? If not, can we offer you another coffee, and will you tell me all about the *Atelier Populaire*?'

CHAPTER 16

Laure drove the winding journey back to Vermeilla almost without seeing the villages she passed through. Her afternoon played before her eyes, warm, complete and yet quite searching in the company of Madeleine and Jordi. Their life was a lesson in how something rewarding could be forged from nothing, turning a raw talent into the foundation for a gainful life – modest but ample.

Jordi didn't talk much about his early life, but she gathered that he'd had little or no formal schooling as a child refugee, and had started out at a young age working for someone else as an assistant potter. He'd finally saved enough to have his own shop and produce some work of his own, and Laure thought that whatever jokes his wife might make, Jordi must have had a focused, organised mind to be able to make that break.

He credited Madeleine with taking the little shop to its current fashionable status, and for encouraging him to paint on canvas, as well as on his ceramics, and giving him the confidence to both seek out other artists and extend his range. It showed that you didn't need the *École des Beaux-Arts* to grow as an artist – what you needed was grit and talent, and Jordi had both of these in spades. He'd had to accept limits to his success, but then so had most of the artists Laure had met. Rare were the international stars in the art world.

Laure drove at last into Vermeilla and parked the van in its usual spot. She stayed for some time behind the wheel, half watching the sea, half thinking. It was time, she decided, to stop feeling sorry for herself, and to get back to work. If Jordi was coming to Vermeilla soon, then she wanted to have something new to show him.

The following day she rose early to help her mother in the bakery through the morning rush, before heading for the beach in the late morning. The day was hot with a fresh breeze, which lifted the water and sent satisfying waves to set the bathers shrieking in their spray. It was a perfect day for sketching.

Laure settled herself unobtrusively in a corner with her sketchpad, sheltered by the rocks, and set to work, seeking out the figures who stood out, either in action or just by being themselves. She sketched a rather gormless looking child splashing in the waves, a sturdy matriarch waving angrily at her troops, and a pair of young lovers walking hand in hand through the shallows. She drew quickly and quite roughly, using simple lines to catch movement and accentuate some of their characteristics.

But she was looking for something more, a subject that would speak to her, and it was nearly an hour before she saw it. Towards the top of the beach a family had laid out a blue baby rug, and on it, under a large parasol, lay a naked baby. He was stretched out on his tummy, with his legs kicking up behind him. A perfection of rounded limbs and slender torso, he had reached the age where he could show off, arching his back and holding his head high to watch the world around him. His gaze was fixed on a man, presumably his father, who lay on the sand in front of him, also on his stomach, propped on his elbows, with his face just a foot or so away from his son in a perfect profile.

The communication between them could almost be touched. The man held his son's eyes as he talked to him very quietly and the baby's huge, round eyes never stirred from his face, but his mouth made little movements as though he was trying to frame a reply. Then the man smiled, and the baby's face broke into a corresponding smile of delight. It was a private, intimate moment, one which it felt almost rude to sketch, as though she was invading their perfection by putting it on paper.

It wasn't the first time she'd felt like this and it always meant you had the makings of a good picture. That feeling of intrusion, of theft, told you that you had found the right subject, and you consoled yourself with the thought that the subject would never know you had sketched them, and wouldn't recognise themselves anyway if they ever saw the finished work.

She worked quickly, conscious that at any time the pair could move and the scene would break up. The father was young and muscled, dressed only in swimming trunks, and it crossed her mind, with humour, to wonder what Lucian Freud would do with so much bare flesh on his canvas.

But this wasn't a picture she would paint in the London style, or indeed in any of the dark styles that she had been experimenting with recently. Laure knew, even as she sketched, that she wanted to paint something very pure and to capture that purity without making it sentimental would not be easy. But if she could do it, then it might be the best thing she had painted for a while.

A woman came up the beach to join the little tableau, shaking water from her hair as she walked, and the private father and son moment came to an end. Laure moved away as quickly as possible, so as not to disturb her memory of them by witnessing a more mundane family scene. She went along towards the far end of the beach, where there were fewer people, since the scattered rocks in the shallows made it difficult to bathe. She sat for a while by the stream that trickled through the rocks to the sea, half watching the horizon, while she began composing the picture already in her head. Then she realised with a start that it was lunchtime, and remembered that Sylvie was coming to lunch with them today.

She pulled herself up and headed home, conscious of a feeling of lightness that she hadn't felt for many weeks. I must do a sketch of Julien too, she thought, before his brother or sister is born and while he is still the only child. A little solo of him, when he's wrapped up in some game, to capture that same concentration. She was sure the baby she had seen was the man's only child. It was what she would paint, that sense of uniqueness.

She found herself studying Julien over lunch, seeing the differences between the toddler and the baby, the bones in

Julien's face were so much more defined and his eyes less rounded, less wide. But she occasionally caught that look, that fixed attention which nothing could distract, and Julien's mouth would open just like the baby's on the beach.

She longed to hide herself away and make more sketches and rough out a plan, recognising with pleasure that driven eagerness which meant she was truly back at work. But she was at home, and at lunch with the family, so she contained her energy by playing 'twitch your nose' with Julien over dessert to make him giggle and then telling him silly stories about bakers who used elves and fairies to help them make their bread. She got that attention from Julien again, that wide-eyed look, and such total belief that his grandfather, the baker, had to promise to show him where the fairies had left a cake for him during the night.

'You're in fine spirits today, Laure,' her sister groaned at her. 'You're making Julien so keyed up that I'll have difficulty putting him down to sleep this afternoon!'

But Papa smiled at her. 'You've washed the Paris lines from your face now, *ma puce*, and you've some colour in your cheeks at last. You've been on the beach, and it suits you.'

She smiled back at her father and gave him what she knew was the biggest present she could offer him. 'It's just being at home that's done it, Papa,' she said. 'It's just being with you all.'

She worked on the picture that afternoon, before helping *Maman* in the shop in the evening rush, and then she worked on it again that evening, rolling into bed late, taking

145

a long time to fall sleep as the lines of her drawings revolved around in her head. It would be a close-up, she'd decided, heads and shoulders and arms only, lifted out of the beach context, so that the father and child communicated with each other in an abstract world of their own, with just the sunlight playing on their faces and giving a hint as to where they were.

She woke the next morning thinking about it and lay for a while, twitching to get painting. But she was going to Perpignan with Martin and art would have to wait. She lifted her arm and could feel her shoulder protesting. It would be a relief to see a physiotherapist, even if today was not the day she would have chosen. And she had questions to ask Martin, didn't she, intriguing questions that Madeleine had told her to ask. The thought got her out of bed, her speculative senses wide awake. The little mystery which had hung over Martin and Daniel's family since her childhood might be about to be revealed, and a train journey into Perpignan could be the ideal moment to tackle him!

Except that when she reached the station, Philippe was there with Martin. 'I've decided to see if this young physiotherapist friend of Martin's can do something for my poor arthritic knees,' he told her. 'I've had enough of old Dr Pujol telling me I just have to live with all my aches and pains. Even if I can just get a bit more movement and go for a walk along the coast without finishing up a cripple, then I'll be happy.'

'You'll neither of you get a miracle cure in one visit,' warned Martin. 'But you'll get some good advice at least.'

'And lunch!' Philippe said emphatically. 'We'll go to old Henri's place by the *Place de la République* and I'll buy you both lunch. I don't often get into Perpignan these days, and I haven't seen Henri for ages.'

There would be no confidences for now with Martin, then. Laure was sure that Philippe must be fully aware of the family story, but Madeleine had told her it was Martin's to tell, so she must wait to have Martin on his own. For now, Philippe was beaming at her and a big smile came to her own face as she looked at him. But she would find time with Martin later. The questions were itching at her.

The train drew into the station, and Philippe leapt forward to open the door for Laure, with his usual sweeping charm.

'Step aboard, fair lady! I'm not sure how exciting Perpignan can be for a woman who has conquered Paris, but for me, this is a day out with two of my favourite young people, and for an old man like me, that's about as exciting as it gets!'

Chapter 17

It was blisteringly hot in Perpignan without the cooling sea breeze they had left behind in Vermeilla. It would be a relief to get into the old town, where the narrow streets stayed in the shade. Like Céret, Perpignan was a mass of yellow stone buildings, but bigger, and with vestiges of an old medieval city wall and an ancient palace from which the Kings of Majorca had once ruled this coast.

Martin's friend Claude lived conveniently on the way into town from the station. He was a tall, seemingly diffident young man in horn-rimmed spectacles, and was at pains to tell them that he wasn't yet accredited, although he had finished his studies and was seeing them only as friends of Martin's, with no question of payment. There was a good physiotherapist at Port-Vendres whom he could recommend if they wanted to continue treatment afterwards.

But he was unerring as he manipulated Laure's back and shoulder. She wasn't sure what she had expected – some massage perhaps – but as she felt her arm twist and her shoulder click, she realised it was a lot more than that and he had found the root problem behind her dead arm. He placed his hands on either side of her neck and stretched it, very gently, and she heard more clicks.

'Do you swim?' he asked her, and she nodded. 'Then I'd like you to swim every day for the next while, using all the strokes you know, and you should do just fine.' He showed her some exercises for the shoulder and left her feeling a little pummelled and sore, just where the arm and shoulder joined, but free in her movement as she hadn't been for two months. She felt like skipping, such was the relief.

Philippe's case was more complex, and Claude made no pretence that he, or indeed any physiotherapist, could do more than alleviate his stiffness a little. But he told Philippe to insist on new medication from his doctor, as there was relief available that the 'antiquarian', as Philippe insisted on calling him, had never thought to prescribe.

'There's no reason to live with any more pain than you need to,' Claude insisted, as he and Philippe came out to the corridor where Laure was waiting.

Philippe's large head wagged in emphatic agreement. 'Can we offer you nothing?' he asked, as he pumped the young man's hand, but Claude shook his head.

'I'll have favours to ask Martin one day,' he said, and bid them goodbye with the most self-deprecating of smiles.

'Martin will know what we can give him,' Philippe insisted to Laure, as they crossed the bridge and made their way under the old Castillet archway into the old town to meet him. Martin had taken a bus out to the hospital, but he arrived at the restaurant only a few minutes after them, oozing success, having found Pierre's father in the register –

149

telephone number and all – and at the same time organised some lucrative night shifts for himself in the weeks to come, covering for doctors who were on holiday.

He told them not to worry about Claude. 'He's right,' he insisted to them. 'There will be lots I can do for him in return, and he won't be shy about asking me. Any gift you could give him would just make him uncomfortable.'

'The medical profession sticking together, huh? You're already scratching each other's backs, and you're neither of you even qualified yet!' Laure said, but all she got was a grin in return.

Meanwhile, there was lunch with Philippe's old friend Henri and lots of salacious stories of the past, mostly about people Laure had never met, but others about people she knew back in the village, which she hoped were exaggerated as some of the details were eye-opening, to say the least. By the time they got to coffee, Henri had called for the brandy and lit a cigar, and the two old men could not have been more ensconced. There was an hour and a half to go before the train and Philippe would no doubt be here until the last possible moment. Laure raised an eyebrow at Martin and the two pleaded shopping to do, and made a dash for fresh air.

And lo and behold, Laure had Martin to herself at last, with time to waste together. They had a couple of purchases to make for Colette, of toiletries she couldn't find in Vermeilla, but after that they made their way into the shade under a café awning and sat down at a table facing the Place de la République. Martin ordered an ice cream and Laure a *citron pressé*, and they settled down to watch the world go by. And Martin himself gave Laure the opening she needed to ask her question.

'So tell me,' he asked her, 'How did you get on in Céret on Monday? You met up with Robert all right? And you gave him everything he needed from you?'

She nodded. 'Yes, he seemed happy enough and he told me not to contact any of the students yet, until he tells me to, just so we're not going against anything his lawyer friend may decide to do. So the details you've got of Pierre's father are for us to hold onto for the time being.' She paused. 'I met Madeleine as well, and she took me to meet Jordi.'

Martin looked surprised. 'She took you to the gallery?'

'Yes, she wanted me to see his work. I'd already admired what I'd seen at the house, you see.'

'And what did you think?'

'It's amazing, very powerful, both the sculptures and the paintings. And I absolutely loved meeting Madeleine and Jordi. They're so open and genuine, and they've made a life which is quite distinctive, really their own.'

Martin agreed. 'I know what you mean. Around here they figure as super-cool, something quite out of the ordinary, and yet they've stayed very simple underneath.'

'Who are they, Martin? I mean who are they to you?' He looked startled, but she continued resolutely. 'Madeleine told me to ask you. It was when I said I didn't see why Robert should do so much for me, and she said that I needed to understand your family story. But she didn't want to tell me herself. She said it was your story to tell.'

Martin didn't blink but raised his eyebrows very slightly, and inclined his head once or twice, as though in acknowledgement of Madeleine's instruction. His mouth opened once and he exhaled, and then he spoke.

'Trust Madeleine!' he said, and his lips twisted into what might have been a smile. 'But she's right. If there is anyone who should probably have known years ago, it's you. After all, your sister has known since she married Daniel. You see, Daniel is only my half-brother. During the war, Madeleine, Robert and their mother had to leave France and go to England, and after they'd gone my mother had an affair with their father.'

It wasn't what Laure had been expecting to hear. She didn't know what it was that she'd expected, but it wasn't this. She stared at Martin in complete silence as she tried to digest his words. She'd grown up with Daniel and Martin, the brothers, one who looked like their father, and the other, Martin, who looked like their mother, or so she had always thought.

But Martin also looked a bit like Robert, and now that she thought about it, a bit like Madeleine. So these people she had only just met were Martin's half-brother and sister? And Daniel, dear Daniel, was his half-brother too.

And now she knew why only Martin could have told her, because while she'd thought that maybe Robert was an illegitimate relative, it was actually Martin who was illegitimate, and only Martin. It was a lot to take in.

Martin seemed to understand her silence and took up the thread again. 'It was when Madeleine came down here ten years ago that it all came out into the open.' He gave a rough laugh. 'It was a bit of a shock at the age of thirteen to find out that I was illegitimate, and had these new, unknown relatives. I was quite messed up about it for some years, but you get over that, and Robert was a real help back then, taking me over to England and letting me see the other side of their lives.'

'And Daniel?' Laure wanted to know.

Martin was quiet for a moment. 'Daniel took it quite hard at the time. Our father,' he hesitated. 'I mean Daniel's father, and my supposed father, had died and our house changed. *Maman* wanted to pretend nothing had happened, but Madeleine was living nearby in Céret and Philippe was trying to bring us all together. It was all very complicated. And Daniel had a bit of a thing for Madeleine too when she first came here, but she chose Jordi. I think that's what made Daniel go away to sea. He needed to get away and it liberated him.'

He had spoken softly, but his voice rang out as he added, 'But he never stopped being protective of me. He's not my half-brother – not to me. Daniel is just my brother.'

Laure couldn't imagine Daniel with anyone other than Sylvie. She thought back to the young Sylvie who had so adored Daniel. That would have been eight or nine years ago. By then Daniel had recovered from any feelings he'd had for Madeleine, surely? He'd teased and courted Sylvie every time he was home and had always seemed on top of the world. A life at sea had definitely liberated him.

But she could imagine them all back then – in trouble and hurting – and she looked at Martin with new respect. He'd never once seemed different to his childhood friends or shown any anger or resentment, and here he was, as whole

153

as could be, telling her the story without an ounce of self-pity.

There was so much she wanted to ask. 'I've never doubted that you and Daniel were full brothers,' she said at last. 'Your relationship is obvious and you grew up together. But what about Robert and Madeleine? Do they feel like your brother and sister?'

Martin scraped his spoon idly over the surface of his ice cream and brought it up to his mouth. He looked thoughtful, as though he was trying to work out the answer himself.

'I don't know,' was his honest reply. 'They feel like close relatives, like cousins, perhaps. Ten years ago it just felt as though they'd been imposed on me and invaded my life just to mess it up, but let's face it, they weren't exactly delighted to find out who I was either! But there were good consequences too. Both of them were happy to have refound their Catalan roots, and I gradually became very proud of the man who had been my father. And they're nice. They've been very good to me.'

Laure had seen how well Martin got on with Robert. They were very natural together. She was very curious now to see him with Madeleine.

'Madeleine and Jordi are coming to Vermeilla soon, too,' she told him. 'We got talking about you, and about Philippe and Sylvie's baby, and Madeleine became quite homesick for here. It won't be this weekend, but I think they'll come with their boys the following Sunday.'

Martin looked pleased. 'I don't see them as often as I should, what with them being in Céret and me in Montpellier.'

'And do Daniel and Madeleine get on well now?' The question was important to Laure.

Martin smiled. 'Oh, yes! You don't need to worry about anything there! They seem to really care about each other, and I never saw Madeleine happier than when Daniel married your sister. I have to remind her sometimes that it's me who's her brother, and not him!'

It seemed they had all resolved their difficulties and found a balance. Laure was still confounded, but her nose told her to wait and see and not assume anything. She would have the opportunity to observe for herself in just over a week's time.

'You're some guy, Martin,' was all she said and finished her *citron pressé*. 'And in all of this, Philippe was pushing you all to get together? Why doesn't that surprise me? Shall we prise him out of his restaurant and go and catch that train?'

She thought of that other bit of gossip, whispered during her childhood in the village, that Philippe himself might be Martin's father. Well, he was in a way, wasn't he? More than any genetic father whom Martin had never known. The thought was vaguely comforting and Laure tucked her arm through Martin's in a homely gesture as they picked up the shopping and headed back through the Perpignan streets.

Chapter 18

Over the next few days, Laure thought a lot about Martin's story. It took some processing, and she would lose herself in little moments of abstraction while stacking loaves or washing the dishes in the kitchen. She could now understand why Madeleine had been interested in her, and why she had wanted her to talk to Martin. She could feel a link to her, like the link she had to Colette, Daniel and all of Martin's family. And it did help to explain why Robert was helping her. She was Sylvie's sister and the association was real.

Robert would be back in Paris now and she wondered what he might be doing, fretting at her own inaction. He had just returned to work and would be busy, and it could be days before he found the time to contact his friend the lawyer. She steeled herself to patience, making herself remember that a week ago she hadn't thought anything could be done at all, and that there were still more than five weeks to go before the University committee would meet to withdraw her place. Robert had told her to trust him and she had to do so.

She submerged herself when she could in her painting, finishing the father and child piece and making numerous sketches of Julien. She didn't see Martin and she felt a strange twinge of jealousy when she thought that he would be seeing Isabelle every day. It was Sylvie who told her they were all going to meet up on Sunday, when Isabelle's brother was coming to Vermeilla. He, Daniel and Martin were going to taking a local boat out fishing. There was no suggestion of an invitation for her, but they were coming back to eat at Daniel and Sylvie's afterwards, and Laure was invited to help eat whatever they caught.

If only Daniel and Martin had been were going, Laure would have claimed her place on the boat without waiting to be asked, but in the circumstances, she buttoned her lip and agreed to lunch instead, and received the inevitable order to bring bread and a tart from the bakery as well. If I stay here for longer than the next month or so, I'll never want to eat a fruit tart again, she thought, as she accepted her instructions.

Since Laure had been left ashore, she met the little powerboat as it came into the quay and quickly made a sketch of the three men as they berthed. Daniel had left the job of berthing the boat to Martin and he made a glorious mess of it, generating some interesting gestures between the brothers that Laure just loved committing to paper.

She'd done numerous sketches of those two over the years, many of them scurrilous, but Isabelle's brother Laurent was new. He was watching them in amusement, but holding back from intervening. He was younger, of course, a good twelve years younger than Daniel, and naturally

157

reticent. She sketched in his curls and his very endearing smile, and reflected again on how much he looked like his sister.

Over lunch, he looked at the sketches with an almost absurd reverence. 'You did these so quickly?' he asked Laure, and she grinned.

'I could sketch these two idiots without them even being present,' she said, 'so all I had to do was capture Martin's ineptitude. It's a good job he's going to be a doctor – he'd make a poor fisherman!'

Martin had been to Paulilles again since their trip to Perpignan. He'd chosen Isabelle's day off, Laure noted, and had lunch with her mother and the children, but he'd also met the union leader that Isabelle's father had introduced him to. He'd come away sobered, for it seemed the nitro-glycerine they'd heard about had life-threatening effects on those who lived and worked with it.

What it did, he explained, was to over-dilate the blood vessels around the heart, which in the long term permanently weakened the heart. There were people dying soon after retirement, and others had died as young as in their thirties. The heart attacks commonly occurred on Monday mornings, after a day away from exposure to the chemical, when the artificially dilated arteries would retract and shrink, choking off the heart's blood supply.

Laure watched as Sylvie went deathly pale. She looked as though she might faint and Laure reached out to hold her arm.

'Daniel doesn't work with that stuff!' she said to her, in a hurry.

'But you go in there, Daniel! You go up to the production units to fix things!'

Daniel moved around the table to sit next to his wife and put an arm around her. 'Don't worry, *ma chérie*, I promise you I'm never in there long enough for it to have an effect on me! It makes your headache, but I get out quickly. It's people who work with it all the time who are at risk, not me.'

Martin was frowning and looked across at Isabelle's brother. 'People like you, surely, Laurent?' he said. 'You work close to the nitro-glycerine, don't you? And didn't your mother and father both work with it, before your mother gave up work to look after the children and your father got a job in maintenance?'

Laurent acknowledged the question with a little, helpless shrug. 'It's true, I work in the production unit, though not as close to the '*matière*' as the women who fill the cartridges. And it's true that you get terrible headaches when you first start working there, or if you come back from a holiday. You just have to work through them, and then when you finish at the end of the day, you need some time outside in the fresh air to take away the feeling of something squeezing your rib cage.'

'Oh my God!' Laure exhaled. 'And do you get that same problem on Sundays, when you're not breathing in the fumes?'

'I don't know. I feel tired sometimes, but it's a long week, so that doesn't surprise me.' He took another sip of water. 'You'll note I refused the wine, too. Those of us who work in the areas with the fumes can't drink alcohol, because it gives you pains, and brings you out in a horrible flush.'

'And yet you stay there?'

'Well yes, because the pay is so good, and I won't be in the mixing department forever. I'm working on getting a transfer to the stores, but I'll have to wait. Nobody dies at Paulilles at the age of twenty-two! And when people do have health problems, the company is good at moving them to other sections. But I haven't been there nearly long enough to suffer any real problems, and overall it's a good place to work. All my friends are there.'

Laure gazed at him, lost for comment. It was Martin who spoke. 'It's true that the number of actual deaths has been small, although the number of people with compromised health is much greater,' he said. 'The union's lawyers are trying to build a body of evidence, but it's not a huge factory, in national terms, and the cases of heart problems are statistically few, poorly documented so far, and difficult to link back to the Nobel Company.'

When Martin got launched on medical matters he could sound as analytical and formal as his half-brother Robert. My little playmate has become a professional, Laure thought to herself.

'And is the Nobel Company working with them to establish if there's a link?' she asked him.

'Far from it! They won't admit there's a work-related problem at all. It's not a recognised illness, and it isn't in the company's interest to admit to it – think of the flood of claims they would get!'

Indeed, and in the meantime, the company continued to pass for a benign, socially responsible local employer, badly needed in a poor area of France. Laure remembered the impression she'd had about Isabelle's family – that they were almost untouched by the world, because of how they lived. She asked Laurent about it, as diplomatically as she could.

'You've had a good life at Paulilles, your father says. How do you feel about the Nobel Company? Are they really the model employer everyone thinks they are?'

Laurent took his time to answer, but when he did, he gave her a slightly wry smile. 'I know what Martin is saying and it's beginning to be understood by all the people who work at Paulilles, even people as comfortable as my father. People don't doff their caps to the Nobel Company the way they used to, especially the younger workers. And in the last few years, they've been taking people on and then sacking them whenever it suits the company, depending on their order book. That doesn't make people very loyal. But for people like my father, Paulilles has been his life and the company is everything. They gave us a magical childhood too, and a great education, if I had paid any attention!'

Daniel still had his arm around Sylvie, whose face was deeply troubled. He gave her a squeeze. 'We're doing a good job of frightening my wife here,' he said, with a warning look at Laure and Martin. 'But what you have to remember is that none of the jobs around here are quite the way they used to be. Look at the fishing – how bitter were people here in Vermeilla when the last of our fishermen gave up trying to make a living two years ago? He even burned his boat, he was so angry. Even in Collioure, there are only a few boats left and they're talking about giving up. All the fishermen now work as crew on the trawler boats in Port-Vendres and they get taken on and laid off just as it suits the owners. How different is Paulilles? At least they pay decent wages!'

'The fishermen don't breathe in toxic fumes or risk getting blown up,' Laure objected.

'But they drown and lose fingers and hands in the ropes, and wreck their backs! And anyway, I don't breathe in toxic fumes!'

'Laurent does!'

'But as Laurent says, he's young. He's made a choice to work at Paulilles and he knows the risks, don't you Laurent?'

His tone was uncompromising and Laure knew better than to continue. It wasn't often that Daniel was anything other than easy-going and complaisant, but for once he was using every one of his years of seniority to end this discussion. God help us all, are you going to turn into a patriarch like all of our fathers, wondered Laure?

Isabelle arrived just then, having finished the lunch shift at the café, and the conversation moved to other things as Laure went to fetch the apricot tart. Laure stood for a moment in the kitchen door, watching the interplay between Martin and Isabelle, but above all watching Daniel.

With his son playing at his feet and his pregnant wife sitting beside him, big brother figure Daniel suddenly looked very serious indeed. But life was a serious business, after all, and earning a living in the sunshine of the Mediterranean was never as easy as it might seem.

CHAPTER 19

It wasn't until the following Thursday that Laure finally heard from Robert. Martin came to the bakery just before they closed for lunch and asked if she could come to the café before the shop reopened that afternoon. So, soon after three o'clock, when *Maman* was putting her feet up and Papa had gone to bed, Laure slipped away to the *Café de Catalogne* to join Martin in the little office section behind the bar, where the phone was discreet from customers' ears.

'He's going to call again at three thirty,' Martin told her. 'I didn't ask him anything. It seemed to me I should leave you to have that conversation in private.'

He stayed with her until the phone rang and then he moved away to the bar, inevitably finding Isabelle. Laure watched the ringing phone for a moment, her hands suddenly clammy, and then picked up the heavy black receiver.

'Hallo?' she said, hoping it would be Robert, as she was feeling too inarticulate to field a business call to the café.

'Laure, is that you? This is Robert.' The voice sounded far away, but it was reassuringly him.

'Yes, it's me,' she answered. 'How are you?'

Do you have any news for me, she wanted to ask, but it was a stupid question. He wouldn't be calling if there was nothing.

'I'm fine,' he said, and moved briskly on from the pleasantries. 'Listen, Laure, we have made some progress, but we have also encountered a problem. Charles Gruet, the lawyer I have instructed on your behalf, has been able to see the statements of the three witnesses who gave evidence for you to the police. Two of them match your story exactly and are very strong in your defence, saying that you were acting to prevent trouble, but there's one which is much more ambivalent. It doesn't exactly say that you were one of those responsible for the stockpile of weapons, but implies that you might have been. It is carefully non-committal, but says that people were reacting in surprising ways at that time, even some of the committee members. It gives the impression that he would like to defend you but is struggling with his conscience.'

Laure heard the words through the static of the phone line and struggled to comprehend them. They didn't make sense. Every one of her witnesses knew exactly what had happened that day. What possible reason could any of them have to tell a different story? Robert was talking about her band of closest comrades – about Pierre, Lolo and Jérôme, and they were all totally loyal, weren't they?

'Who?' she asked, and could hear her voice trembling. 'Who gave that statement?'

'It was one of the students, Jean-Louis Lavignière.'

Laure brought her left hand up to her face as the blood drained from it. There was a chair behind her and she sank into it, unsure of her legs. Her right hand still held the phone receiver, loose in her lap, and she found herself taking deep, deliberate breaths. Lolo, her Lolo, had given a statement to the police in which he'd implied that her motives might be untrustworthy? She shook her head as if she might be able to make it untrue. Could Robert be mistaken? No, of course not, you didn't make allegations like that lightly, she knew that. She knew it, but she couldn't take it in.

'Laure? Are you still there?'

She heard the voice coming faintly from the receiver in her lap and made herself lift it to her ear, holding it with two trembling hands.

'I'm sorry, Robert,' she said, controlling her voice as tears suddenly threatened. 'I'm still here. It was just a shock, that's all. Lolo… Jean-Louis… is a good friend of mine, and I'm trying to get my head around what you've just told me. So he made a statement which was deliberately meant to cast doubt on my story? You're sure of that – that it was deliberate, I mean? It couldn't have been a misunderstanding?'

'No, it was deliberate, we're sure of that. But it was done very subtly, you understand? I haven't seen the statement yet, but Charles called me today and described it to me. It was a series of answers to police questions that were written down very faithfully, and Charles says the responses sound very plausible and very concerned, and make the other two witnesses' statements, in contrast, look like very partisan efforts to clear your name. Because your story and the other two matched, a decision was made not to take the matter further and to let you off with a warning, but not to drop the charges completely against you. You've benefited from the general amnesty, but there's a taint of suspicion still around your name.'

'So what can I do?' her voice broke as she asked the question. Robert must have heard it, because he came back instantly reassuring.

'Don't despair, Laure, there's a long way still to go yet. It seems that Charles Gruet, the lawyer, is a member of some exclusive dining club frequented by the Rector of the *Beaux-Arts*, and he's hoping to get a word with him this weekend.'

'It's not the Rector who's dead set against me and my work, it's Professor Duchamp, and he heads the awards committee!'

'I know,' Robert came straight back. 'But everything helps and Charles may learn something more, as well. But, in the meantime, we have to work on correcting that statement of Lavignière's. Did you get contact details for the other student? Yes? Well, can you call him and tell him what I've just told you, and see what he says? He'll probably be as astonished as you, since he gave a completely different account of the day, but maybe he'll have an inkling as to what Lavignière's motives might have been. I'll do the same here in Paris with the other witness, the artist – Jérôme Delmas, wasn't it? And don't worry, if necessary, we'll go and confront your supposed friend Lavignière together and make him rewrite his story.'

'How?'

Robert laughed. 'Don't ask! Just make your phone call and find out what you can, and we'll speak again at this time tomorrow, if that's all right?'

Laure could only agree. It had all been too quick and there was so much she would have liked to say, but she couldn't keep Robert on a long distance call for nothing. He rang off and she sat cradling the telephone long after he had gone, gazing uselessly at the wall and the cluttered wooden desk in front of her. It was Martin who took the receiver out of her hand and placed it back onto its cradle, and she didn't even notice that he'd come back until he put a coffee into her hand with a brief instruction to drink it. She did so mechanically and the hot, pungent liquid gradually worked its way through to her brain, clearing the fog and allowing her to focus. Robert had given her a job and she needed to act on it. She looked up at Martin and gave him a rather limp smile.

'Phew,' she expelled. 'Martin, how do you feel about negotiating Lyon hospital's telephone system for me?'

Even Martin could not be expected to get straight through on the phone to a busy hospital doctor. It took him three hours and when he did finally get to speak to the doctor, Laure wasn't there to help him. Not knowing Pierre himself, Martin couldn't really ask for his home telephone number, so he simply told the father that Laure Forestier needed very badly to speak to Pierre and asked him to pass on the café's phone number to his son. Then that evening, Laure came and sat with him in the café, playing cards, waiting without much hope for a call to come through.

She was so knotted up she couldn't eat or concentrate on her cards, but she muzzled all thought. Call me, Pierre, she willed, again and again, for surely Pierre would tell her it was all nonsense, and that Lolo's statement had been forged or altered. Wasn't that what everyone had said about the flics throughout the events of May? They couldn't be trusted and she held on to the thought.

But when Pierre finally did call, at around nine o'clock, he listened to her frantic explanation in troubling silence, and gave her an equally troubling reply when she had finished, sounding as though he was mulling his words as he spoke.

'I can't imagine why Lolo would write a statement like that, Laure, but he did change at the end. You weren't with us in those final days in the *atelier*,' he reminded her. 'You had to stay away. But did you know that Lolo also stayed away a lot? I got the impression that he didn't want to be seen with us there when the inevitable police clear-out came and he seemed to be withdrawing from us. It was strange after he'd been so much at the centre of the *atelier* throughout.'

'But that doesn't explain that statement!' Laure was adamant.

'No.' Pierre's voice was hesitant. 'I don't have any explanation for that. But I'm not sure I believe the police forged it either. You're just not important enough to them, Laure. But listen, I know you care about Lolo and he seemed to care about you too, but do you remember that night when you fell to the ground by the barricade, and people were trampling you?' He stopped and seemed reluctant to continue.

Laure was puzzled. 'Of course, I remember. You saved me, I'll never forget that.'

'Yes... but Laure. Lolo saw you go down too. We were standing on the barricade, the two of us, and I never saw Lolo more euphoric, it was as though we were intoxicated, and then you were hit by that tear gas canister. I grabbed Lolo and showed him, and he waved at me and told me to go and help you. I yelled at him that he should come too and he just laughed, and said one of us would do. "I've got a revolution to run, man! You go!" That's what he said to me. I was shocked but afterwards, I thought maybe he'd been right. You only needed one of us and Lolo was such an inspirational figure.'

Laure was silent. He was telling her that Lolo was self-serving and would never care about other people as much as he did about himself. But she'd known that, hadn't she, underneath it all? It was just how he was and he could be that way because he had a magnetic character, and people would always revolve around him. Pierre was one of them – he had been one of Lolo's followers, although not, it seemed, blind to his faults.

She swallowed the humiliation of learning that Pierre had been so casually dispatched to tend to her lying on the ground.

'I'm just glad you came to help me, Pierre,' she said. 'Lolo would never have found that medical unit for me. But if we accept that you're a nicer person and a better friend, does that mean we also have to accept that Lolo wrote a statement designed specifically to damage me? Why would he? What on earth would make him want to?'

But there she got no further. Pierre had no explanation and nor did she. Lolo might not care about Laure, but he had no reason to do her harm. But again, before they finished their call, Pierre repeated that the police wouldn't have done it. He believed the statement was Lolo's work. He said again that Lolo had changed, withdrawn at the end.

'Something happened to him,' was the last thing he said to her.

She took Pierre's phone number and thanked him. She wanted to cry, not because she'd loved Lolo, for she hadn't, but because it seemed he hadn't cared at all. She had been a mere dalliance for him, while it had been something so much more for her. It seemed so callous.

And why had he lied about her to the police?

Laure dreamed again about Lolo that night, bringing that first night of theirs back so vividly to mind that she came out of sleep with the taste of his lips still on hers. The feeling of well-being stayed with her for a moment and then left her with a thud as she remembered. On that Monday morning, Lolo had made her an intimate breakfast, and then on the following Friday night, had seen her fall, crushed by a fleeing crowd. And she now knew that he couldn't even be bothered to come and help her.

They'd had just two more nights together during the whole of May and June, but the student occupation explained that. They were so busy, so engaged, and there would always be time later. They knew that. Laure felt it. And meanwhile, Lolo had always stayed charming, always caressing, and always singled her out with his smile.

And then she'd been arrested, and since then she'd seen Lolo only once. Pierre said Lolo had withdrawn from the student occupation but Laure hadn't known that. For the few days between her arrest and the end of the occupation, she'd assumed that he was still living in the *École des Beaux-Arts* and that was why he hadn't come to see her. And because she couldn't visit the *atelier*, she'd had no way of knowing that wasn't true.

And then the *atelier* had finally been closed and she'd gone looking for him, trawling their favourite cafés. She was in trouble and hurting, in need of both moral support and Lolo's smiles. She'd found him at the *Deux Magots* with just a couple of their friends. He had been very sympathetic and very concerned, but he was leaving the next day, he'd told her. He was under pressure to go home, to help in the vineyards, and he couldn't justify staying on in Paris any longer. Unlike Laure, who had to stay, for she was still waiting to hear what was going to happen to her.

He took her out that evening, bought her dinner and made her laugh, and told her everything was going to be all right. The University would never withdraw her award, he told her – not with her talent. She'd believed him for a few hours because she wanted to, and at the end of the evening he'd kissed her and told her not to despair. In September, they would both be back in Paris to share some more of that wine.

'We saw some action, didn't we?' he'd said. 'It was fun, *n'est-ce pas, ma puce?*'

And looking back, she could see that was what it had been for Lolo – fun. Make a noise, go on a march or two, preach, build a fan base and your own ego, and when the revolution fails, go home with a light heart to grow grapes. Make love, not war, but make it lightly, because what mattered to Lolo was really Lolo.

It left a hollow feeling, hollower this morning than ever before.

CHAPTER 20

In a brief call from Robert the next day, Laure learned that he hadn't yet managed to contact Jérôme, but was hoping that evening to call by the gallery where his work was displayed. But they both agreed that he was unlikely to add much to what Pierre had already told her. Robert felt that they now had to make plans to go and confront Lolo and Laure could see the sense, but not how she could travel all the way to Bordeaux without money, and without telling her parents what she was doing. She didn't say so, but Robert must have caught her hesitation.

'If you can't get away, then I'll go and see him myself, as your lawyer,' he told her. 'But one way or another, he has to retract his statement. Otherwise, there will always be some doubt hanging over you.'

'What if I found some other committee members who knew what I was doing that day and why?'

'Could you?'

'I don't know. Maybe Pierre has some contact addresses. I could ask.'

'It would take time, though, and we're already at the end of July. Let me trace Jérôme first, and you take the weekend to think whether you can come to meet me in Bordeaux.'

'But what about you? How can you leave Paris? You have a full-time job, after all!'

He laughed. 'Don't worry about me! I'm owed a lot of leave and I'm on a mission now. I don't like what this so-called comrade did to you, and I want to know why.'

So do I, thought Laure. Lolo's behaviour was worse than Robert knew, for he had no idea they'd been anything more than comrades. Lolo's betrayal would need some very serious explanation indeed.

She trod bleakly through the next two days, burying herself in her artwork. A strong northerly, tramontane wind whipped the sea into an ice white frenzy that suited her mood and she painted a furious seascape, sitting on the rocks for hours while spray flattened her hair.

By Sunday the wind had calmed, and Sunday brought Madeleine with her two boys. Laure was helping in the shop when Madeleine came to visit, wafting the boys before her to choose their favourite macaroons. They were striking, handsome boys of eight and six years old, with Madeleine's dark, oval eyes and quirky, cheeky grins that reminded Laure of a younger Martin.

'I've come to see your work,' Madeleine told Laure. 'I'm so sorry Jordi isn't here. There's a group visiting the art museum this afternoon, some art club from Lyon, and Jordi wants to keep the shop open for them. But you'll show me your work, won't you? And then you're coming to lunch at Colette's aren't you?'

174

She turned to Laure's mother. 'You must be Madame Forestier. I don't think we've ever been introduced, but I'm a friend of the Perrens family, and I've been into the shop several times, very often to get bread. My family absolutely love your macaroons!'

Madame Forestier shook hands. 'I remember you and the boys. They have such long lashes, wicked on a boy! They look very like you.'

She brought out the tray of macaroons and offered one to each of the boys, who took them with shy thanks.

'We don't make these ourselves,' she told Madeleine, 'Because they're so special. But we have a very wonderful supplier who makes them for us, just in the summer, when we have our visitors who appreciate them.'

She brought out a pastry box and the boys selected enough different flavours to fill it, and *Maman* tied it ceremoniously with silver ribbon before presenting it gravely to the elder of the two boys. And then she shooed Laure out to take Madeleine upstairs. The boys followed, the older one carrying the precious pastry box carefully in two hands.

'Can we open this?' the younger boy asked his mother when they reached Laure's sitting room, pointing to the box of macaroons.

He spoke in Catalan and she replied in the same language. 'Before lunch? No way, Luis. It's already eleven o'clock, and we'll be eating soon. And then we'll go to the beach, okay?'

Young Luis agreed and he and his brother sat themselves quietly on the sofa to wait. Laure turned to Madeleine and congratulated her.

'They're beautifully behaved, your boys. And they have Catalan names?'

'Yes,' Madeleine gave her boys a quietly happy smile. 'The older one's called Enric, for Jordi's father, and the little one is Luis, for mine. They're great boys and they're even kind enough to help their poor mother when she has a block in Catalan. I had to relearn the language, you know, when I came back out here to live.' She shifted her gaze from the boys to Laure.' So tell me, how is your campaign going with my brother? Has he got you back into the Sorbonne yet?'

Laure grimaced. 'It's not quite as simple as that.'

Madeleine took a long look at her and then nodded. 'I'll let you tell me later, when we're alone,' she said. 'That's if you want to. There's a lot I'd like to catch up with. Meanwhile, could you bear to show me some of your work?'

Laure had never liked showing her work, though she'd got used to it over the years. She brought out the recent paintings from the corner where she had them stacked and placed them upright against the wall. There was the seascape from yesterday, plus a man swimming nude in a still pool, which she had done last summer and finished this week, plus two studies of little Julien and, of course, the father and child close-up from the beach ten days ago. She had photos too of other work she'd done in Paris but, for now, she just let Madeleine look at the five canvasses, holding her silence and withdrawing slightly to one side.

Madeleine moved along the line and took time in front of each painting. Then she whistled.

'My God, you can see why you won that award, Laure. These are outstanding!'

She knelt in front of the father and baby portrait, and held out a hand to trace the outline of the baby's chin, not quite touching the canvas.

'You could stroke this,' she said, and Laure blushed beetroot red at her hushed, slightly awed voice. 'How could that professor of yours think you weren't the right person for the award?'

Laure shrugged. 'Can't you see? He wanted someone who is working in the style of the French schools, New Realism and those following on from *Art Informel*. He can cope with American Pop Art influences because they're leading in the same directions, but unless you're deconstructing machines, using collage techniques, creating metal sculptures or huge abstract murals, then he doesn't want to know. My influences are German and British, and he doesn't think I am promoting the French art world. I had a professor at Toulouse who loved the London School and who had established a significant reputation in the field as well, and he encouraged me to go to the *Beaux-Arts* to work with a couple of lecturers there after I'd finished my first four years of study. He told me I should go because he knew I wanted to do research and I would be more likely to get funding and contacts in Paris, but he warned me that I wouldn't necessarily always find the resonance I was hoping for up there.'

'And have you?'

'To an extent. There are a couple of lecturers at the *École des Beaux-Arts* who have been incredible supporters. They've helped me to be less imitative and to find my own style. What I'd love would be to work in London for six months or so, but if I don't finish my Diploma course then I can kiss all hope of that goodbye.'

'Well, then you must. Frankly, Laure I haven't seen talent like this ever outside of the major galleries and I speak as one whose husband is in the field! But Jordi would be the first to say that you have a talent beyond his dreams. The only advantage he has on you is age! You capture texture, light and depth, and the flesh, and through the flesh, you reach the soul. Have you sold any of your work?'

Laure shook her head. 'Nothing important. I've been working towards exhibitions and have needed all my good work.'

'Would you let us sell any of these?'

'In the gallery, you mean?'

'Why yes, we would love to sell your work, and it could only be good for the gallery to have the work of one of the top students at the Sorbonne!'

Laure grimaced again – she was doing too much grimacing these days. 'Well, you may be able to say that of me for another month. I could do with the money, that's for sure. I guess I could give you the portraits of my nephew because I can do more of those for my sister. And the man swimming is last year's work, so you can have that.'

She studied the seascape. It was good, but it wouldn't fit into any selection she made for an exhibition, and she had done it in a hurry, in a black fury. The only one she couldn't sell was the father and baby portrait. She went over to the paintings and took that one away.

'There you go. Do your worst! You can sell these and at least I'll have some cash again. If anyone wants them, that is.'

Madeleine nodded, very satisfied. 'You've kept the best one, but you're right to do so. Do you have a price you'd like for the others?'

'No,' Laure shook her head emphatically. 'You decide what they're worth. I'll trust you and if any of them sell, you can just let me have what I'm owed.'

'Sounds good to me.' Madeleine held out her hand and they shook on the deal. 'Shall I bring the car around here later to collect them?'

She nodded to the boys, who had been looking through some collectable action men cards they had in their pockets, and they got to their feet to join her. Madeleine reached over and kissed Laure on both cheeks.

'Thank you for showing me these,' she gestured to the paintings. 'You have made my day.'

Laure smiled, feeling warmed and valued. 'You're as bad as Philippe, with his partisan defence of my work!'

'Uncle Philippe is always right,' Madeleine assured her. 'I must get him to come and see your paintings this afternoon before I take them away. We'll see you at Colette's in an hour and I'll boast of the new talent I've managed to secure for the gallery!'

Chapter 21

It was a merry group that Laure joined in the apartment above the café that lunchtime. She was the last to arrive, having stayed to help her mother for as long as possible, and they were already grouped around the long table, having an aperitif of sweet muscat wine which Madeleine had brought with her.

Madeleine's two boys were sitting on the floor with little Julien, helping him to build a simple racetrack for his inevitable toy cars. Madeleine, Daniel and Martin were talking rugby and Philippe was half listening while he poured more wine for Colette. He held Colette around the waist to keep her with them, laughing as she protested and tried to head for the kitchen. She shook her head at him in mock anger but accepted the glass, before passing it on to Laure as Philippe poured another one for her.

It was a family scene, happy and at ease, and in stark contrast with the lunch group that Laure had joined when Robert had been here. Then, everything had been formal and correct, and Colette had watched from behind a wall of reserve. Madeleine was part of this family, it seemed, in a way that Robert hadn't achieved.

They ate pan-fried squid, a Sunday roast chicken with a potato gratin and Colette's very special crème catalane, and finally the macaroons so carefully chosen by Enric and Luis. Laure found herself watching everyone, trying to understand their relationships. Colette, she thought, was genuinely fond of Madeleine, while Philippe clearly loved her, and Martin treated her with the same unceremonious affection he had shown to Robert.

And Daniel? How did he feel towards Madeleine? Laure observed him with particular attention; her brother-in-law who had no blood relationship to Madeleine himself, and whom she had passed over for Jordi ten years ago. Laure sat close to Sylvie, ready to feel protective of her sister if she saw the slightest sign of lingering fancy in Daniel.

But she needn't have worried. Daniel's relationship with Madeleine, she thought, was almost the best of them all, for they were nearly the same age and dealt as equals, as though she was a preferred sister-in-law, perhaps. I'm the one who's really his sister-in-law, she grumped inwardly, but not seriously. Daniel and Madeleine had a history that went back to before she was born.

And as for Madeleine's boys, Colette, in particular, treated them like favourite nephews. She offered them all the best bits of everything and cajoled them to eat in much the same way as she did her own grandson. It all fascinated Laure so much that she sat silent herself, a state so unusual in her that Philippe asked her, with some humour, if she was feeling all right. Martin caught her eye and raised a quizzical eyebrow, and she raised one back. Don't worry, she thought, I'm not brooding about Paris. Your family are far more interesting today!

At the end of the meal, Daniel took all of the boys off to the beach, ignoring Sylvie's protest that Julien would soon need his sleep.

'You go for a siesta yourself, *chérie*, and I'll keep Julien with me. I can always bring him home if he gets crotchety.'

Martin backed him up. 'Don't worry, Sylvie. I'll just help *Maman* here for a bit, and then I'm sure Madeleine will come down with me to the beach as well. Then we'll be there for Madeleine's boys. If Julien needs a sleep, Daniel can bring him straight home.'

'You're sure you don't want to wait around the café for a while?' Daniel asked suggestively. 'I see that Isabelle is working today.'

He got a frown from his mother and an interested look from Madeleine, but Martin didn't reply, merely blushing a little as he went to the kitchen with some dishes.

Daniel picked up Julien and kissed his mother, giving her a wicked grin. 'You know, *Maman*, I really think it's time that Sylvie and I invited Isabelle to stay over with us one night, so that she can join us all for dinner for once, instead of only being in Vermeilla when she's working. I must suggest it to her.'

Colette gave him a light slap on the backside. 'Stop embarrassing your brother! You're not too old to wallop yet, my boy,' was all she said, as she ushered him and a smiling Sylvie down the stairs after the boys.

Madeleine and Laure made light work of helping Martin to clear up, refusing Colette access to the kitchen, and then they all headed off to the beach. Philippe, naturally, was already slumbering in his chair.

There was no sign of Isabelle in the café when they came downstairs but they found her outside, clearing tables. She smiled when she saw the three of them, and the way she looked at Martin took Laure slightly aback. She'd been too preoccupied to watch Martin and Isabelle much in the last few days, but there was a welcome in Isabelle's eyes today which was beyond warm, and Martin went straight to her and put his arm around her.

He turned Isabelle slightly to face them and said to his sister, 'Madeleine, can I introduce you to Isabelle Bariol, my girlfriend.'

So there it was, out in the open! And then, in a further bombshell, he turned to Isabelle and said: 'I've told you about Madeleine, haven't I? She's my big sister who lives in Céret.'

Phew! So what had taken him ten years to tell Laure, he had told Isabelle in a matter of weeks. Laure could feel her own eyes widening, but Isabelle took the introduction in her stride.

'It's lovely to meet you,' she said, holding her hand out to Madeleine. 'Were those your little boys who went by just now with Daniel and Sylvie? I gave them both a chocolate from the bar – I hope you don't mind.'

She spoke with the natural courtesy of a nineteen-year-old speaking for the first time to a woman more than ten years older, but without the slightest awkwardness. Martin

183

watched on enraptured and tightened his arm around her waist.

Madeleine moved forward, ignoring Isabelle's outstretched hand, and kissed her on either cheek. Her long, dark mane brushing against Isabelle's golden curls as she pulled the girl down to sit at the table she had been clearing.

'Martin, it must surely be time for Isabelle's break. Why don't you go and order us coffee? I'd like to talk to your girlfriend.'

'And do I get to join you?' Martin was amused.

'If you like, when you have the coffee.'

Laure backed away. This was a family affair and no place for her. Her best friend Martin was moving into new territory, and Laura suddenly realised how wary of life she had become, for this was all going too fast and all the unreserved happiness in front of her just made her want to run away.

'If you think you can handle these two on your own, Isabelle,' she said, as playfully as she could, 'then I'll head down to the beach and see if Daniel is okay with the children.'

'Tell the boys to be good,' Madeleine said briefly, and then turned back to Isabelle. Laure smiled fleetingly at Martin and then whisked herself away.

She was in the water when Martin and Madeleine finally made it to the beach. She was sitting in the warmth of the shallows, giving advice to Enric and Luis, who were on the beach in front of her trying to build a fortress out of the rather pebbly sand. They had reached the stage where they were starting to bicker, so she was pleased to see their mother and uncle arriving.

'Daniel gave up waiting for you and took Julien home for his sleep,' she told them. 'And the boys are struggling a bit with their castle here because the stones won't stick together to make a tower.'

Martin swung himself down onto the sand beside his nephews. 'Well, it's not bad,' he said. 'But if you have a bucket you should come with me because I know where the best sand is, further up the beach. And you need some flat stones to make a road up to it, and some shells too, to decorate it afterwards.'

He pulled off his trousers and shirt as he spoke and stood up in his trunks. 'Got your buckets?' he asked them in Catalan. 'Then come with me, soldiers, because our army needs a castle!'

Madeleine grinned after him. 'What a good-natured person he is,' she said. She took a rug out of her beach bag and threw herself down onto it, heaving a contented sigh. 'And what a lovely girl Isabelle is. I'd say it's quite serious, wouldn't you?'

Laure frowned down slightly at the sand she was sifting between her hands. 'I hope so,' she answered. 'It's all very new, but Martin's a serious soul underneath his banter and he wouldn't have made the kind of declaration he did this afternoon unless it really mattered to him. But Isabelle's young and he's studying a long way away. She's a lovely girl, as you say, but we don't know that much about her really, do we? Will she stay in love from a distance, do you think?

I'd say he's the first person she's ever fallen for, but will he be the last?'

Madeleine knitted her brow, twisting a long strand of hair slowly through her fingers, as though she was thinking back through the meeting she'd just had with Isabelle. After a moment she nodded. 'I agree about her age – what is she, nineteen? And she has never been away from here, she told me. But on first meeting, she seems to me to be just the kind of person Martin needs. He's serious, as you say. In the past, he's got burned by falling for women who are too hard-edged, which is something you could never say about Isabelle. And she doesn't come across as a silly young girl. She has a lot of maturity about her, and she's intelligent.'

'But sheltered.'

'Do you mean she's had a nice, uncomplicated life? That can only be good for Martin. She'd be a very welcome addition to our complicated family!'

Laure was silenced. This family always seemed to make her feel as though she was too prickly and negative. She tried to work out her own thinking. If Martin was ready to come back to Vermeilla and become a village doctor, then she didn't think it would matter to him whether his wife had as much experience of the world as he had. The key issue was that he wasn't yet there, and had at least two more years to go before he would be qualified for general practice, plus he would then probably work in Montpellier for a while, while he waited for a place to become available in this area. It could be a long time.

She nodded at Madeleine in acknowledgement of her last point. 'Yes, you're right. Isabelle is genuine and nice, and could be just what Martin needs, but will she wait two years for him, or possibly four or five, until he moves back here?'

'Does she need to? Doesn't she have plans to study? Why can't she study in Montpellier?'

'You haven't met her father. He doesn't want her to go anywhere. He point-blank refuses to let her go so far away, and has a job lined up for her at Paulilles.'

'Then she and Martin will just have to get married!' Madeleine caught Laure's gape of surprise and grinned. 'All right, I'm jumping the gun! They announce that they are going out and I have them married off already. It's the big sister in me.'

Laure grinned back. She stretched and rolled over to lie on her front in the lapping waves, flattening herself to immerse her shoulders, which were beginning to feel the heat of the sun.

'Isabelle has younger siblings too,' she remarked. 'Perhaps that's why she's so mature.'

Madeleine put her head to one side. 'Possibly, though I'm not sure how mature I was at her age. But let's talk about you. Tell me how things are going with Robert's legal battle for you.'

Laure sighed and told her about Robert's calls and Lolo's statement, and was surprised by how mechanically the story came out, after so many hours anguishing over it. Madeleine watched her closely, but she said nothing and allowed her to finish the story.

'And Robert wants you to go with him to confront this young man?' she asked at the end.

Laure made a face. 'Yes, but I can't.'

'Why is that?'

'Well, I can't just travel to Bordeaux without any excuse. You and Martin are the only people here who know about my problems in Paris, and I can't leave here without my parents asking where I am going. And anyway,' she added, 'I don't have any money.'

Madeleine looked along the shore to where Martin and the two boys had finished their beachcombing and were making their way back.

'Here come three of my favourite men,' she said with a smile. 'Let's talk about this before they get here. Do you know, Laure, I don't think Robert would have asked you to make this journey if he didn't think your presence was important.'

'He said he could go alone if I couldn't make it.'

'Yes, but can't you? Let's think. You're about to work in partnership with Jordi at our gallery. Well, what if I were to invite you to spend a couple of days with us this week to work with Jordi? That would seem quite natural, surely, and would cover your absence? And as for money, well Jordi and I would happily advance you a suitable sum on your paintings, to be redeemed when they are sold.'

Laure pulled herself up suddenly onto her elbows. 'Oh, but I couldn't! I couldn't take your money like that!'

'But why not? Your paintings will sell, don't worry about that. In my opinion, we're the winners in this partnership, in being able to display your work. And it's what Robert would want me to do. He's one of my favourite men too, and I've learned that he isn't often wrong.'

Laure was silenced. With all obstacles lifted to her journey to Bordeaux, all that was left was her own reluctance. *I don't want to see Lolo*, she realised with a sudden intensity that clenched her stomach. But she would go. She knew that she would go. Between them, Robert and all his family were trying to give her back her future. Madeleine and Robert were as generous as Martin, and as he came up to them, followed by the boys carrying two buckets that were heaving with construction materials, she greeted him with a smile and got to her feet to help them build the sand castle.

'Robert was going to phone again this evening, wasn't he?' she asked Martin. 'Well, when he does you can tell him I'll join him in Bordeaux. For it seems I have a sponsor!'

'You do, but I think we can add to that as well,' Madeleine came in. 'We'll take Martin and Philippe to see your paintings in a while, and I know what will happen when Philippe sees those studies of Julien. He'll want one, the one where Julien is so intense in concentration, and he'll buy it for Colette, I know. You can then have some cash from a real sale, as well as the advance we'll give you.'

Laure paused in the act of cupping water in her hands to mix with the sand. 'Oh no, I couldn't do that! I'll give them the painting, if they want it, or do them another one. I can't take money for painting a picture of my nephew for his own grandmother.'

Madeleine shook her head. 'Back me up, Martin. If you offer the painting to Colette, then it's your gift, Laure. You can do that anytime, another time. But when Philippe sees that picture, he will desperately want to give it as his own gift. He's always trying to find ways to spoil Colette, to make her happy and there's precious little you can do for a woman who needs so little.'

'Madeleine's right,' Martin assured Laure. '*Maman* always refuses gifts, but she wouldn't refuse that one. You don't have to charge Philippe the full price but if, as I gather, this money is to pay for your journey to Bordeaux, then I'd take it if I were you. Use it to buy some wine or something for Robert because, knowing him, he'll refuse to let you pay for anything once you're there.'

Oh, help. Of course, Robert, with his fancy salary, would plan a trip to Bordeaux on a different scale from her. She would need some cash just so that she didn't feel even more like a penniless, rebellious, troublesome student than she already was. The whole trip filled her with dread on so many levels. No, she thought, I won't go empty-handed with no more than my train fare. I'll go dressed, I'll go made up, and I'll find some way not to look like a pauper.

She looked across at Madeleine and Martin. 'All right then,' she assented. 'I'll take your advance and I'll also sell a picture to Philippe if he wants one.' She had a rueful smile for the passionate rejection of commercial values so embodied on the barricades of May. But it had ended with pay rises for the workers, hadn't it, and part of their fight had also been for proper funding for the University and proper facilities for students. It all needed money and so did she. Long live the commercialisation of art!

CHAPTER 22

Wednesday morning saw Laure on the train for Bordeaux. It would take her more than six hours and Robert's journey from Paris would take perhaps five, and she marvelled more and more that he was taking the best part of three days off work to fight her campaign.

She felt like an errant teenager today, like a much younger Laure who had to make up stories to her parents. She hadn't enjoyed telling them lies, but her whole life was a pretence at the moment, and the only way to resolve it was to go to Bordeaux. Today was the last day of July and there was precious little time left to build her defence before the University committee would meet.

She'd had only a five minute chat with Robert on the phone since Sunday, and he told her he'd found Jérôme, who it seemed was flabbergasted by what Lolo appeared to have done. I'll fill you in on everything when we meet, was all Robert had said and she was impatient to have more news. Robert would be waiting for her at Bordeaux station and he'd hired a car to take them the few kilometres to Saint-

Emilion, where they would sleep since it was close to the Lavignière vineyards. It was unknown territory for Laure, and at any other time, she would have been excited to be visiting the most famous wine-growing area in the world. But today, there was no excitement, only apprehension.

Until Toulouse, the train route was familiar to her. It followed the Canal du Midi and passed the beautiful medieval city of Carcassonne, but the terrain changed after Toulouse. Her journey now traced the path of the river Garonne down towards the Atlantic, away now from the vineyards, through rich farming country dotted with ancient fortified villages.

And then, as they came closer to Bordeaux, the vines reappeared on flat, sweeping plains that bore no relation to the craggy hills behind Vermeilla. At home, the vines clung claw-like to steep, terraced slopes and everything was small-scale, but here around Bordeaux, the vines stood tall and in straight rows, rolling away to the horizon on huge plantations. Here there was money in wine, serious money, of which the Lavignières had their share. You couldn't help but be impressed.

As the train drew into Bordeaux station Laure knew another moment's apprehension, wondering what she would do if Robert wasn't there to meet her. But as she stepped down with her overnight bag, she saw him immediately on the other side of the barrier, smoking one of the American cigarettes that she'd seen him smoke in Vermeilla, and which made him stand out from his Gauloises-smoking fellows. His city suit and tie looked less incongruous here than in

Vermeilla, but he still looked daunting, and Laure drew a determined breath as she made her way towards him.

He greeted her with a conventional peck on each cheek. 'I'm very glad that you could make it,' he said. 'It will be much harder for Lavignière to brazen things out with you in front of him. I have a hire car parked outside.'

He took her bag and led the way through the station to where a classy looking Citroen DS was parked. He opened the passenger door for her and she slid nervously inside. It felt very strange indeed to be here alone with Robert Garriga.

He seemed to understand this because he made idle conversation throughout their drive, pointing out some famous landmarks as they crossed the river in Bordeaux and a couple of vineyards whose names she recognised on the road to Saint-Emilion, chatting generally about the Bordeaux vintage. Within an hour, they had Saint-Emilion in their sights; the stunning hilltop town with its old yellow stone buildings and red roofs bathed in late afternoon sunshine. They threaded their way through its historic narrow streets and as they neared the centre, Robert pulled over to the right and parked in the courtyard of a small, elegant looking hotel.

'I stayed here a couple of years ago,' he told her, 'when I came down with some friends for a tasting tour. It's a fairly small hotel but they have a nice restaurant.'

Laure nodded, still annoyingly mute, and followed him into the hotel reception. As they filled in their registration forms she heard Robert refer to her as 'my sister', which helped, for this was a role she could play without discomfort.

'Shall we meet for drinks before dinner? At seven o'clock perhaps?' Robert asked.

She agreed, as naturally as she could, and he carried her bag for her up the stairs to the first floor and along the deep-carpeted corridor to the door of her room, where he left her. Laure opened the panelled door and found herself in a lovely, airy room with a private bathroom and a balcony, which looked down onto a spacious, green inner courtyard where a small stone fountain cooled the air. The sheer gentility of the place held Laure immobile for a moment, but it was peaceful too and the sound of playing water came through the open window and soothed frayed nerves.

She had an hour and she took her time, washing away her stress in a long bath, taking care over her makeup. It made her feel insensibly better and by the time she came downstairs she had reminded herself that she was a woman who lived an independent life in Paris and she began to see the funny side of this situation. She wondered what Madeleine would think if she knew she had a new sister. She too, Laure thought, would be quite amused.

She found Robert already at a table on the small terrace which gave onto the courtyard. There were other guests taking early evening drinks on the terrace and behind them was the restaurant, its full-length glass doors open to the evening air. As she approached Robert stood up and a waiter appeared to pull out her chair. She wasn't used to such treatment but it was undeniably pleasant, and when the waiter filled two champagne glasses from a bottle of Dom Pérignon, she decided just to sit back and enjoy it.

'Well, it's not from Bordeaux, but there's nothing wrong with a glass of champagne,' Robert said to her. 'Here's to families!'

He raised his glass and she smiled. '*Santé*,' she said and took a sip. It was vintage champagne, super dry and super smooth, with a host of the tiniest bubbles that misted the glass, and she remembered Dom Pérignon's own words when he first tasted champagne. 'I'm tasting stars,' he had said, and in truth, that's what it tasted like.

The waiter came back with a plate of savoury canapés and then left them alone. Laure bit into a miniature pastry filled with a delicious tapenade and gave a sigh of satisfaction. Then she took another sip from her glass and decided the time had come to talk business.

'So, how did your meeting with Jérôme go?' she asked Robert. 'Did you find him easily?'

Robert put his glass down on the table and settled himself in his chair. 'It wasn't too difficult,' he said. 'The gallery owner wouldn't give me his contact details but he passed on a note for me, and I think my message intrigued Jérôme because he phoned me quite quickly. He couldn't believe what I had to tell him and wanted to meet me to hear more. He's a nice guy, isn't he?'

Laure was surprised. 'I wouldn't have thought he was your type,' she said.

'Why? Because he's an artist?'

Laure conjured up Jérôme in her head, with his old cotton trousers and baggy shirt, and the great, shaggy beard he grew because he couldn't be bothered to shave. She looked again at Robert, but he was there before her.

'I think you're forgetting whom I have as a brother-in-law. Jordi would give Jérôme a good run for his money! I think I said to you back in Vermeilla that I keep my feet firmly on common land, Laure.'

Laure gestured idly at the terrace around them and raised one eyebrow, and he grinned in acknowledgement. It made him look far more disarming. 'Okay,' he admitted, 'I do like to eat and live well! But I can do simple too, believe me. Or, in fact, don't bother because tomorrow I'll take you to lunch at a very modest little *brasserie* near here which does great omelettes.'

'Truffle omelettes, perhaps?' She was teasing him now and enjoying it. Would he remember his little exchange with Madeleine in Céret over truffle oil?

'No! This is a little *brasserie* we're talking about! You don't have to have truffles to make a good omelette. Fresh herbs are all you need!'

He had reddened slightly and she relented. Leave the poor man alone, she thought. 'All right, tell me about Jérôme,' she said.

'Well, he reiterated what he'd said in his statement, of course, that you were acting to prevent trouble when you removed the weapons and that they had nothing to do with you. He has an interesting outsider's view of your student group since he isn't a student himself, and he clearly likes and respects you.'

'And Lolo?' Laure made herself ask.

Robert hesitated. 'Well, he seemed to think Lavignière was rather full of himself and would always look after his own interests,' he said at last, and then stopped.

'He isn't wrong,' Laure admitted. 'But you say he was surprised by what Lolo did?'

'Yes. You see, he seemed to think there was a particular reason for Lavignière to be loyal to you.'

He spoke gently, watching Laure as he did so and she looked quickly away, fixing her eyes on her glass of champagne.

'Yes, well, he isn't totally wrong there, either,' Laure said when she had herself under control. 'But there was no established relationship between us.'

She heard the protest in her voice and cringed. It made her sound very pathetic. She felt so foolish now for the role she had played in propping up Lolo's ego, for doing what she'd been so determined not to do, in becoming one of his conquests. She made herself look directly at Robert. Stop squirming, she thought, and let's address this honestly.

'I've realised now,' she told him, 'that Lolo had no interest in me beyond the idlest amusement. I think he liked being with the "top" student, if you like. He is very conscious of his own image.'

Robert nodded. 'You're also very beautiful, remember, and you have a kind of gamine chic which must have appealed to him. I can imagine that he would have enjoyed everyone knowing that you were with him.'

Laure grimaced. 'How unflattering to think that I was just an adornment! And then at the end, when I was in trouble, he disappeared completely from my life. I thought he was busy with the *atelier*, but Pierre told me Lolo had pretty much withdrawn from the student occupation at the end. He was still in Paris because I found him at our regular café, just after the *atelier* had closed, but he was keeping himself to himself it seems. Pierre found him changed and it troubled him. But Lolo was charming to me that evening. It's all very strange.'

Robert frowned down at his glass. 'Laure...' he started, and then stopped abruptly. He took an almost angry swig of the champagne and then started again.

'I told you about the dining club, didn't I, that your Rector belongs to? Well, Charles Gruet, the lawyer, caught up with him there at the weekend and he told the Rector he was representing you.'

He hesitated and Laure drew a breath. Something was coming that he was having difficulty telling her. The silence extended between them and eventually she prompted him.

'And?' she said.

He toyed with his glass, then looked up at her again and spoke with a careful lack of emphasis. 'The Rector told him that your Professor fellow has put a formal proposal to the committee for Lavignière to take over the prize you won. He said Lavignière had asked for it.'

It hit Laure like a cold shower. She just gazed at Robert, frozen, as the implications of what he had said worked their way through the passages of her brain. So that was it! It all made the most horrifying sense. Lolo had seen his opportunity as soon as she was arrested, when he knew that she'd been caught by the very Professor who so much preferred his work to hers. And from that moment, he'd acted quietly to unseat her, and to put himself in her place, first writing that false, damaging statement, then what? She could picture him visiting Professor Duchamp to build a case for himself, and as she thought about it a deep anger gripped her.

What would he have said, at that meeting with the Professor? That his statement to the police had actually been over generous because he didn't want to damage Laure? That she was actually hand in glove with the anarchists? That he, Lolo, had only been at the *atelier* himself to try to keep things stable? He could have invented practically anything because he was speaking to a man who wanted to believe.

She remembered Lolo commenting once that it would be much better to send him to New York in the autumn, rather than her, because his work was American influenced, whereas hers was profoundly European. He'd laughed as he said it, but she'd known he was envious underneath, of that trip to New York and of the prestige her award gave her. She'd just never believed he would do anything about it.

And then after he'd met with the Professor, he'd backed away from the *atelier*, away from the limelight he'd previously sought throughout the events of May and away also from Laure. She thought back to the one evening where she had hunted him down, when he'd told her he was heading home the following day. Had he really left or did he just want her to believe he had gone, so she wouldn't seek him out again? He'd been so charming too, so reassuring. So false, as she now realised.

She'd been dreading confronting Lolo, but now she wanted more than anything else to see him. She couldn't wait to see his face when he realised they knew everything. Without Robert she would never have known the content of that police statement, or that Lolo was the new proposed prize holder. But now she did know, and if he didn't change his statement she would make sure every student at the *École des Beaux-Arts* knew what he had done. She could make his life at the Sorbonne unliveable.

She looked over at Robert, who was still watching her with that same concern, worried by the news he'd had to break. He'd certainly managed to dumbfound her! She breathed out in a long, soundless whistle and then grinned at him a little limply.

'Well, well, well! So Jean-Louis Lavignière is just quite simply a complete bastard.' she said, shaking her head slowly to try to stop it spinning. 'Don't worry, Robert, you haven't upset me. In fact, you've just liberated me! I can't thank you enough. Now it all makes sense and I can see what Lolo's motives were, and I don't need to make any more excuses or wonder what I did wrong, or if I'm in some way responsible. He's just a slimy slug and I'd like to squash him under my heel.'

Robert smiled back at her, relieved. 'Attagirl! And you think you can?'

'Oh yes, now I know I can! There's no way that piece of low-life would ever have imagined I'd find out what he'd done. And the last thing he'd want is for anyone else to find out among the students, his public!'

'So you'll give him your silence in exchange for a letter?'

'Exactly. And I'll tell Pierre we were mistaken about the police statement too, but only after I get my University place back in full.'

'Then it looks as though Lavignière is in for an unpleasant shock tomorrow.' Robert raised his glass. 'Shall we make a toast to his discomfiture?'

'No. I want to make a toast to you. You've saved me, Robert.'

He blushed and shrugged uncomfortable shoulders. 'Not yet, I haven't.'

'Yes, you have.' Laure felt a surge of confidence and wanted to shout out her exhilaration, but the select surroundings of the hotel terrace stopped her. 'You've changed everything and I don't know how I'm ever going to be able to repay you.'

'You can paint me a picture.'

She grinned at him, shaking her head. 'One picture? Oh no, *cher* Monsieur, for what you have done I'll paint you a whole private exhibition!'

Chapter 23

Saint-Emilion had a population of only three and a half thousand, but it seemed so much bigger as they drove out of it the following morning. It was even more magnificent than Laure remembered from their arrival yesterday, when she'd been too tense and uncomfortable really to register anything. Today everything felt different and she could appreciate the beauty of ancient yellow stone, cobbled squares, monasteries and cloisters covered with ivy, alleyways which snaked upwards towards the ancient church, and everywhere cool greenery in the midst of the stone.

It wasn't the cheerful, colourful charm of her Catalan village, with its painted houses and sparkling blue sea. This was more refined, elegant and sober, and it was hard to imagine such class ever quite letting its hair down. The summer festivals here would be a great deal more restrained than the street parties of Vermeilla!

And that kind of majesty persisted in the surrounding country. Saint-Emilion dominated this whole corner of Aquitaine from its hilltop position and from the town, in every direction for as far as the eye could see, extended the vines, groaning now with fruit.

It was only a short distance north to where the Lavignière vineyard sat, in an area which Robert assured Laure was renowned for its 'Bordeaux Supérieur'. Her nerves returned as they neared Lolo's home. She'd been so curious about it for so long, but now it was more daunting than intriguing.

The road took them through acres of vineyards belonging to the Lavignière domain before they reached the chateau itself. They drove in through ancient high gates and were immediately in a huge deserted yard surrounded on three sides by closed doors, some small ones leading to offices, she thought, and some huge ones that presumably hid the wine cellars and winemaking facility. The door to one of the storerooms was open, and a couple of men were loading boxes unhurriedly into a small lorry. It was a sleepy scene in the summer heat, but the yard would presumably look quite different in a few weeks' time, when the grape harvest would be in full swing and tonnes of grapes would arrive to make Bordeaux Supérieur.

In the distance, hidden behind some trees, was a rambling old mansion, baronial but discreet. Lolo's home. Laure gulped but refused to feel humbled. She had done with being humbled by Lolo Lavignière. But there was an explanation in that house. It explained why Lolo always felt so comfortable at the top, in the lead, surrounded by the less assured. And it explained why he thought, just as Professor Duchamp had, that a provincial girl from the far south should never have won a prestigious award when he hadn't. She took one last look at the house, then turned away and stepped determinedly out of the car, following Robert as he approached the two workers.

The men greeted them courteously and asked if they were looking to buy wine. When Robert asked instead for Jean-Louis, they looked a little surprised, but not greatly interested. He was not there, they told him, but should be back very soon, since he had left some time before to take a delivery to a valued local client. In that case, Robert said, with his most urbane smile, they would take the opportunity to taste some of the Lavignière wines while waiting for him, if it was possible.

It was all very civil and unhurried, and Laure, still silent behind Robert, followed in his steps as they were ushered through one of the doors into a small room with a discreet counter and a huge old upturned barrel, beautifully varnished, which served very appropriately as a tasting table. It was surrounded by four high stools, and Robert and Laure were invited to be seated while one of the men went to fetch someone to help them.

There followed a very civilised wine-tasting, led by a young woman with practised skills, who offered them one by one a series of four red wines, increasing in age and smoothness, and of course, in price. Robert was very knowledgeable and engaged the young woman in a lively discussion which Laure followed with interest. She knew her wine, but not at this level, and her purchases were limited by her student budget. But Robert was clearly ready to buy and the saleswoman gave him the respect his bank balance deserved. He was just concluding a purchase to be despatched to his address in Paris when Laure spotted Lolo passing by the window.

She tensed but he passed straight by, and she wondered if he hadn't been told he had visitors. But it seemed the workers had done their job, for a couple of moments later Lolo came into the room by an inside door. He smiled at the young woman before he addressed himself to Robert.

'You were asking for me, Monsieur?' he said, and then he spotted Laure. He looked genuinely shocked and by no means delighted.

'Laure!' he exhaled and then he pulled himself together, although his attempt at sangfroid didn't quite come off. 'How lovely to see you! Are you on a visit to our region?' He looked speculatively from her to Robert, as if trying to decide what their relationship might be.

It was Robert who replied, before Laure could speak. 'Mademoiselle Forestier and I would be grateful if you could spare us a moment of your time, Monsieur Lavignière. We have come specifically to see you.'

He spoke very neutrally and Laure thought he was deliberately not giving any information, not saying anything that might put Lolo at his ease. He's a lawyer, she remembered and smiled inwardly. If Robert wanted to play with Lolo, then he was welcome to do so as far as she was concerned.

Lolo looked different here in rural Aquitaine. He had abandoned his coloured trousers and patterned waistcoat, and his little goatee beard looked less provocatively original above a conventional white linen shirt. She wondered if he still painted during his time here at home or whether he left his whole artist's persona behind when he left Paris.

Lolo looked over at the young woman who had served them and at the order she had just written out, which was lying on the counter with Robert's cheque next to it. He'll be registering that Robert has money, thought Laure. That can only help.

'I see you've bought some of our 1961 vintage, Monsieur,' he said, injecting ease into his voice. 'You have excellent taste. It was a very fine year for Saint-Emilion wines.' He then turned to the young woman and suggested that she could leave if she wanted to.

'Mademoiselle Forestier is a friend of mine from the Sorbonne, Anne-Marie,' he told the woman. 'If you've finished all the details of the sale, then I'd like to spend a little time catching up with her.'

The simper the young Anne-Marie gave him suggested that she too was one of his conquests. She shot Laure a speculative look, then handed Robert the receipt for his purchase, wished them a good day and left them alone in a silence that seemed to hang suspended in the room. Little motes of dust hung with it in the sunlight that filtered through the ancient window. Laure looked at Robert and thought he was waiting Lolo out.

Lolo stood for a moment just watching them, as motionless as they were, and then he came over to the tasting table and deliberately leaned down to kiss Laure on both cheeks.

'There's no need to ask you how you are, *ma chérie*,' he murmured to her. 'You look radiant. How happy I am to see you.'

Laure reeled at the absurdity of such a comment, at the hypocrisy in his words, when for the last six weeks he had condemned her to live through a period so far from radiant. But in a way he was right. She was not the same crushed creature who had left Paris in July. Her back gave her no more pain, she had regained some weight and the sun had given her back her colour. And she had also gained the weaponry with which to defend herself – physically and mentally she was different.

Her smile back was just as false as his own, and she gestured to the seat next to hers. He sat down. 'And so you decided to drop in to see me?' he continued.

Laure looked at Robert, who gestured to her to take the lead. 'Why yes, Lolo. May I introduce my lawyer, by the way? This is Robert Garriga, who is representing me in my attempt to clear my name in Paris. Monsieur Garriga has, of course, met with the police who arrested me and has been given access to the witness statements they took that day.'

She could have sworn Lolo changed colour. She kept her voice unemotional as she continued, but made her statement a question. 'It seems that Pierre and Jérôme gave accounts which matched with what I had told the police, but that your account was strangely different?'

'Different? How was it different?' Lolo demanded.

Laure hesitated and looked at Robert, realising suddenly that she hadn't ever seen Lolo's testimony. It hadn't occurred to her to ask whether Robert actually had the transcript or had even read it himself. I wouldn't make a lawyer, she thought with an inward grimace, but she needn't have worried. Robert was already sliding a folded document from the inside pocket of his jacket.

'I think you'll agree that there were some significant differences,' he said. 'Would you like me to read you a short extract from your discussion with the police, Monsieur Lavignière?' He smoothed out the sheets of paper, perhaps three in number, and ran his finger down, clearly looking for some specific passage. Lolo now looked deeply uncomfortable but said nothing.

'Yes, here we are!' Robert continued, with a satisfied nod, and began reading.

'Lavignière: *I told the most militant students that they should remove all weapons from the occupied building and Laure Forestier offered to carry them to the store, to stock them there.*

Officer: *Did she do so with the agreement of the militant students?*

Lavignière: *I'm not sure, but it seemed to me that she might have.*

Officer: *Would you say that Laure Forestier was close to the militants?*

Lavignière: *Yes, I would.*

Officer: *And was she one of those in charge of the weapons?*

Lavignière: *I couldn't say that, I couldn't really be sure of that. Laure Forestier is one of our committee members, and we've had no real reason until now to doubt her good intentions. But many of the students have been acting with increasing extremism recently, even some of the committee members.'*

Robert paused. 'I could continue if you like, Monsieur Lavignière. Or perhaps you would like to read the transcript for yourself?'

He pushed it across the table, but Lolo didn't touch it. He kept his eyes on Robert, his expression veiled.

'If you have read the whole of my testimony, you'll know that I defended Laure and said she wasn't responsible for those weapons.'

'No, you said she might or might not have been, with an implication of guilt.' Robert's voice was no longer so urbane. He was clipped and angry and Laure could feel her own anger growing to match his. Hearing Lolo's false statement made her boil.

'You said the anarchists knew I was taking the weapons away! How could you?' she threw at Lolo. 'You knew, just as all of the committee did, that I was removing the weapons to a place where the militants wouldn't find them. You were the one who called them out to a meeting, remember, so that they wouldn't know what I was doing? It was all agreed between us to prevent any trouble.'

Lolo looked at her and shrugged contemptuously. 'Did we really know that you hadn't already met with the militants that morning?' he asked her. 'You came in late to our committee meeting upstairs and made out that you had found your way into the building without any of the other students seeing you. It occurred to me afterwards that might not have been true. It was important not to get you into trouble, but in what I said to the police I was just obeying

209

my conscience. I couldn't, in all honesty, say that you were clear of all suspicion.'

Laure couldn't believe her ears but as his cynical lies sank in, she could feel a new dread creeping up on her. If this was the line that he was going to take, then all except her closest friends in Paris might believe him.

'You know that's not true!' she gasped.

'Do I? Does anyone?' Lolo was smiling again now. 'But you're free, aren't you? That I just wanted to obey my conscience didn't harm you, Laure, as anyone can see.'

'But it did, Lavignière,' Robert interjected. 'Your lies have meant that Laure's name hasn't been properly cleared, and have left a damaging element of suspicion hanging over her at the University. But you didn't stop there, did you? Tell me, how long did you wait after Laure's arrest before you went to see Professor Duchamp, to put in your bid for her prize?'

The complacent smile disappeared from Lolo's face and he inhaled sharply, recoiling slightly on his stool. Laure saw him swallow and crossed her fingers. He'd bounced back so successfully from their first challenge that she was beginning to wonder whether anything they could throw at him would shake him for long. She decided to let Robert handle things from now onwards. She was just too vulnerable to Lolo's barbs.

Lolo pulled out a Gauloises and lit it, drawing deeply on the cigarette before he finally answered.

'I'm sorry, but I really don't know what you're talking about,' he said.

He offered a cigarette to Robert, who waved it away. 'We have our information from the Rector, Lavignière,' he replied, never taking his eyes off Lolo.

'But what information?' Lolo wanted to know, keeping his voice supercilious.

'That Professor Duchamp has put your name forward to take over Laure's award and the internship place.'

Lolo visibly relaxed. 'Well, how kind of him! I know he has always appreciated my work, but it is really very flattering that he should think of me for the award.'

He took another drag of his cigarette, watching closely for Robert's reaction.

'Except that the Professor didn't think of it on his own, did he? It seems you visited him to request it. I'm looking forward to asking him for the details of that meeting.'

Lolo flinched slightly. 'But the Professor is on holiday,' he retaliated.

'How do you know that, I wonder?' Robert spoke contemptuously now and didn't wait for a reply. 'You needn't worry though, he'll come back before the University committee meets. I gather from the Rector that he himself isn't as convinced as the Professor about your candidature. Do you think if he learns that you have lobbied in an underhand way that he'll agree to you getting that award? Or any other of the committee members, for that matter?'

Lolo looked uncomfortable now. 'All right, so what if I did ask for the award? If Laure can't have it, then the place is vacant and there is nothing wrong with me putting in an application.'

He threw his cigarette on the floor and ground it out with his foot, then he looked viciously at Laure and almost spat at her. 'What do you think to gain coming here to throw a load of accusations at me, you stupid bitch? Don't assume that if I don't get the award it will come back to you. You can take it from me that Professor Duchamp has written you out of the University completely. Either I'll have the award next year, or no one will – it certainly won't be you!'

Robert held out a hand to stop Laure replying. 'Ah,' he said to Lolo, 'but when Laure has your letter to the University, explaining what you have done, then I think they may well change their minds, don't you?'

He got a leer in reply. 'Why on earth should I do that, Mr Lawyer?'

This time Laure leapt into the conversation. 'Because if you don't, then I'll publish everything that we know among the students, and among the lecturing staff as well. How much fun do you think your life would be at the *Beaux-Arts* if no one wants to know you, and without even the award to make up for it?'

'I could cope.'

'Could you?' She conjured up an image of the young American lecturer who had brought so many New York art world connections to the University. He was a modernist and had been a supporter of the student occupation at the Sorbonne. He was Lolo's academic supervisor, but also very friendly with Laure, and he and she had spent many hours already planning her New York internship. She raised one questioning eye at Lolo.

'And if Dr Longfellow were to find out, do you think he would still agree to supervise your dissertation? I think not! And then, Lolo dear, not only would you not have the internship you desire, but I think you might find yourself struggling to finish your diploma at all, don't you?'

She'd scored a hit and they all knew it. The young woman Anne-Marie came back into the room and Lolo almost snarled at her to get out.

'I just wanted to ask if you'd like coffee,' she stuttered, and Lolo shook his head.

'Our two guests are just about to leave,' he said to her, in a tone that made her scuttle back out.

'Are you telling me,' he snarled at Laure, 'that you propose to go into the *École des Beaux-Arts* even if you're not a student, and seek out Dr Longfellow to talk to him about me?'

'Most certainly Lolo! And do you know what, I would have the utmost pleasure in doing so. To repeat what you said just a few moments ago, I would really only be obeying my conscience.'

There was a silence while he digested this, and then his face twisted in an angry snarl. 'So tell me, *salope*, you snooping bitch, since you know so much,' he spat at her, 'what is it exactly that you and your fancy lawyer want me to do?'

It was Robert who answered, quick as a flash. 'I will give you very precise instructions, don't you worry Lavignière! And the next time you call Mademoiselle Forestier a *salope*, this same fancy lawyer will shove your foul tongue where you won't be able to speak for many days.'

Chapter 24

Laure had rarely been so pleased to get out of anywhere as she was to leave the Lavignière winery that day. The further away they drove, the more she was able to banish Lolo's angry face from her mind. Her every nerve had been on edge, and as the tension slid slowly away, it left behind the inevitable reaction and an incipient headache knocked dully at her drained mind.

Robert drove slowly and she thought he too must be worn out. He hadn't finished with Lolo yet either. It had been agreed that Robert would return to the Lavignière estate later that day to collect the documents Lolo had to prepare. Robert had insisted on two handwritten documents. The first would be a new statement for the police, and to make it sound plausible, Robert had suggested that Lolo should say that he had recently met one or more of the militant students, whose account of that morning when Laure was arrested had completely confirmed her innocence and made him realise that all his doubts had been unfounded.

'You can tell them your conscience won't allow you to leave Laure's reputation tarnished in any way,' Robert had told him with unmistakable irony.

And the next document he'd demanded was a letter to the Committee, in which Lolo was to say that in the light of the new statement he was copying to them, which cleared Laure of any wrongdoing, he hoped that any threat to her award would be removed and that he himself was withdrawing his candidature.

Lolo had argued that it was no easy task to frame such delicate documents and that he would write them over the next few days, and then send them directly to the police and to the University, but Robert was having none of it.

'I'll stand over you and give you the words if you want,' he'd told Lolo. 'But one way or another, I want those two documents in my hands before I leave here tomorrow morning. I can call for them at your house this evening if you like?'

Never had anyone looked less keen. Lolo clearly had no desire for them to pitch up at his family home, with all the explanations that would involve.

'No, just come here to the office at around five o'clock,' he said through gritted teeth. 'I'll find time to write the stuff this afternoon, and then I'll leave the documents with Anne-Marie.'

Robert acquiesced, before adding with a smile that if the documents didn't meet their needs, then he would just stroll up to the house anyway.

'And if you're out, of course, then I can just go through them with your parents!' he said as they moved towards the door. He'd held the door open for Laure and then they were both outside. The two men had finished loading the lorry and were sitting on a wall smoking a cigarette in the midday sun. One of the men raised a casual hand in greeting and Robert wished them a *Bonne journée*. The sleepy scene seemed strangely unreal compared with the hostility they'd just left behind, and Laure trod almost gingerly over the cobbles to the car.

As she slid into her seat and closed the door she let out a long sigh. 'Phew,' was all she said, and then, 'Thank you!'

Robert smiled. 'You're welcome!' he replied. And then they were silent, both lost in thought until they came to the outskirts of Saint-Emilion.

It was Robert who broke the reverie. 'Well, Laure, I think we've earned ourselves lunch, don't you?' he said.

She laughed. 'An omelette?' she asked.

'The best omelette in the world,' he agreed. 'And with a glass of fine Bordeaux to accompany it.'

'I fancy a chilled glass of white, so cold that it has little beads of moisture on the glass,' Laure said, and could taste it already.

'Then you shall have one!' Robert agreed.

He drove straight past their hotel and took them a bit further around the town to where a little brasserie sat, with its terrace giving directly onto the road. A honeysuckle covered its yellow stone frontage and was threatening to invade the white painted windows, and some simple wooden troughs filled with geraniums separated the terrace from the road. It looked friendly and shaded, and from the number of people already sitting at the tables, it must serve good food as well.

Robert parked and they found a little table for two at one end of the terrace, where they were unlikely to be overheard. Laure realised suddenly that she was ravenous, and looking at her watch, saw that it was nearly one o'clock. Their trip out to the vineyard had taken much longer than she could have imagined.

They ordered green salads and omelettes, and Robert chose a half bottle of Sauternes as an aperitif. It came on a bed of ice with all the dewy beads Laure could have asked for, and she felt a rush of pleasure as the luscious, sweet liquid eased over her dry throat muscles. She raised her glass to Robert and he touched it with his.

'Well, I think that was a good morning's work, don't you?' he said.

'Thanks to you! You were brilliantly prepared, and you handled Lolo like a professional.'

'I *am* a professional,' he said immodestly, but then gave her a disarming grin. 'He wouldn't have buckled though if you hadn't been there. You had the inside knowledge of what to threaten him with. Bringing in his academic supervisor was inspired.'

'So it was a joint effort.' Laure leaned back in her chair and contemplated her glass. 'It's not won yet though, is it? Lolo's statement has to be accepted by the police and the charge against my name has to be dropped, and then old Professor Duchamp has to get over how much he dislikes me, and give me back my prize.'

Robert topped up her glass. 'If Lavignière writes what I've told him to, then Charles Gruet will have no trouble arguing your case with the police. They've had enough of the whole student protest thing now and if the donkeys at ground level won't close the case, Charles has good connections higher up who will listen to reason.'

'And the University?'

'Your Professor is not the only one on that committee, and he'll look pretty churlish if he maintains his case against you. They don't have to give you back your prize, remember – they haven't actually taken it away. They just have to leave things as they are. But we'll see once I get back to Paris, and once Charles has the letter to work with. Charles ought to be able to attend the committee meeting to represent you, even if briefly, and if we think it would help to have you there too, then we might ask you to come up to Paris.'

Laure felt herself tensing up again and took another sip of the wine. All she wanted was for this to be all over, but she had to be sensible. And she had to be positive too. Robert didn't seem to harbour any doubts that they would bring this off successfully, and he had the patience of the legal mind. Well, she would be patient too.

'It will be all right, Laure, trust me,' Robert was saying, watching her face.

She smiled at him as the waiter appeared with their omelettes. 'Oh, I trust you, don't worry. And if you believe things are going to be all right, then I do too! My goodness, these omelettes look amazing. I can't believe how hungry I am!'

The omelettes were indeed amazing. Robert had stuck to his faith in a simple herb filling, but Laure had opted for mushrooms and the creamy omelette was bursting with them, little brown field mushrooms flavoured with parsley and a little garlic. It was simply presented with a sprinkling of crisp sautéed potatoes, and in the middle of the table the waiter placed a bowl of green salad and a half a baguette freshly cut in a little wicker basket. Laure attacked the food as though yesterday's cordon bleu dinner had never happened, and as she ate all her courage returned, along with her sense of fun.

'Are you trying to get me drunk?' she laughed at Robert, as he poured her a glass of red to go with the omelette.

'What, on a glass and a half of Sauternes and a single glass of Saint-Emilion? And you a girl brought up in Vermeilla!'

'Mmm,' she said, tasting the wine. 'I'm not sure that we drink anything quite as fine as this in Vermeilla. It goes brilliantly with the omelette.'

'And with cheese – you will have cheese, won't you? They have a great blue cheese here which goes like a dream with this wine.'

Laure let herself go. With the wine came a lassitude which crept through her muscles and left her limp. She'd slept badly for days now, ever since Robert first phoned her last week to tell her what Lolo had done. She was bone tired and now that the tension was gone all her energy had gone with it.

She had offered to go back with Robert to the vineyard this afternoon, but she wasn't sorry that he'd said no.

'It's tougher for you than it is for me,' he'd said as delicately as he could, and she knew he was referring to her relationship with Lolo. She wanted to talk about that, but not now. She was still digesting her disgust at Lolo's behaviour this morning and trying to get over how degraded she felt to have been so fascinated by him. It was humiliating to have been so wrong and so gullible, like a stupid teenager with a crush on the cockiest boy in the class.

She closed her mind to it and ate cheese, and dessert, and took yet another glass of wine, and when they got back to the hotel she made her way straight to her room and stretched out fully dressed on her bed.

The room was cool and the bed was soft and comfortable. She nestled her head into the thick feather pillow and breathed in the scent of fresh linen. What I really feel most of all is thankful she thought, and within minutes she was asleep.

Chapter 25

After dinner that evening, they went for walk into the incredibly mellow light of Saint-Emilion. There was a group of young people celebrating in one bar as they passed, but the little streets were quiet apart from that as they made their way up to the top of the village, with just a few other couples out strolling in the silken evening air.

They carried on climbing, and when they reached a little square at the top of the village they were alone apart from a solitary cat out on its night-time prowl. There was a special hush up here. They made their way over to a stone wall that bordered one side of the square, and there, suddenly exposed below them, was an amazing, panoramic view down over one whole side of the village. The stone buildings spread below them were lit up by the street lights in the softest yellow, their deep red roofs providing a dark canopy, and beyond them, plunging down the hill, a deep inky blue showed where the miles of vineyards took over. It was a cloudless night and the air was balmy, with the merest hint of an evening breeze lapping around them as the half-moon lit the square. It was extraordinarily special and Laure stood wordless, drinking in the view.

Sleep was an amazing healer and Laure felt more positive this evening than she had felt for a long time. She felt serene and back in her stride, even verging on dismissive when she thought of Lolo. He was a nothing, a cheat who'd been found out, and now she needed to move on and write her brief infatuation off to experience. I'm the one who won the prize, she thought with a first feeling of triumph. I'm a better artist than him, and now he'll have to live with it.

She twirled around in pleasure, stretching out her arms to the night air. 'What an amazing place!' she said, exultantly.

'Better than Vermeilla, perhaps?' Robert asked, and she heard rather than saw the smile in his voice. But such a suggestion could not be allowed.

'Nowhere is better than Vermeilla! There's no comparison!' she threw back, also grinning, and then added more soberly, 'Vermeilla is where I go home.'

'And will you live there, do you think, when you've finished your studies?' he wanted to know, and this time the question was serious.

Laure leaned back against the wall and faced him, and gave him a serious answer. 'And do something like Jordi, you mean, with a gallery or something? It's funny, Martin and I were talking about that just the other week. He would love to have a medical practice somewhere near Vermeilla, I know. But to answer your question, no, I don't think I could return to Vermeilla full-time, at least not for a long time.'

'So what would you like to do?'

'In my dreams? Well, if the truth be told I'd love a place at the *École des Beaux-Arts*.'

'As a lecturer?' He was surprised. 'Haven't you just been occupying the place, to protest that the University is too rigid and stultifying, and failing its students?'

'It's still an amazing place to be if you're a senior student like me. For first year students, it's pretty dire and a lot of them fail, but isn't that what the protests wanted to change? We need better resources and for people like old Professor Duchamp to retire, and more new blood to come in like the American lecturer I was talking about, who has brought us new international links and new energy. That's what I'd love to share in. But I'd have to get a research place first after my diploma and get my doctorate. And I'd love to spend some time in London, if I could, on the way. Hopefully, the University would give me some junior classes to teach so that I could support myself while I study, but it would be a long road of some years.'

'Worthwhile though,' Robert said thoughtfully. He seemed to disappear into himself in the way he did when Laure had first known him. Was he thinking about his own career, which Madeleine had said was such a compromise?

'What about you?' she asked, after the pause had gone on for some time. 'Where would you like to finish up? Do you see yourself staying in Paris, or would you rather be in the south with your sister?'

He shook his head. 'I'm kind of stuck in the big cities and really I need to be in Paris, or perhaps Brussels or Geneva. But for me, Paris is the best option. I can't see how I could ever live in the south, unless you can find me a big international company down there that wants a legal adviser with my kind of qualifications.'

He hooked one leg over the wall and stared down at the village below.

'Madeleine told me it was your grandfather who made you study law,' Laure ventured, tentatively. 'Would you rather be doing something else?'

'Often, yes,' he answered, giving his answer full weight. 'But you know, I didn't actually mind my studies. Law can be interesting when it's about people, but corporate law is not what I wanted to do. Did Madeleine tell you more, then, about what her little brother is doing? I know she doesn't approve and thinks it has changed me, dried me up.'

'She just told me you wanted to be in France, rather than England, which is why you followed the corporate path.'

'Yes, our mother was half French and it's where both Madeleine and I wanted to be. And I like being in Paris. My mother's cousin and her husband are Parisian, and we have a lot of connections, so it feels like home. But our father was a Catalan, a refugee from Spain, so the south always draws me back.' He looked at her speculatively. 'I think you know about our family story now, don't you?'

Laure nodded. 'Madeleine got me to ask Martin.'

'I'm glad he told you,' he said simply.

'You all seem to handle the situation incredibly well,' she commented. 'I can't believe I knew Martin so well all his teenage years, after such difficult revelations, and yet he never showed any sign of a problem in his life. He never seemed anything other than completely carefree, though he took his studies very seriously.'

'He's some guy, that half-brother of mine.' There was real pride in Robert's voice. 'He had a lot of issues though for a good few years about who he really was. He wasn't as carefree as he would have the world think. He even went down to Spain to look for our father's family.'

There was another surprise. Laure had never known that Martin had made such a trip.

'And did he find them?'

'Oh yes, an aunt, an uncle, cousins, the lot! And they loved him, of course, and he could really be a Garriga with them, unlike in Vermeilla, where he has to pretend all the time to be a Perrens. That was when he started to relax, I think, and stop worrying about his legitimacy. They gave him so much acceptance and confidence.'

'He told me you helped him a lot too, taking him over to England,' Laure suggested.

'Did he?' Robert sounded unsure. 'But those trips came before the one to Spain, and he still had many issues. I'm the closest to him in age you see; of Daniel, on the one side, and Madeleine and myself on the other, all his half-siblings. So I thought I could help, and be close, and I wanted to make him feel that he had a place wherever we were, myself and Madeleine, but I was never sure how much those UK trips really helped in the long term. It wasn't there that he was going to find our father and his roots, after all.'

He paused, thinking. 'So all I could do was try to be a brother, and of course, in Vermeilla I've always been handicapped.'

'Handicapped?'

He nodded. 'Let me show you a photo.'

225

He brought out his wallet and drew out two small black and white photos, and held one out to Laure.

'This is my mother. She was fair skinned with blue eyes, very unlike Madeleine's deep colouring, but there's nevertheless quite a lot of *Maman* in Madeleine, I think. And this,' he held out another photo, 'this is my father.'

It was too dark to see either of the photos very clearly but even in the gloom, the likeness was close enough to make Laure gasp.

'My goodness, you're his image!'

'I know, I look exactly like him, and my mother was always very proud of it, but because of it, Colette has never found it easy to handle me being around. She was very much in love with my father, you see. The first time she saw me, I thought she might faint and her eyes just followed me everywhere. It doesn't help us to be easy with each other, and she is my little brother's mother.'

Laure listened and so much began to fall into place – why Colette had been so ill at ease at her own lunch table that day when Laure first met Robert, and why he'd been so stiff as well. How sad for Robert that the village of his birth was so complicated for him.

She found it immensely touching that this urbane city lawyer should carry photos of his parents in his wallet. He'd lost them both young and ploughed a fairly solitary, if highly successful and competent furrow ever since, unlike Madeleine, who had met Jordi.

The Robert she was here with this evening was far from the man she'd known hitherto. Why had he chosen to share all this with her? Was the cradle of the Saint-Emilion night responsible? This gentle, beautiful scene with all its peace that encouraged confidences?

In part, perhaps, but she thought principally it was because he'd seen her own fragility exposed, and his humanity drew him to respond and share with her in his turn. It made them equals and he had given her a great gift.

She gave him back the photos. 'Thank you for showing these to me. Could I look at them again in better light some other time? Your mother was a very beautiful woman.'

Even in the dark, she could see his face soften. 'She was. Come, we'll see if that bar is still open down the road, and I'll buy you a coffee and a cognac. It should be light enough there for you to see her properly.'

'All right,' Laure replied. 'But this time I'm buying, okay?'

They strolled together back down through the village, which was now deserted; the few couples they'd seen out walking earlier having evidently retired for the night. Laure herself felt keenly awake after her unaccustomed sleep that afternoon and was very glad when they found the bar still serving, with a few of the young revellers still inside, but no one at the outside tables. They installed themselves outside, where the music reached them in light flurries and Laure ordered a cognac and a coffee for each of them. It amused her to think that in their day and a half in Saint-Emilion they had tried pretty much every fine drink this corner of France had to offer.

Tomorrow they would be leaving, each of them to their own home, and in their short time here everything had changed. Laure felt an overflow of gratitude to Robert, so great that she couldn't even imagine how to express it. But in a way she thought she didn't need to. He knew and they were bonded, by family and by friends, and now by shared fragilities.

He brought out the photos once again and she studied them deeply this time, feeling curious, so curious about this family. Robert could have been mistaken for his father if he walked into the bar right now, so exact was the likeness and, of course, the photo was of a young Luis, before he was killed in the war. So he had the same youthful beauty, the same cheekbones and the same almost arrogant masculinity as this son who sat before her in Saint-Emilion.

And his mother? She was indeed beautiful, in the style of an English rose, but she didn't have the same passion in her picture as Robert's father did. Laure looked at her for a long time, without comment. It would mean that when people talked about her later, Laure would have a vision she could apply to her.

So she said nothing more to Robert and just gave him back the photos. There were no more confidences this evening and they took their coffee in near silence, with just a few desultory plans for the journey tomorrow. Robert looked tired and it occurred to Laure that he had done all the planning for this trip and all the driving, and had rigorously prepared the whole assault on Lolo, and gone back to the vineyard while she rested. He had obtained the documents and had checked them in detail, while Laure hadn't even read them.

She dunked a sugar lump in her brandy, letting it soak up the spirit and offered it to Robert. It was a favourite trick of her father's and gave you a little burst of alcoholic sweetness at the end of a long day. Robert took it and raised an amused eyebrow.

'I thought you might need a pick me up,' she explained. 'You've had quite a day!'

He laughed. 'You know what, Laure, it has been a pleasure,' he said. 'There's something intensely satisfying about what we've achieved today. It makes one hell of a change from a normal day at the office.'

As they sauntered back to the hotel the church clock chimed midnight. 'Thank you for a lovely evening,' Laure said.

'No, I have to thank you, Laure. It has been special.'

They walked up the hotel stairs together and when they separated, Robert took her hand and held it for a moment.

'Sleep well,' he told her. 'I know I will.'

For some reason, she felt tears pricking at the back of her eyes. 'Thank you again, Robert,' she said and felt her throat constrict, so that she had troubling continuing. 'There's so much to thank you for, and I don't know what to say.'

'Then don't say anything *ma puce*,' he answered very gently. He brought her hand to his lips and then let her go.

'*Bonne nuit*,' he whispered and then left her.

Chapter 26

Madeleine met Laure as she stepped onto the platform to change trains in Perpignan. It was the last thing Laure had been expecting, and she was astonished to see her.

'Madeleine! What on earth are you doing here?' she asked.

Madeleine laughed. 'Did you expect me to sit quietly in Céret waiting for news after you've been on such an odyssey? Anyway, you're supposed to have spent the last few days with us, remember, and I think it looks only natural that I might drive you home, rather than sending you all the way via Perpignan by bus. And we've already sold one of your paintings, I'll have you know! The seascape sold yesterday to one of our regular buyers, and he wants to know what more you'll be painting for us. That's some news that you can carry home with you.'

It was hot in the station, but there was a strong tramontane wind blowing again outside, less than a week after the last one, when Laure had painted that wild sea last Saturday. Madeleine had tied her hair in a tight chignon, but

Laure's hair whipped around her eyes as the emerged from the station, and the two battled their way to the car that Madeleine had parked in the shade.

'Phew!' Madeleine exhaled as they closed the car doors behind them. 'This started yesterday, so you've missed the best part of it. They say it will ease off tomorrow sometime.'

'It'll be fun in Vermeilla,' Laure commented. When the wind was this strong it set the old wooden shutters banging furiously and could lift boats out to sea. It was a bitterly cold wind in winter, but in this summer heat it brought some freshness and sent clouds scudding out to sea, cleaning the skies, and leaving the world bluer and fresher. You just needed to sit it out.

They drove slowly along coastal roads full of summer traffic. It would have been quicker to take the train, but Madeleine wanted to talk, or more accurately to listen, and Laure found it cathartic to tell the story. There would only be Madeleine and Martin to tell since nobody else here at home knew that she'd been to Saint-Emilion, or that she'd ever been in such trouble in Paris.

And even Madeleine and Martin had only part of the story. Neither of them knew that Lolo had ever been anything more than a fellow student to Laure. And as Madeleine heard the story, she exclaimed and swore, 'But how despicable! *Quelle infamie! Quel salaud!*' Laure was infinitely grateful that Madeleine need never know the whole. What Lolo had done was more than exceptionally vile, and not for a moment had she seen it coming, or had the remotest inkling of quite how ruthless that egotistical side of him would prove to be. Even Pierre had been less surprised than Laure, and Jérôme had mistrusted Lolo's narcissism, realising he would always look after his own interests. Only she was the real fool.

But if you had been a fool it helped if no one else had to know. The only person who knew was Robert, and that was the way it was going to stay. Robert could know. Robert had the right.

Madeleine was delighted when Laure told her how brilliantly Robert had prepared and executed his confrontation with Lolo. 'Atta boy, my brother the lawyer!' she exclaimed. 'I bet he just loved winning that encounter.'

Laure looked at her in some amusement. 'You're more alike than I realised, you two. When I tried to thank Robert for what he'd done, that's exactly what he told me, that he'd had fun, and that it was ten times better than a day at the office.'

'Well? Wasn't it? Don't tell me you don't feel pretty elated by what you both achieved?'

Laure exhaled. 'Sure, I do now, but I'm not sure I would call it fun, nevertheless. Remember, I had rather a lot to lose.'

'Yes, but between you and Robert, you seem to have had all the weaponry and skills you needed. A top team! Lavignière didn't stand a chance. Anyway, what comes now?'

'Well, Robert will put the two documents into the hands of his lawyer friend in Paris, and he seems to think that within a couple of weeks they'll have my name completely cleared, and then it's just a question of persuading the University not to throw me out.'

'Will you have to go to Paris?'

'Possibly, but they may be able to settle things without me.'

'Well, if you do, you can always say you're coming to Céret again,' Madeleine offered.

Laure shook her head. 'Thanks, that's very kind, but I wouldn't need to do that if I was going to Paris. There's always something I could be needed for there – not now, perhaps, bang slap in the middle of the summer holidays – but by the end of August, when the administration people return, I could well have something I need to do at the *Beaux-Arts*. Preparing my internship, for example. *Maman* and Papa don't really understand how things work up there anyway, and they certainly don't interfere.'

She thought for a moment and then smiled at Madeleine. 'But I would like to earn some money, just in case I have to go, so I'd better get on and paint you guys some pictures to sell for me.'

'Paint that for us again!' Madeleine cried suddenly, as they rounded a corner and saw the sea for the first time.

Laure looked and smiled because the wind-whipped sea was almost identical to the angry cauldron she'd painted last week, and which had already sold. Madeleine had an eye for a commercial product, it seemed.

'I'll see,' she answered diplomatically. 'I don't normally paint seascapes, but last week it suited my own angry mood. I'm not saying I never paint the same thing twice because, of course I do, like the series of studies I want to do of little Julien, but I probably feel too cheerful right now to do that sea justice.'

'But this sea is bluer than the other seascape,' Madeleine protested. 'You could do it differently, find Matisse's light! Look at that sky!'

Laure took another look, and indeed the sea was bluer than last week because there wasn't a single cloud to grey the sky. The summer sky today was of an impossible azure, nothing silvery or hazy, just that deep, hot shade known as Persian blue. And so the sea below it was also blue, messed with lashings of white, more headstrong than angry, and there were lights of yellow in it which Matisse would have loved.

She glanced over at Madeleine and raised a shoulder in mute acknowledgement that she might be right. 'Let's see what the wind is doing tomorrow,' she said. 'But remember, I don't paint seascapes, or landscapes, except for their mood. Can I paint you a vine?'

'Isn't that landscape?'

'Not the way I want to do it. I want to paint something almost sexual, a warped vine with dripping fruit.'

'Wow!'

'What you've seen of my work so far has been it at its most figurative,' Laure told her. 'There's a lot of weirder stuff to come. It was all those neatly trained, well-behaved Bordeaux vines that made me think of it. Here the vines are so misshapen in comparison, because they have to grow on such craggy hillsides, and I just love their scruffiness and insubordination. They kind of match the Catalan temperament, don't you think? I think I could have some fun painting vines this summer.'

'Bring it on, then,' Madeleine retorted, 'but please, can I have that seascape as well, just one, *please*?'

She eased the car into the narrow streets of Vermeilla, and as they drew up behind her father's bakery van, Laure stretched her muscles and rotated shoulders stiff from sitting for so many hours on a rattling train. It seemed a little unreal to be back in Vermeilla. She got out of the car and thanked Madeleine for the lift, hooking her bag out from the back seat.

To her surprise, Madeleine got out too. 'I have leave of absence for an hour or two this evening,' she explained. 'So I phoned Martin and he was helping in the café today because Isabelle isn't there, but it's after six o'clock now, so he should be finishing soon. I'm just going to pop round and see him. Will you come along? He'll want to hear how you got on.'

Laure frowned. Martin never worked in the café if he could avoid it. 'Is it just Isabelle's day off then, or is she unwell?'

'Martin said it's her mother who's unwell, or rather not so much unwell as injured. She seems to have sprained her arm, or something, and Isabelle is at home to help with the house and the children.'

That didn't sound too serious, but it would be a shame if it lingered on and Isabelle was stuck at home. Martin was due to start some night shifts at the hospital next week as well.

Laure had been stuck on a train all day with no other company than a book, and the idea of company was appealing, plus her curiosity had been piqued, and she wanted to see how Martin was handling his role as waiter. She wanted to be served by him!

'All right, I'll join you,' she told Madeleine. 'I'll follow you in a minute. Tell Martin he can pour me an ice cold beer.'

She went into see her mother in the bakery and everything was just as it had been when she left, just as it had always been, every time she left home and every time she returned to her well-ordered family life. Her mother had not the slightest suspicion that Laure hadn't been in Céret, which was both a relief and a source of guilt, and the only piece of news was that the first of little Julien's molars had finally come through, and another was on the way.

He would be a cantankerous little soul for the next few days then, and not much fun to sketch, Laure thought. She'd go and have a look at a vine or two tomorrow instead, up on the hill behind the village, and if the wind held she might even paint the sea from up there.

She stole a *mille-feuilles* pastry from underneath the counter and dodged as *Maman* rapped her knuckles. Laure then promised to be back for dinner and left her mother doing her daily stocktake prior to closing.

She walked around to the café the long way and sat on the quayside wall for a moment to eat her stolen cake, loving the feel of the wind as it blew away all the remnants of her journey and woke up her brain. Robert would be home by now, she thought. Or maybe in his office, for he had told her he would pass by there to check his mail before signing off for the weekend.

What did he do at weekends? Would he see Charles Gruet, the lawyer, to give him Lolo's new statement and the letter to the University? He'd promised to call Martin when there was more news, but had told her to be ready for a week or more of waiting. Life was all about waiting at the moment and she envied him his more active role. She wasn't used to being passive or patient, and now that she was no longer frightened she felt restless and tired of being on 'holiday'. Three days in Saint-Emilion had stirred up something new in her, and she felt twitchy and strange in her skin.

She leaned her head back and let the wind toss her hair. She had been sitting here too long, and Madeleine and Martin would be wondering where she was. She stood up from the wall and turned to look one more time at the sea, which last weekend had been an icy white, angry mass, and so had she. Today it was wild and turbulent, but not angry, and the restlessness in her loved it. She would get up early tomorrow, while the wind was still strong, and go up the hill to paint it. And now? Well, she was at the end of a long and very dramatic three days, and she wanted to see Martin, and she wanted him to serve her that ice-cold beer.

Chapter 27

It wasn't Martin who actually served Laure when she got to the café. He was clearing tables and gave her a brief, rather dismissive wave as he gestured to the barman to serve her beer. She wondered whether it was deliberate. He was grumpy and Colette was running around after him so much, she wondered how beneficial it was him being there. Martin would look after twenty seriously ill patients for twelve-hour shifts without a moment's complaint, but he had always hated working in the café.

He was grumpy too, Laure thought, because he was worried about Isabelle. He didn't seem to have the same concern for the mother's injured arm. A sprain's a sprain, was all he said, and she'd get over it. But he was sure that Isabelle was being turned into a domestic drudge and he wanted her back in Vermeilla. And on the Monday, after a weekend spent serving the tourists with ever diminishing civility, he got her.

Laure had spent an equally busy weekend both painting and working in the bakery, but Monday was quiet everywhere. So she went for coffee to the café and found Isabelle happily taking an order from a single occupied table. Martin was hovering, waiting for her to be free, and joined Laure at the bar, where their friend the barman had made her a *noisette*, the little espresso with just a shot of milk that Laure loved to drink in the morning. One café in Paris made the best *noisette* in the world, Laure always said, but the Café de Catalogne came a very close second.

She raised an eyebrow at Martin. 'So how are things with Isabelle?' she asked.

He waved over the barman and ordered a coffee for himself. 'I haven't had a chance to ask her yet,' he said. 'There was a group in for breakfast, but here she comes.' His face changed, and a light came into his eyes as he greeted her and kissed her on both cheeks.

Isabelle perched herself on a stool next to him. 'Phew,' she said. 'How nice it is to be back.'

'How's your mother?' Laure asked.

'She's not too bad, but she seems to have hurt her shoulder somehow. It started off with pains just in her arm, and then it moved to her shoulder. It was really sore last Thursday and our doctor gave her a sling and some painkillers, and told her to rest. When she does as she's told it's fine, but you know what mothers are like. They can't easily sit back when there's work to be done, and she keeps using the arm and the pain comes back.'

'And you've spent the weekend trying to stop her, I bet!'

'Yes,' Isabelle sighed. 'My aunt has come to stay for a couple of days, so I can come back here and work again. But oh, Martin, if you'd seen my father over the last few days, it made me want to despair! He kept telling me how glad he is to have at least one daughter amongst all his sons, and gave me money to do the shopping, and praised my cooking and told me over and over how much *Maman* depends on me. I even heard him boasting to our neighbour that he could trust me to run the house for the whole family. I was almost tempted to burn the dinner, just to prove him wrong. Thank God *Maman* only has a sprained shoulder. She needs to get better soon, before Papa decides that my role is permanently in the house.'

Martin frowned. 'You haven't spoken to him again about Montpellier then?'

Laure perked up at this question. She knew that Martin had taken to driving Isabelle home each evening on his moped, no doubt with various stops and detours along the way, and her family must think she worked late every day here in Vermeilla. So Martin and Isabelle had begun making serious plans for Montpellier? She listened for the reply, but Isabelle merely raised both hands in a helpless gesture, and Martin shook his head in frustration.

'He can't be allowed to ruin your future!' he muttered.

'Just wait until *Maman* is better, Martin, and I will speak to him. I just need to find the right moment, that's all.' There was nothing Martin could say.

He had a night shift that night, and the following afternoon Laure called round to see if he had woken up, and would like to go to the beach. Isabelle waved at her from across the café and mouthed a 'Hi', and when Laure came back down the stairs from the apartment, towing a sleepy Martin behind her, Isabelle met them at the door.

'How's your mother today?' Laure asked. 'Is she feeling any better?'

'Well, she was,' Isabelle said, 'or she would be if she was just be a bit more careful. *Maman* can be so frustrating! The pain had completely gone yesterday, but then in the evening she walked up to Cosprons to see old Claudine, and by the time she came back she had pains going down her arm again and even over her chest.'

Martin came almost to attention. 'Over her chest?' he said. 'What kind of pains were they, do you know?'

Isabelle looked at him curiously. 'Well, she said they were kind of pulsing pains, and I know she was sore. She had to sit down and put the sling on again.'

Martin's brows knit together. 'You know, Isabelle, that doesn't sound like a sprain to me,' he said. 'First, her pain disappears completely, and then when she does some exercise it comes back in the chest. Tell me, did she feel any tightness or pressure in the chest, do you know?'

Isabelle looked curiously at him. 'Well yes, she did say the sprain seemed to be pushing against her ribs. But then she closed her eyes for a while and I made her a tisane, and she seemed better. But Martin, what are you suggesting?' She sounded really alarmed and Martin took her arm. He pulled her to an outside table and then sat down opposite her. He spoke very gently, but without mincing his words.

'Isabelle, sweetheart, if I was your mother's doctor I would want to test for angina.'

'Angina?'

'Yes, it's a disease of the coronary arteries.' He saw the look of horror on Isabelle's face and took her hand and held it. 'Don't get distressed, *chérie*, it's something that can be treated, but I don't think your mother should write off her pains to a muscular strain anymore. She needs to see her doctor again and describe the pains to him in proper detail, and she also needs to tell him that she worked with nitroglycerine for years when she was younger. That way, he'll know at least what he needs to investigate.'

Laure had been standing by the table all this time listening, as horrified as Isabelle, but now she moved around and put her hands on Isabelle's shoulders. Isabelle's spare hand came up to clutch hers and she squeezed it hard.

'Does your mother have another visit planned to the doctor?' Laure asked. 'Has he asked to see her again about her shoulder?'

Isabelle's voice when she answered was tight with distress. 'No. Why should he? It was just a sprain... that's what we thought.'

'It could still be, surely?' Laure asked Martin, with a little challenge in her voice.

He shook his head, standing his ground. 'It could be, but I wouldn't bet a single franc on it. Isabelle, *ma chérie*, you need to suggest to your mother that she goes back to see the doctor again. Will she listen to you, do you think? Could you suggest that she doesn't seem to have just muscular pain, and ask her to go back?'

Isabelle was shaking her head. 'There's no way she'd listen to me. She'll just say that a sprain doesn't go away in five days and I'm being silly. She hates bothering the doctor.'

There was a silence and then Martin nodded. 'God help doctors!' he muttered. 'The patients who need help won't go to the doctor at all, and the ones who spend their lives in doctors' surgeries are the ones with nothing wrong with them. And anyway, even if your mother did go back to her doctor, it might not do any good, because let's face it, unless she agreed to take you with her, we'd have no guarantee she'd tell him everything.'

He looked at Isabelle for confirmation. 'It's Dr Molard, isn't it, that your family sees? Well, he's a reasonable kind of guy, from what I've heard.'

'He's an old dear,' Isabelle agreed.

Martin made a face. 'We might have been better if he was younger, and a bit hotter on diagnosis, but at least if he's friendly he won't bite my nose off. I'm going to have to chance his wrath at the presumption of a mere student medic and call him, I think. He won't be in his surgery yet, though – he'll probably start his afternoon session at around three o'clock.'

'What will he do?' Isabelle asked.

'Well, I'm hoping he'll call in to see your mother. He can always say he was just passing and wanted to see how she's getting on, and then he can ask all the right questions. It's the best solution and it doesn't involve upsetting your mother in advance. And if Molard suspects I'm right, he won't hang around before he calls on her.'

'And there's definitely a treatment? *Maman* will be all right?'

'Angina can be managed with medication, if that's what it is. Ironically, patients are given nitro-glycerine to expand the arteries. But Isabelle, I'm not going to jump the gun. I could be very wrong here, and the only thing I can say with certainty is that your mother's symptoms warrant further investigation.'

Martin could sound very like Robert, Laure thought, when he was on his professional soapbox. Isabelle looked up at Laure and smiled rather wanly before she withdrew her hand from where it was still lying in hers.

'I'd better get back to work,' she said, as a couple arrived and settled themselves at a nearby table.

'You don't think you should sit down for a while? I could get you some water or a coffee? Martin could serve here instead.'

Isabelle shook her head. 'No, I'd rather get on thanks. You go to the beach and have a swim, and take this guy with you, since he can't call Dr Molard for at least another half an hour.'

Laure looked at Martin, who shook his head. There was no way Martin would go to the beach just now, and he and Isabelle didn't need her hanging around. She looked from Martin back to Isabelle, who was already standing up and picking up her tray.

'I think I'll leave Martin here,' she told Isabelle with a smile. 'Too much sun is bad for him anyway. Good luck to you both, and I'll call by tomorrow to see how things are. Let her go early won't you, Martin? You never know, Dr Molard may even call to see Madame Bariol this evening, and it would be good if Isabelle was there.'

She gave Isabelle a kiss and then eased her way out of the café. There was nothing light or easy about this summer, for any of them, she thought. Would the Nobel Company help Isabelle's mother if she had a work-induced heart problem?

Not at all, was the obvious answer, any more than they had helped anyone else or ever admitted any responsibility for any illnesses. Instead, no doubt, they would give Isabelle's father some compassionate time off, and consider themselves the most benevolent of employers. It made a mockery of all Isabelle's father's loyalty, which he had shown them for all those years. Laure wanted to kick something, very hard.

CHAPTER 28

By the end of the week, they knew that it was indeed angina. Madame Bariol was admitted for tests to the hospital in Perpignan, and Isabelle looked more and more harassed as the week went on, working her shifts and then running home.

'If only it wasn't the school holidays,' she wailed. 'All the younger boys are at home, and the twins are only nine, so they need to be watched. Jean-Claude is seventeen, but they don't always listen to him, and he's none too happy anyway at having to stay at home. He has been helping Papa at work for a few hours each day, and he'd rather do that than look after his younger brothers.'

She made a wry face. 'Papa would have me at home full-time and keep Jean-Claude with him, but thankfully *Maman* put her foot down. She told him that Jean-Claude isn't really needed in the factory; he's just doing work experience, whereas if I don't come to work I'm letting Colette down. *Merci Maman!*' she said fervently. 'At least this way I get away from time to time, and the rest of them have to get on and manage.'

She was grabbing a late lunch after the restaurant service was finished, and Laure had joined her for coffee. 'And when do you expect your mother to come home?' she asked.

'Hopefully tomorrow. Papa is visiting this afternoon, so we should know by this evening.'

'How is your father taking this?' Laure conjured up an image of Monsieur Bariol on the beach at Paulilles, a man quietly sure of his world and determined to keep it just so. His security depended on everything staying the same, and she could imagine that his wife's illness would shake him badly.

Isabelle confirmed this. 'Oh, he's far worse than *Maman*, of course. She has been quite calm, especially since Dr Molard told her they'll give her medication. *Maman* never thinks her own state is particularly important anyway – she just wants to know that she can still look after her family. But Papa is beside himself! I want Martin to come to Paulilles after *Maman* gets home and talk to Papa. The more people who can try to convince him to stop panicking the better. Will you come too?'

Laure was taken aback. 'You don't need me,' she objected. 'Your family hardly know me. It's Martin who needs to visit. Or do your parents not yet know about you and Martin?'

Isabelle held up a hand. 'Oh, they know all right! He's been driving me home, remember, and I've taken him a few times into the house. Papa likes the fact that he's Daniel's brother, and he told *Maman* that if his daughter was going to encourage any young man, he was happy for it to be a doctor. But he does feel it's his duty to play the stern father a bit when he sees Martin, just for form's sake, and Martin is kind of building him into an ogre in his head, particularly because of Papa's expectations of me as the daughter of the house.'

It was something Laure had seen herself. Martin cared too deeply for Isabelle not to want to leap to her defence, and he was becoming increasingly fretful about her future.

'So how can I help?' she asked.

'Just by being there,' Isabelle answered. 'Poor Papa is so stressed and worried, and he could take it out on Martin, but he won't in front of you.'

So two days later, on the Monday, Isabelle finished work early and Martin borrowed Philippe's old car and drove them all to Paulilles. Isabelle's mother was home and doing very well, Isabelle told them, with the entire workforce of Paulilles rallying around her, and indeed when they entered the house they found her sitting at the table, teaching the boys how to prepare vegetables, while a neighbour stirred a pot of stew through in the kitchen.

Madame Bariol sat Martin down next to her and thanked him for his intervention with Dr Molard. She had her tablets next to her, in case she should need them, and was nervous but determined to manage her illness properly. Laure found her dignified and homely at the same time, and thought that she was keen to welcome in the young man who had entered her daughter's life.

'You remember Laure, don't you *Maman*?' Isabelle asked. 'Daniel's sister-in-law, who was with us for the beach picnic on the fourteenth of July?'

Her mother smiled and welcomed Laure, asking after her sister, and inviting her to a seat next to Martin. She dismissed the boys from their chores and Isabelle took the vegetables through to the kitchen, where the neighbour was preparing to leave. It all seemed very quietly organised and comfortable, though there was no sign of the father of the house.

It was while Martin and Isabelle's mother were deep in conversation that Monsieur Bariol came in. Madame Bariol was admitting that for a long time she had been feeling pains, but it just hadn't occurred to her that they could have anything to do with her heart.

'I now need to lose weight,' she said, rather ruefully. 'And then the doctor has given me a very easy exercise regime. I've got to take better care of myself, for the sake of the family.'

'We're all going to go without the home baking,' Isabelle joked, coming back into the room. 'It's no better for Papa than it is for you *Maman*, and if you need to lose weight then so does he, *n'est-ce pas* Papa?'

She kissed her father, who had been hanging up his hat by the door, and he put his arm around her. Martin had got nervously to his feet and Laure stood up beside him, shoulder to shoulder, an elbow just touching him in tacit support.

Monsieur Bariol came towards them with a rather mechanical smile on his face and shook hands with both of them.

'Welcome, Mademoiselle Forestier,' he said. 'And Martin?' He raised a quizzical eye at him, and then turned to his wife, placing a hand on her shoulder.

'And how are you, Marie? Shouldn't you be resting? Surely it's not good for you to be sitting up like this?'

There was worry written all over his face, and it took all of his wife's reassurance to comfort him. She drew him down into a chair on the other side of her from Martin, and gestured to both Martin and Laure to be seated.

'I'm fine Henri,' she insisted. 'I even have a young doctor here, so what can happen to me?'

Monsieur Bariol looked hard at Martin. 'It seems we have to thank you for recognising that my wife was more unwell than we thought,' he said, with grudging respect. 'So tell me, young man, is she right that she needs to get back straight away to normal life or should she be resting, like I say?'

Martin didn't twitch, although Laure heard him take a deliberate breath before he replied. 'I think Madame Bariol is right,' he said. 'She has good support from your own doctor, and from the hospital, and their advice is exactly on the mark. To lose some weight can only help, and her pills are designed to dissolve very quickly under the tongue and dilate the arteries if she feels any pain. Perhaps no long hikes over to Cosprons, though, or any heavy lifting, for example.'

Monsieur Bariol chewed at this for a moment. 'The union guy has been asking after you, Marie,' he said after a moment. 'He wanted to document your case for their records.'

'Document my case? But why?'

'I told you, remember? The union are trying to prove that working with the *matière* causes heart problems.'

'But I haven't worked in the factory for years!'

'I know,' he said. 'That's what I told him, but he seemed to think your years there could have caused damage which you're only feeling now.'

Madame Bariol scoffed. 'What rubbish! The people who've had trouble have all been working full-time with the *matière*. And Dr Molard didn't say anything of the sort, or any of the doctors at the hospital either. Anyone of my age can have heart problems, especially if they've put on weight like I have.'

Her husband didn't seem quite so sure. 'You're probably right, Marie,' he said, with a note of concern in his voice. 'But those union guys got me worried today with all their talk. I'm going to work on getting Laurent out of the production section as soon as possible and into the maintenance division, or the stores, perhaps.'

At mention of her son, Madame Bariol drew in a breath and gripped her husband's hand hard. She looked over at Martin, her eyes wide with something like panic. 'Is it true?' she asked him urgently. 'Why haven't the doctors told me if this heart trouble came from over there?'

Isabelle was in the room with them now and she came over to stand behind her mother, placing her arms around her. She looked over at Martin, and there was a clear message in her eyes. Martin nodded and Laure knew he would not want Isabelle's mother to work herself up in any way. He spoke very reassuringly, in his special doctor's voice.

'Please don't distress yourself, Madame Bariol. There is no way that working with nitro-glycerine could have affected your son's heart by the age of twenty-two. You really don't have to worry. It probably did damage your own arteries somewhat, but Isabelle tells me you worked at the factory for seventeen years, which is a long time to be exposed to the chemicals. That doesn't change anything now though, does it? Like you say, lots of people from all walks of life have heart damage and live with angina, and from now on, you'll have all the help you need to manage it fine.'

'But my husband! He worked with the *matière* for years as well!'

'Not as closely as you, *Maman*, surely?' Isabelle urged.

Martin looked over at Isabelle's father. 'Have you ever had any pains, Monsieur, or any tight feelings in the chest?' he asked. Isabelle's father shook his head.

'Then I'd say you're fine,' Martin said and smiled at Madame Bariol. 'I think you're the only invalid in this family, Madame, and by the looks of it, you're going to be very well looked after. And I'm sure your husband will be able to use his influence to get Laurent moved quite soon to a different part of the factory. Laurent himself said just a couple of weeks ago that it was his plan.'

Madame Bariol had recovered her colour and managed a smile. 'You're a good, kind boy, Martin,' she said, 'and my daughter is a lucky girl.'

Martin blushed deep red and shot a nervous look at Isabelle's father, and for the first time, Laure found this meeting amusing. Martin the doctor might come across as knowledgeable and self-possessed, but Martin the suitor was a less confident case altogether.

Monsieur Bariol's lips had twitched at his wife's words, but he took his daughter's hand in his before he commented. Laure linked arms with Martin and as Monsieur Bariol glanced at her, she gave him her sweetest smile.

Monsieur Bariol chuckled. 'It seems you have a lot of fans, young Martin,' he said at last. 'Well, if truth be told I think they're right. You're a bright young man and if you're anything like your brother, then you'll be a good worker too. If my Isabelle and you make a go of things then I'll be happy enough. But don't go thinking you're going to take her away from here anytime soon. We need our daughter even more than ever now that her mother is unwell.'

Martin paled and Laure could see him visibly summoning all his dignity. 'Monsieur Bariol,' he said, after a moment. 'I'm entering the final stages of my studies, but I still have two years minimum to do before I qualify for general practice. It's all going to be quite serious for the next two years, and I don't know how often I will get home. But if Isabelle came to study in Montpellier I could help her, and look after her as she starts out on her studies, and she could fulfil her potential. Isabelle tells me you have a cousin in Montpellier with whom she could live, so she wouldn't even have that worry. She would be with her family and protected. She has excellent grades and it would be such a shame if she couldn't study.'

There was a silence and then Isabelle's father spoke again, this time without the slightest chuckle in his voice as he spoke the most uncompromising of words.

'I have as much respect for my daughter's brains as anyone,' he barked at Martin, 'and so does the Nobel Company. The opportunity being offered to Isabelle is exceptional, and will allow her to gain a very creditable qualification while she works. Isabelle is still a minor and needs her family, her mother, and not just some second cousins whom she hardly knows and who will never watch over her as we do.'

He gave Isabelle a challenging look at as he spoke, and Laure thought this must not be the first time those cousins had been mentioned and angrily dismissed. And then he looked fiercely back at Martin.

'You walk into this family and within weeks are trying to tell me what is best for my daughter! Well, my young doctor, when you qualify you can come back to me, but until then you won't interfere in my family's life, do you hear? Isabelle has brothers who love her and a mother who is unwell, and this is where she belongs. We'll have no more talk of her going to Montpellier. Isabelle stays here.'

His voice had risen even further, and he almost looked as though he was going to thump the table, but he controlled himself. He finished with a flashing accusation. 'And what's more, young man, until you appeared on the scene, we heard none of this nonsense from my daughter. You'll stop right now putting preposterous ideas into my daughter's head, do you understand, otherwise Isabelle can stop working at that café of yours, and you'll no longer be welcome in this house. That is my final word.'

Laure looked over to Isabelle and could see that she was holding back tears. Madame Bariol was twisting her handkerchief nervously in her fingers, and Martin sat as still as a stone beside Laure. Outside the house, they could hear the Bariol boys playing, and Laure could have sworn she heard the evening birdsong as well, providing the most surreal backdrop to this awkward scene.

Then it was broken as Laurent and his brother Jean-Claude came in. Immediately Laure could smell the nitro-glycerine from Laurent's overalls. It hit her head and set a tic twitching behind her eyes. Under cover of their arrival, Isabelle fled to the kitchen and only emerged ten minutes later, eyes suspiciously red, as Laure and Martin prepared to leave.

They refused polite offers to stay to eat and kept the civilities to a minimum, for Laure could tell that Martin really needed to leave. As they reached the door Madame Bariol came after them and took Martin by the hand.

'Thank you again, my dear boy,' she said, and then to Laure, 'Give my best to your sister, Laure, and look after this young man! My husband wouldn't normally be so harsh, but he has had a real fright in the last week and he's feeling very insecure. Hold hard for just a few months, Martin, and Henri will come round. If Isabelle still wants to go away to study next year he'll feel she's older, and he'll have seen too that I'm not the terrible invalid he believes me to be.'

She shooed Isabelle out with them as she spoke and left her daughter to accompany them to the car.

'Oh God!' Isabelle burst out, once they were out of earshot of the house. 'I'm sorry, Martin! I didn't think he would do that with Laure here. But what persuaded you to tackle him this evening about Montpellier? You'd just reassured him, and made him feel more comfortable, and then you threw that at him just in the same week that his wife has been diagnosed with heart disease!'

Martin sighed. 'I know, I'm sorry, but I needed to say something! We're well into August already, and if you don't apply now for a University place it will be too late. I had to have a try! I made a mess of it, but I just wanted him to understand that I'm serious about you and about life, and I thought if he believed me, then maybe he would have a change of heart.'

'But to talk about my family in Montpellier! They gave a room to my cousin from Perpignan when he needed one, and they've always offered, but there's never been any mention of me. It will make Papa think we've been plotting behind his back.'

'I'm sorry Isabelle,' Martin repeated helplessly.

He took Isabelle into his arms as he spoke, and Laure made her way ahead of them and slumped into the car. Where was the happy ending, she wondered? It was going to take a long time and a lot of patience.

And it was already the middle of August. Her stomach tightened. So much was unresolved and she hadn't heard from Robert either, not a word since he'd seen her onto the train in Bordeaux. She looked back at Martin and Isabelle, heads cradled together, and felt a lump in her throat for them. It had been a nasty little scene and they all felt raw, even Isabelle's father, she was sure, whom they'd left sitting completely silent at the table. All over France, there were men like him – good, normally quiet men – who became tyrants in the name of family love.

But they didn't all live at Paulilles, this special, idyllic cocoon with its tight community and one single, compromised employer. Laure looked around her at the row of houses and the gardens, and then across the road to where the factory sat quietly with just a few lights coming on, up on the hill. And as Martin got into the car beside her, she looked at him and sighed.

'Shall we get out of here, Martin *mon ami*?' she said, and he nodded.

'I've still got a night shift to do at the hospital tonight, after I've dropped you,' he said, leaning back exhaustedly against the driver's seat, and then slowly he started up the car and turned it onto the road for home.

Chapter 29

The following days passed in an atmosphere of gloom, although the sun outside had reached heatwave proportions. Isabelle hurried to and from work without much time to breathe, as had become usual. She reported that her father had apologised for the way he'd spoken to Martin, but not for what he'd said. His attitude seemed to have been hardened by Martin's visit.

Martin had two night shifts in a row, and spent most of his daytime hours sleeping.

The rest of the time he struggled to break a smile. Isabelle was due to start her new job in September, and by the time Martin left again for Montpellier, Isabelle would have her head firmly in a set of Nobel Company account books. Preaching patience to either of them seemed inappropriate at the moment.

This Thursday was the fifteenth of August and the week would bring the Feast of Ascension and another national holiday. There would be festivities all weekend in the neighbouring village of Collioure, for the feast day of their own village saint. Friday evening would see dancing and corridas, and fireworks in Collioure bay. Every year since Laure could remember, she and Martin and all their friends had joined the celebrations on the beach. Would that happen this year, Laure wondered? It didn't seem likely. She was longing for some simple fun and wondered what had happened to the sparkling summers of their past.

She still had no word from Robert either, nearly two weeks after their confrontation with Lolo. What was happening up in Paris? The question went around and around in her mind and nearly drove her crazy. And how was Robert? The special bond that had existed between them seemed very far away, left behind in the hushed streets of Saint-Emilion. She asked herself endlessly why he didn't call and spent her days restlessly escaping Vermeilla for the vineyards with her sketchbook and easel.

By Thursday, Laure decided that Martin had rested enough, so she rooted him out of his house in the afternoon and dragged him off to go snorkelling again. He came willingly enough and she thought that he too must be feeling the need for some exercise and fresh air. No sooner had they reached the beach, then he plunged into the water and headed off in his usual fashion, miles out to sea, even more aggressively than usual. Laure made her way in a more leisurely fashion around the bay to their usual sunbathing rock.

There was nobody else there today in this punishing heat, and she sat for a while quietly watching the comings and goings of boats in the bay. To her left along the beach, she could hear the shrill noises of children playing, but it seemed far away. Here she was islanded in her own world of private sunshine, where all ordinary stresses were held at bay, so she relaxed and closed her eyes.

When she opened them Martin was swimming back into the bay, heading towards the beach. He'd been a long time, so presumably had swum even further than usual. Laure waved to attract his attention, and as he turned towards her, she jumped off the rock to meet him.

Martin circled her, then came to a halt, and let himself float idly in the water. 'Phew, that feels better!' he said, with a look of release on his face, and Laure thanked the stars for his naturally buoyant temperament. They spent half an hour snorkelling, lazily at first, and then diving down to touch the bottom, racing each other as they had as children. Martin stayed down, cruising the bottom, and then came back up carrying two cockles, which he insisted on carrying ashore with them, much to Laure's amusement.

'It's not exactly a great treasure. How are you going to cook two cockles?' she asked him.

'Who said I'm going to cook them?' he asked, in his turn. 'These little devils aren't going to survive two minutes when I get ashore.'

Laure made a face. 'You're going to eat them raw, right now? You can't do that! You need to soak them first to get rid of the sand.'

'Hah!' scoffed Martin and made for the main beach.

Laure made after him, determined to catch him, and she was nearly by his side when they reached the shallows. She stood up and looked down at Martin, who was sitting in the water, happily using a flat stone to open the cockles.

'You're sure you don't want one?' he asked, as he broke open the first cockle and pulled out the live flesh.

'They'll be full of sand, you know,' said a voice from a couple of metres away.

Laure was still looking downwards, but she knew that voice. She froze, watching Martin, whose head swivelled instantly towards the beach. His face lit up.

'Robert!' he yelled 'What on earth are you doing here?'

A smile came unbidden to her own lips, and she turned slowly and caught the same smile reflected from Robert.

'I came to tell Laure that everything is all right,' he said. 'I thought it might be nicer to do so in person than on the phone.'

Laure stood in the water and just looked at him. She could feel her salty hair sticking to her head, and the sun burning her bare back, and Robert in his crisp pressed shirt seemed to have come from another planet. What had he just said?

'All right?' she repeated blankly.

His face dimpled into a broad smile as he answered, and for a moment he looked so much like Martin that it was uncanny. He was obviously delighted with what he had to tell.

He almost purred at her. 'Not only has Charles Gruet had your case closed by the police, but he has also received confirmation from the Rector that he is removing your professor's proposal from the agenda of the all-important committee meeting in two weeks' time. You will no longer even be discussed.'

Laure brought her hand to cover her mouth. Her throat tightened and she wondered whether she would be able to speak. She heard Martin getting to his feet beside her, and turned to catch an unholy smile on his face. She couldn't yet smile herself. She could barely believe it was true.

'And you came all this way to tell me?' she managed to ask, incredulously.

Robert was still smiling. He gestured to the beach around them. 'Why yes! I had an urge to get away from Paris. It is a long weekend, after all, and Martin may have forgotten, but Monday is Madeleine's birthday. So I thought I would get the sleeper train down last night, and head back on Monday night.'

'You're staying with Madeleine?' Martin asked. He had stood up and moved forward to the beach, where he grabbed his towel and started scrubbing himself dry.

Robert nodded. 'She picked me up in Perpignan this morning and lent me her car to come over this afternoon. But I was wondering whether Colette could be persuaded to offer me a room for the night tomorrow? It's been a long time since I saw the fireworks in Collioure, and I would love to go there tomorrow evening. You'll be going, won't you?'

He spoke to Martin, but then he turned and looked a question at Laure, still standing motionless in the shallows. Laure's mind seemed to have stopped working and she felt suspended between now and a moment ago, when everything had been different.

Then something broke and bubbled through her chest, and up her throat, fixing a smile on her face that she couldn't control. She stood watching Robert, nodding slowly.

'Yes, I'll be going,' she said, and the words were just for him.

Martin had thrown on his shorts and shirt but hadn't answered Robert's question. He glanced rather curiously at Laure, and then back at Robert, and seemed to be thinking hard. In the end, it was Laure he spoke to.

'Could you give a room to Isabelle tomorrow night?' he asked her.

She was surprised out of her reverie. 'Why yes, of course we could! Or even Daniel and Sylvie could. But could she stay over at the moment, do you think, with everything that's happening in her family?'

'For one night?' Martin's voice was hard. 'If they can't spare her for one night then she might as well give up all hope of a life. She needs to come with us to Collioure. *Maman* has given her four full days off next week, while that younger brother of hers Jean-Claude goes off to some cousins or something. Well, if young Jean-Claude has the right to disappear for four days, then Isabelle can surely disappear for one night, and I think she's ready to tell them so herself if necessary.'

Despite everything that Laure had already observed of the Bariol family, this latest piece of information still shocked her. 'You mean Isabelle has to stop work for four days just because her seventeen-year-old brother is going away?' she asked, stunned. 'I thought the Bariol family lived in this amazing community where everyone looks after everyone else. Is there no one in Paulilles who could help Isabelle's mother during the day? They're turning that girl into a slave!'

Curiously, the level of her indignation seemed to appease Martin. 'I know,' he said, in a calmer voice. 'But actually her mother is beginning to rebel against her father's attitude and she's insisting on getting on with life more normally. I think she'll stick up for Isabelle over tomorrow night.' He grinned. 'I want one night out with my girlfriend! In nearly two months, we haven't had a single one.'

He looked at Robert, who'd been standing rather perplexed during their exchange. 'You've missed our Paulilles drama,' he told him. 'Isabelle's mother has been diagnosed with heart problems, definitely associated with her time working at the factory, some years ago.'

Robert raised a quizzical eyebrow. 'And the girl is being turned into a drudge in consequence? A traditional family, I take it?'

'Very. And I've had the temerity to suggest that Isabelle should come to Montpellier with me to study.'

'I see,' Robert reflected. 'Things have moved on then, between you and Isabelle?'

Martin flushed slightly but nodded. 'Yes,' was all he said.

Robert smiled and reached out a hand, which Martin took. They shook in what could have been too formal a gesture, but which actually seemed very intimate to Laure. She realised that she was still standing in the sea and moved forward onto dry land. Robert turned towards her and now held out the same hand to her. She took it, and he closed his around hers. A little moment passed, during which Laure felt all the affinity between them from that evening in Saint-Emilion two weeks ago today.

She looked at him almost shyly. 'Thank you for bringing me such wonderful news,' she said. 'I can never repay you.'

'Remember the painting you promised me,' he said, with that smile which made her think of both Martin and Madeleine, except that neither of them had the power to make her hold her breath. 'I'm holding you to that painting. But, for now, how about we go sit in the shade, and if you insist, you can buy me an ice cold beer!'

Chapter 30

Martin and Isabelle and Laure and Robert walked over to Collioure the following evening by the coastal path, the same path which they had taken, Laure remembered, on the day she had first told Robert about her problems in Paris. That was only a month ago, but it seemed a lot longer now.

The past month had been such a waiting game, full of long and frustrating periods of fearful inactivity. In the middle, there had been the intense disappointment of learning about Lolo, followed by that Saint-Emilion moment of horrible confrontation, and hard-won success. Safe now from Lolo, Laure walked with her friends along the cliff path by a sea made the softest blue in the early evening light, and as the others joked and laughed she trailed a little behind them, thinking about Lolo.

He seemed very remote now, and at this distance, it was too easy to see him as merely an insignificant, unpleasant toad, but she faced the reality that he was actually quite ruthlessly self-serving and heartless, a venomous snake in the grass. And the other reality, which she made herself face head on, was that she had been completely duped and had allowed herself to care, however superficially, for a man who frankly despised her.

She had to face it, so that she could move on and allow the revulsion she felt towards him, and occasionally herself, to develop into something much easier to live with. She'd made a mistake, but then so had many others, for there was no denying Lolo's charm or his talent.

Let it go, she told herself. Self-flagellation is a pointless exercise which harms only yourself, and anyway, you don't need to despise yourself. You're a better artist than Lolo, with infinitely more real commitment, and when you return to Paris, it's you who will have the upper hand.

It would have been easier if she didn't need to see him, of course, but she would handle it, and she would be going off to New York just a few weeks after term started. At the thought a rush of excitement went through her, and an equal rush of gratitude to the man walking in front of her, Robert Garriga, who had gifted her back her amazing adventure.

Martin had been leading them in single file along a narrow part of the pathway, but just now the path widened and Martin turned to join Isabelle and Robert. Robert looked around for Laure and paused as he saw how far behind them she had dropped. He stopped to wait for her and she picked up her pace to join him.

So, if she was being rigorously honest, how did she honestly feel about this man who had saved her from Lolo? There was no denying the effect Robert had on her or how drawn she felt towards him. It had happened when she had allowed herself to see past the lawyer's mask, or perhaps when he had himself chosen to let it slip. Which had come first? It was hard to say, but what she did know was that the Robert she now saw was as genuine as Lolo had been fake.

They walked companionably behind Martin and Isabelle, leaving behind them the bay where she had first told Robert her story, and headed on towards Collioure, around past the old fort and down into the village. It was still early evening but the festivities were in full flow on the beach, and would be up at the bullring, where bull fights and displays would dominate the weekend.

They paused for a while to watch some mock jousting taking place on a colourful jumble of boats out in the harbour, while a group of youngsters were preparing to run a sprint race along the beach. There were clear favourites among the boats and the runners, and the gathered villagers were loud in both their encouragement and hoots of derision as some burly men fell into the water. Martin and Laure knew one or two of the competitors, and as the holiday mood caught them, Laure found herself shouting and waving along with the crowd.

After a while, Martin eased a path through the mass of spectators and they made their way along the quayside and around the corner, along to the famous Café des Sports, with its collection of paintings covering every wall.

Inhabitants of Vermeilla didn't like to compliment their bigger, more famous neighbour Collioure, but Laure loved this village, and she loved this bar. Matisse and Derain had drunk here during the summer of 1905, during the frenzy of crude, wild painting that had redefined colour forever in Art and created the Fauvist movement. They were followed later by other artists like Dufy, Chagall and Picasso, who all came to dip their brushes in the town's now famous light and take refreshment at the Café des Sports.

The light in Collioure was no different from that of Vermeilla, Laure maintained, but it was Collioure that artists mostly flocked to. Its medieval castle dominated the harbour, a honeyed, yellow mass of stone, and opposite it sat the clock tower that had been immortalised in surely more paintings than any other building in France. It was all undeniably beautiful, but Martin always maintained that it was really the bars of Collioure which had brought in the artists, and none more so than the Café des Sports, where impoverished artists had paid their tick for nearly a hundred years by handing a painting over the bar.

During the Fifties, Picasso was a frequent guest. It was said that he wanted to buy a house here, but couldn't find anything grand enough for his megastar status! It was a good job he hadn't tried Vermeilla, Laure thought! But nobody defined Collioure like Matisse, who had come here as an unwanted, unknown artist, and had stayed for such a brief time, but who had left here famous and had made Collioure known to the world.

They took their drinks on the terrace outside the Café des Sports, and ate a small plate of salted anchovies, as you must in Collioure. Isabelle was sparkling tonight like a child let out to play after a long confinement, and Martin and Robert were in rollicking form, exchanging ribald stories, and providing a running commentary on the passers-by that would have created a scandal if their victims had heard them.

All the time Robert sat by Laure, his bare arm so close to hers that she could feel the hairs tickling her flesh. She was content to let them all talk, hardly believing how she felt compared with yesterday, before Robert had arrived. With the end of her worry she was letting go, a semi-abandonment that would have brought fatigue but for her heightened senses and her awareness of this man by her side.

They sat for a long time, watching the crowds and listening to the sounds of the travelling funfair erected in the village square. Laure could have sat forever, but as hunger began to bite, they made their way back to the quayside. The sun was setting behind them, lighting the harbour in Matisse's orange, and as they watched, the horizon grew purple and an orb of moon rose from the sea. They made their way down to the beach, past a group of dancers in traditional dress, dancing the *sardane* to the music of a *cobla* band. They'd brought a picnic with them and they threw down a thick rug within a metre of the lapping waves and ate cold chicken, ripe tomatoes and soft goat's cheese with hunks of fresh bread, washed down with copious amounts of local red wine.

The beach around them had now filled up with tourists and villagers like them, who had come from all around to watch the fireworks. They cleared the remainder of their picnic and poured the last of the wine into their paper cups before the fireworks started. As all eyes turned to the sky, Isabelle leaned into Martin, and in a gesture that seemed completely natural, Laure leaned her shoulder against Robert's. His hand came around her waist and together they watched as the skies lit up all around them, and a river of stars poured down from the castle walls.

They walked back very slowly along the coastal path after midnight, all four of them with torches, mindful of the fall down to the rocks below. A helpful moon was nearly full and shone pure silver on the sea, which was almost drunkenly calm. Laure always felt that the sea was never so deep as at night. I could paint this, she thought, and catch that silence. The only sound was the noise of male crickets attracting their mates in the brush to their left, and below them to their right the hushed, deep swish of the barely moving swell. No one said much, but Robert held Laure's hand all the way home, even where they walked in single file, walking in front of her with his torch fixed firmly ahead.

Laure felt cocooned. It could have irked her to have such a protector, but there was nothing proprietary or domineering about Robert's actions. Instead, it was a sharing, as if he felt they were safer together than alone.

'We walked out of France, you know, when I was just a kid,' he told her, speaking in a low tone which seemed to sit well with the night. 'It was in 1942, when the Germans took over this coast. My mother and we children had to leave, and we walked over a pass in the Pyrenees to get to Spain. Or Madeleine did anyway. I was only three and I think I was carried all the way!'

'Was that when Jordi's father was your guide?'

'Yes.'

And they'd left Robert's father behind, to have an affair which produced Martin, and then to be killed by the Germans, while Robert lived a childhood far from here. It made her own existence seem very tame, but Robert wasn't telling her in order to be dramatic. He was just feeling the night, and the silence, and their little procession. She squeezed his hand, and he squeezed hers back.

When they reached Vermeilla, the two men walked Laure and Isabelle back to Laure's home and there they left them.

'Will you walk with me tomorrow?' Robert asked Laure, as she stood beside her open door, and she nodded.

'I'd love to,' she answered. 'I'll show you the vines that I've been painting, and then you can see what I've made of them. It might surprise you!'

'I think you will always surprise me,' he said, with a hint of a smile, and then kissed the hand he was holding.

'*A demain, belle artiste.*'

'*A demain, cher avocat. Dors bien.*' Sleep well, dear lawyer!

He grinned and touched her cheek, and she turned to the waiting Isabelle and went quietly into the house.

Chapter 31

It felt astonishing to wake up the next morning with something so special happening in her life. And from the look on Robert's face when she met up with him, he was feeling exactly the same. It was that little sense of amazement, which sharpened everything you looked at and set fingers tingling.

They walked up the path to the vineyards, dodging several grasshoppers, who at this time of year hopped right under your feet. They were so well camouflaged that you would only see them when they took flight, arching themselves high into the air to land a metre or more away. Laure longed to sketch their movement, but it was over in an instant and you had to follow intently with the eyes to catch where they landed.

Around them, the vines were heavy with fruit, grapes hot with sugar that attracted bees and insects of all kinds. In a couple of weeks the harvest would start, and within a month or so these vines would be stripped bare, but for now, huge bunches of the black grapes weighed down the twisted branches, nearly brushing the dry, shale soil.

As they climbed, Robert stopped time and again to drink in the views behind them. You could see for miles along the coast towards Perpignan, and out to sea, it was clear right to the horizon, with just a hint of mist where the sea met the lavender sky. Below them, the village nestled in its little bay, almost out of sight.

'God, how I miss this when I'm in Paris!' he sighed.

Laure thought for a moment. 'Me too, but you have to be free to love it. When I felt excluded from Paris, I would come up here to escape because I felt as though the village was confining me. But even up here I felt restless, and it felt as though I was chained to the ground, while freedom was out there.' She gestured to the open sea.

'And today?'

She held her face up to the sky and reached for it, grinning deliriously. 'Today, it feels as though I'm up there.'

He smiled and she looked at him, catching her lip slightly with her teeth to hold a bubble of excitement and laughter in check. He held out his hand and they continued their walk, fingers interlaced.

The more they climbed, the more they caught the light sea breeze that cooled hot cheeks. At the top, they found some shade from the huge fig tree that was so often Laure's destination. She could work here, out of the sun, and still have the vineyards within a couple of metres of her easel. Most of the figs were still green, but Robert picked one which was already deep purple in colour and peeled it open experimentally. It was surprisingly ripe inside and he offered it to Laure. She sucked at it, closing her eyes.

She sensed rather than heard him coming to stand beside her. She waited for him to touch her but he didn't. The only sensation on her skin was the movement in the air. The stir that might have been the breeze, or might have been him. After a moment he spoke.

'Laure...' He broke off, his voice uncertain, and she turned towards him, her face a question. He seemed to collect himself and then continued.

'Laure, I don't know how to kiss you. You've been hurt by a guy who wanted you without caring, and I don't want...'

'You don't want to be like him.' It was a statement and it came out quiet but sure. Laure wanted to say the right things to Robert now. She reached her hand out as she spoke and touched his hair.

'You couldn't be. You don't know how to be. Listen, Robert. I wasn't in love with Lolo. I was flattered because he was so courted by all the other girls, and I thought I was being really clever by holding him at bay for a long time which, of course, made him pursue me more. And in the end, I allowed myself to be convinced because I wanted to be, but I held back from letting my emotions go completely because he clearly had his own in check. I have felt mortified since I've learned what he's really like, but it's just that – humiliation, rather than real hurt. Whereas with you...' Now it was Laure who was lost for words.

She looked to him for help and thought, here we are again, exposing our vulnerability. It took courage, but when Laure caught the expression in his eyes she felt a strength passing between them, and she felt sure and fearless. She moved that little step closer to him and took his face into her hands. As they kissed, his arms came out to circle her bare shoulders and then to hold her very hard.

They stood for a long time and when they finally broke apart Laure spied tears in Robert's eyes. Never mind worrying about me, she thought, this man has been through so much more than I've ever had to deal with. First, in his repressed childhood, and then while trying to prove himself to the world and find a path which allowed him at least to make the first steps back towards his Catalan roots.

She wondered what relationships he'd had, and if any of them had given him the support he needed to be himself. Or had they all been with upper-class women with fashionable pretensions, looking for what he could give them, rather than what they could give him? Madeleine might be able to tell her, but Laure knew she wouldn't ask, and one day maybe Robert would tell her himself. It only mattered for his sake. To her, he was open, flaws and all, and she would touch very gently on his bruises.

They found a piece of scrubby, shaded grass to sit on and talked idly, or not at all, Laure lying with her head on Robert's lap while he grazed her chin with the soft flower of a dry grass.

She looked with some humour at his upside down face. 'You know, I'd love to paint you,' she said. 'Although maybe not from this angle!'

He looked down and raised disappointed eyebrows. '*Mais* Mademoiselle, are you telling me this isn't my best position? I've been told I have a rather fine chin!' He lifted it for her to admire, and she laughed.

'I wonder who told you that, Monsieur the lawyer! Anyway, you haven't seen any of my recent portraits, they don't always flatter, believe me!'

'Yes, but they presumably show the beauty of the inner soul,' he said.

She laughed again. 'Or the inner idiocy, perhaps!'

She could have lain there forever talking nonsense, but as lunchtime approached she remembered that she was due at sister Sylvie's for lunch. She pulled herself regretfully to her feet and dusted down the back of her skirt. She'd been tempted to wear shorts for their walk, but on second thoughts had decided not to tempt local comment, so she had dressed in her floatiest off-the-shoulder dress in Robert's honour.

He himself was dressed as usual in cotton trousers, but he'd swapped the usual pressed cotton shirt for a soft Lacoste polo shirt, in a deep red that sat well against his dark skin. No one Laure had ever been out with had dressed like Robert, and she had a moment of panic as she wondered whether it could ever work out to be with someone living in a world so many chasms away from her own. He was getting to his feet and must have seen the tightening of her face, because he pulled himself quickly upright, and planted himself in front of her.

'What is it, Laure?' he asked. 'Are you okay?'

She began to nod, but then stopped and shook her head, determined to be honest. 'You know we're from different worlds?' she asked him, with a little tense challenge in her voice.

He didn't pretend to misunderstand her. She didn't mean Vermeilla, or even their very different upbringings.

'You're talking about Paris, aren't you?' he said, and she nodded.

He grimaced. 'Old fashioned, dull corporate lawyer meets exciting, avant-garde artist and builds unrealistic hopes of a future,' he said. 'It would make a good theme for a comedy film, perhaps.'

There was sadness, even bitterness in his voice, and it propelled Laure into speech.

'That's not what I meant! You're not dull! There's more to you than to anyone I know. But what will your fashionable friends make of you being with an impoverished student living in University digs? Where do you live in Paris, in the 16th *arrondissement*? A few metro stops from where I live, but it might as well be in a different country.' She looked at him, willing him to understand. 'I'm not ashamed of you. It's the other way around. You have friends who mix with my Rector, for goodness sake.'

He smiled and shook his head. 'Not friends, Laure, acquaintances. And I may live in the *Seizième*, but on the very edge of it, in a small bachelor pad above a restaurant. I do have three rather posh relatives, my ancient and revered *Tante* Louise, and her daughter and son-in-law. They live near me, which is why I chose that neighbourhood, and they have been incredibly good to me and Madeleine. *Tante* Louise has old money, and has always been a patron of the arts with a deep distrust of the commercial world I work

278

in. In her heyday, she used to invite all of Paris society to her house. Anyone interesting, she would say, including the most free-thinking radicals. It was at one of her salons that my left-wing father met and ran away with my mother. Dear Louise had no trouble accepting Jordi when Madeleine took him to Paris, and she will welcome you with open arms, and invite you to save my cultural soul!'

Laure frowned, trying to visualise this world of elegant salons, but Robert persisted.

'People respect talent and character, Laure, that's what you have to understand, and as for my wider circle of acquaintances, well, firstly, I don't care too much about them anyway, and secondly, they will take you exactly as they see you. You're chic, charming and intelligent, and you can run rings around most people I know, so you'll deal with them just right – if you want to. And that touch of the wild child in you will go down just fine – the artistic temperament is very fashionable, you know, and Parisians think they're a good deal more in the groove than they actually are!'

'And if I mention the barricades?'

'Go ahead, it could be very amusing! You might even boost my exotic profile. I already feature as rather different anyway, with my mix of English and Catalan backgrounds, and the Spanish surname, and I like the fact that the people I least care about never know quite how to take me.'

Laure could believe it. Robert had his tentative side, the side he showed to those close to him, but she had already experienced the urbane side of him that he reserved for his public life. It was a mix of charm and cool reserve, and some unpredictable commentary designed to keep people guessing.

While the persona may originally have been assumed for his own protection, she thought that it was a very comfortable skin for him nevertheless. So his Paris world amused him, it seemed. Well, if she followed that lead, then maybe it would also amuse her if she took it in small quantities.

'No,' Robert continued, 'it's your friends who will have the most difficulty with your new man, if you introduce me. I'd need to bring Jordi up to Paris to give me some credentials!'

Laure grinned. 'Jordi would certainly help. And I'll have to buy you a new shirt or two. But I know a few gallery owners who might take me a good deal more seriously if I was with you when I visited. I wouldn't worry about my friends if I were you. They mostly come from bourgeois families anyway, and most of them will disappear from my life in a year's time when they finish their studies. There are some really serious artists whose work I admire, and they'll judge you by your intellect rather than your cover.'

She struggled to imagine Robert in some of the scruffy cafés they frequented in the Latin Quarter, but why should he bother to fit in with a bunch of students anyway, with all their quixotic behaviour? Take it as it comes, she thought, and don't create barriers on roads we haven't even trodden yet. She found Robert's eyes and held them with hers as she spoke.

'I think we'll need to respect the differences in our lives, and give each other space. I'm off to New York for a while anyway in a couple of months, so we won't have the chance to live in each other's pockets. But if you think I won't disgrace you, then I'd really like to be part of your life.'

She bit her lip again, her breath coming shallow as she saw how he was looking at her. He reached for her.

'Sweet Laure,' he said, 'I hope to heaven you already are.'

Chapter 32

Martin joked that Madeleine didn't get to see much of her brother that weekend. For a man who'd come down for his sister's birthday, he told Robert, he had left her very much to her own devices. Robert retorted that Madeleine would be only too glad to learn how he had been spending his time. But on Sunday afternoon, he tore himself away from Vermeilla and went back to Céret, safe in the knowledge that Laure and Martin would both be there for Madeleine's birthday lunch the next day.

The new romance had given Martin something else to think about apart from Isabelle's problems. He'd shopped them with unholy glee to *Tonton* Philippe and Laure remarked that Robert had better tell his sister before Martin arrived in Céret, otherwise Martin would give him no chance.

Robert had grinned. 'Martin's a toad,' he said, 'but it's only good news he's telling, after all. Anyway, I can't wait to tell my sister. She's been so afraid that I would get hooked up with some arrogant *Parisienne*, and she will be happier than I can tell you that things are happening for us.'

Laure had taken him home to look at her paintings, but she'd stopped short of making any declarations to her parents. It wasn't the moment. They were so frantically busy over this holiday weekend, as it was peak summer, and *Maman* never stopped moving. She'd refused Laure's help though and had taken on a young girl from the village so that Laure didn't need to be there all the time.

'I know you need the money from your painting, *chérie*,' she'd said to her, 'and it's a waste of your talent to have you closed up in here.'

Laure felt grateful and guilty in equal measure as she stole that weekend for herself and Robert. They swam and lazed in the sun, and walked back along to Collioure to eat a fish stew on the festive seafront. And they talked, non-stop, about anything and everything, about childhood, studying and Laure's future, which Robert was sure would be brilliant.

'Do you speak good English?' he asked her, as they discussed the New York trip.

'Not bad,' she confirmed. 'It's always been a part of my studies, and I like the language. I've been taking extra classes ahead of going to America, of course, but I lack practice.'

So he set himself to speak nothing but English to her for a day, until her head was aching and she called for a break.

On the Sunday, she asked Robert to help her sort out some paintings to take to Jordi's gallery. 'I may not have done any actual painting this weekend, since *Maman* released me from the bakery,' she said, ruefully, 'but I can at least sort and pack the canvases for sale, and between that and my English lessons, then maybe I'll feel I've done some work these last days.'

Robert was reverential as he handled the paintings. Laure was pleased with the vines she had painted and felt she had achieved the voluptuousness that she'd spoken to Madeleine about. You could only paint the grapes so heavy and full at this time of year and Laure had taken liberties with her subject, and made the grapes darker and fleshier than they could ever be in real life, almost spilling open. There was nothing muted about these paintings!

'Look how you've brought out the surface texture. You paint their skins the way you paint flesh.' Robert murmured. He ran his fingers around the grapes, as though he could feel them. But he lingered the longest over her painting of the man and boy on the beach, the piece she'd given her heart to, immediately after she met Jordi.

'I can see why you haven't put this up for sale,' Robert said. 'It's heartbreakingly special. If I were you, I'd never want to part with this one.'

'Then I've found the painting that I want to give to you,' Laure said happily.

He looked up at her, startled. 'But you can't give me this!'

'I can give you anything I like!' she grinned. 'It's a professional fee for services rendered, remember. And nobody could have earned this more. Can you take it on the train? Then, I'll bring it with these others to Céret tomorrow.'

She brooked no argument and they spent a good half hour packing up the various canvases before Robert headed off on the rather beat-up motorbike he'd borrowed from Jordi when he came back from Céret on Friday, so as to leave his sister her car for the weekend.

'You look quite normal on a motorbike, quite like the rest of us,' Laure teased him. 'It makes a change from that flash car you hired in Bordeaux!'

'Flash? That was nothing! I happen to like cars.' He had that look she loved – part humorous, part unsure – as if he was appealing to her not to blame him for the bourgeois life he lived.

She shook her head in mock disapproval. 'Are you telling me you have an even posher car in Paris?'

He grinned in reply. 'A Jaguar convertible. It's rather good fun when the weather's fine. Will you come out in it with me, *ma chérie*.'

'With pleasure! I can sell my soul with the best of them. Now off you go on this old soldier, and try to remember you're just a common man until you get back to Paris.'

'With you in my life, my girl, I'm unlikely to forget it.'

On the following day, Martin and Laure laid the carefully packed paintings in the back of the bakery van and headed off together for Céret. It was becoming easier for Laure to give her work away for sale, but at the last moment, she took back one of her favourite vine paintings. It was the one that Robert had traced with his fingers, and she didn't want to sell it. It was experimental enough to be worth exhibiting one day.

The roads were slow and the sun was hot. I'm beginning to know this route quite well, she thought as they crawled through villages choked by summer traffic. Martin was quiet beside her and she remembered that this was the week when Isabelle would be confined at home for four days. Martin told her that Isabelle had sent her application off in secret to Montpellier, just in case her father should change his mind, but it was a forlorn hope as Martin's depression made clear.

They kept the windows wound down, but there was only a breeze when the van was moving. When they were stuck in traffic the van was like an oven and by the time they wound their way into Céret at around midday, they were both hot and sweating. They made their way directly to the gallery, where Robert, Madeleine and Jordi were all waiting for them.

It had been a long time since Martin had been to Céret and Laure was glad to see his face light up when Jordi came out of the shop. It didn't take too much to lighten Martin's mood and these people were the right ones to do so.

In the melee of birthday greetings, Robert's kiss for Laure might have gone unnoticed, but this family were an observant bunch. It won a smile from Madeleine, who gave Laure a special hug of welcome.

'So, you've taken on my little brother, have you, Laure? Well, it's very kind of you to embrace that challenge.'

'Oh, she's embraced the challenge all right!' Martin put in quickly, and Laure aimed a quick punch at his arm.

'Wretch!' she said. 'You know, Madeleine, he's spent the weekend telling everyone he can find about Robert and me, and yet when he was dating Isabelle at first, did I tell you about it? No! I left him to tell you in his own time.'

Martin was undaunted. 'Yeah, but you just bagged my brother, buddy. That's my family you're mixing with. And I already have your sister for a sister-in-law. I'm being invaded by bakers.'

Madeleine cocked an amused eye at Laure. 'Give him the occasional free patisserie and you never know, that might keep him quiet. And your case in Paris has been resolved, Laure? I was so delighted when Robert told me. He has his uses, doesn't he? Now you'll be able to go back up to Paris and keep an eye on him for us.' She looked at Martin. 'How are things with Isabelle? Has her father agreed to her going to Montpellier?'

He frowned. 'No, it's worse than ever. I seriously messed things up when I saw him. Did you know her mother has been ill?'

Madeleine put her arm around him. 'No, *mon coco*, I didn't know. And her illness has aggravated your problems? I need to know, but let's close up the shop first and you can tell me over lunch, because we have to reopen by two o'clock. Laure, my dear, Jordi has unloaded your van, but do you mind if we open up the paintings after lunch? We'll have more time to view them then, and we can tell you about the sales as well – your stuff sells well!'

She wafted them out and around the corner to a nearby restaurant, leaving Jordi to lock up the shop behind them. The waiter brought them menus and Robert ordered champagne, ignoring Madeleine's protests that this wasn't a special birthday.

'I'm thirty-two, for heaven's sake, and I'm not sure I even want to celebrate. But you can trust Robert to be extravagant. You'll see, Laure.'

'I already have,' Laure replied, raising one eye at Robert, who was sitting close beside her, but he merely grinned.

Madeleine pulled Martin into the seat next to her and he began to tell her about Isabelle's mother and, meanwhile, the champagne arrived and there was still no Jordi.

'What has become of my husband?' Madeleine wondered, as the waiter filled her glass. 'It only takes a moment to lock up the shop.'

'Would you like me to wait to pour for your extra guest?' the waiter was asking.

Robert nodded. 'Perhaps a customer arrived just as he was leaving,' he suggested.

'Perhaps,' Madeleine agreed, but she didn't sound convinced. They sat for another moment or two, not knowing whether to make the toast or wait, and then just as Robert made to get up, Jordi came hurrying in, wafting the heat in behind him. He looked very grave.

He stood by the table, making no move to take his place. 'I'm sorry to keep you all waiting,' he said. 'Philippe phoned just as I was shutting the door.'

He looked down at Martin in his seat by Madeleine. 'Martin, Philippe says that you have to go to Perpignan immediately. Isabelle called the café to tell them that her brother has had a serious accident.'

'Her brother?' Martin ripped back. 'Which brother? What has happened?'

Jordi sat down next to him and placed one hand on his arm. 'It's her older brother, Laurent, is that his name? He was at work this morning and a piece of machinery fell on him and injured his leg. Philippe said Isabelle talked of it being quite badly crushed.'

There was a just a moment's silence, then Robert spoke. 'How long ago did this happen? He's in hospital already?'

Jordi nodded. 'Yes, in Perpignan, and Isabelle is there also, with her mother and father. The accident happened early, at around eight o'clock this morning, Philippe said. He told me Isabelle is distressed because they can't get any information. Her brother has been taken into the operating theatre, and no one will tell them what is happening or if he's going to be all right. She thinks if Martin was there he would be able to find out for them.'

Martin was already on his feet. 'Laure, can I take the van?' he was asking.

'Woah, Martin, if you're going to Perpignan then we'll come with you. You'll come too, won't you?' Laure asked Robert hopefully.

'Of course,' he answered, and she felt a surge of relief. She instinctively felt that Robert's presence could be very helpful, and she wanted him there.

'What about your train?' Martin asked, and Robert waved dismissively.

'Never mind my train. Let's go, shall we? Madeleine, can I take your car in case we have people to ferry around?' He leaned over the table and took her hand. 'We'll do your birthday lunch another time, *ma belle.*'

'Pooh!' Madeleine replied. 'Take the car, of course. I won't come with you because we could become too much of a crowd, but you will let me know what's happening, won't you?'

Robert squeezed her hand. 'Of course, and you and Jordi should drink the champagne and eat something. The young man's not dead, you know,' he said, addressing these words partly at Martin. 'It's just his leg that's injured and they're operating now. And Isabelle's right, Martin can really help them all, and we'll be there in under an hour. Thank God Jordi hadn't left the shop when Philippe phoned.'

Madeleine rose and hugged Martin. 'Give Isabelle my love.'

'I will,' he answered, but he was already on his way to the door.

CHAPTER 33

Isabelle and her parents were huddled in a corner on some wooden benches, as close as they could get to the corridor which led to the operating theatres. They had that helpless look of people out of their depth. As Martin, Robert and Laure entered, Isabelle jumped to her feet, but her parents didn't move.

'He's been in there for hours!'

The words burst out of Isabelle, almost hysterical, and she grabbed Martin's arm with a complete disregard for her father sitting behind her.

Martin was exceptional. He eased Isabelle back down onto her bench next to her parents and sat facing them, greeting them calmly, before asking patient questions, while holding Isabelle's hands in his the whole time. Madame Bariol looked so pale that Laure wondered how her heart would cope with the pressure, but she sat quietly with her inhaler in hand, quite clearly not thinking for one moment about herself. And Monsieur Bariol looked blank, in shock, his face unreadable.

He managed to answer the questions though. He'd been called out from his workshop that morning to be told that Laurent had been injured. He described the machine which the men had been manoeuvring into place, a huge mixer rather like a baker's kneading machine, only bigger. Everyone knew those machines were dangerous. They were so heavy and moving them caused sparks, so they had lined the room with a kind of shockproof asphalt. But they moved them daily without accident, such was the vigilance of the teams who worked together.

So what had happened today? Well, it wasn't clear, but it seemed one of the men doing the lifting had a seizure and let go of his side. The machine had toppled and its full weight had come down on Laurent's leg. The man who'd had the seizure was also at the hospital. Was it yet another heart attack? Who knew, but it seemed likely.

They'd left Laurent for a long time under the machine, which upset Monsieur Bariol most of all. It took them too long to bring in other men to get it off him, he said, and then when they did pull him free they hadn't been any too gentle.

'At Paulilles they said they could hear him screaming from outside the building,' he said, with tears on his cheeks. Madame Bariol clutched the folds of her skirt and looked at the wall.

'Well, he'll be under anaesthetic now,' Martin said reassuringly. 'He won't be feeling anything at all. Let me go and see who I can find, someone who might know what's happening, and then I'll come back. But don't upset yourselves too much. Have you had anything to eat or drink?

No, I thought not. Well, we haven't eaten either. Robert can get everyone a sandwich from the canteen.'

Martin was in charge here and Robert didn't question his authority. He simply nodded and headed for the main door. Martin pulled his badge from a pocket and fastened it to his shirt, and then he too disappeared, off down the corridor leading into the bowels of the hospital. Laure took his place on the bench facing Isabelle. She wanted to make normal conversation, but there wasn't much she could think of to say.

'Is someone at home with your younger brothers?' she asked at last.

Isabelle nodded and answered in her normal voice.

'Yes, they're all right. Jean-Claude has gone off for a few days, as you know, so there are just the four young ones at home. When they came from the factory to tell us what had happened, our neighbour took them in. She has young ones of her own, and she'll keep them for as long as we need.'

'And is anyone from the company here with you?'

'From Nobel, you mean?' Isabelle asked. 'Well, Georges the driver brought us here, and he said he thought someone from personnel would be coming along once they sort out the panic that followed at the factory. Georges went back to Paulilles in case he's needed.'

'Well, we have two vehicles here for when you want to go home later,' Laure said. 'We were at Céret when we got the call from Philippe with your message, and Robert brought Martin here in his sister's car, while I followed them in the bakery van.'

'It's kind of you, Mademoiselle Forestier,' said Isabelle's father, 'but we don't want to trouble anyone. The company will take care of us.'

A silence fell again among them, the kind of silence that just waited. Robert provided a diversion when he came back with several baguettes, filled with cheese and ham, and some little glass bottles of fruit juice. Isabelle at first refused, but her father grunted his thanks and took a sandwich. Breaking it into two, he put one half in his wife's listless hand and the other in his daughter's.

'Listen to that doctor of yours,' he told Isabelle. 'He said you should eat and he's right.' He watched as his women mechanically obeyed him, and then accepted another sandwich for himself.

'Thank you, Monsieur,' he said, and it occurred to Laure that he had no idea who Robert was. She introduced him and watched as Monsieur Bariol took in that Martin had a Parisian lawyer for a relative.

'You have some fancy qualifications among you all, don't you?' he muttered, but without any malice. 'You're down on holiday, Monsieur? Well, thanks again then, for giving up your day to bring your young doctor here.'

'It was the least I could do,' Robert said, opening up the fruit juices and offering them around. He sat next to Laure and they ate, and she finished her sandwich in record time, aware suddenly of the lunch they had missed.

As she finished her last mouthful, Robert made a suggestion. 'If you'll come with me Laure, the canteen sells a decent looking coffee in paper cups and we could bring one for everyone.

Laure didn't want to be gone too long in case Martin came back, but the thought of coffee was very inviting indeed, so she jumped up and collected the little juice bottles. Isabelle was still chewing valiantly at her half sandwich, while her mother had given up eating. Coffee, thought Laure, might pick them all up a little.

As they emerged into the hospital courtyard, Robert took Laure's hand. 'It doesn't sound very good for that young man's leg, sadly,' he sighed.

'You don't think so?'

He shrugged a little despondently. 'My bet is that if they whisked him into the operating theatre and have been so long already, they're fighting to save his leg. It sounded like such a brutal accident.'

Laure brought Laurent to mind, with his ready smile, his blue eyes and that mop of blond hair, which made him look so much like Isabelle. What had he told them? That he would be well away from the nitro-glycerine before it affected his health. Well, he was right, but something almost worse had happened. Those words 'they'll be fighting to save his leg' meant that Robert thought there was a threat of amputation. Save his leg, she breathed to herself, clenching Robert's hand. For God's sake, let them save that boy's leg.

They bought six coffees to take away and then had to buy two more, as both of them downed their first cup in one go. The hit did her good, and Laure drew a more positive breath as they headed back with the six small cups held carefully between them. There was still no sign of Martin when they got there, and Isabelle's parents were sitting exactly where they had left them. Isabelle had walked over to the window and was idly watching a car manoeuvring outside. She accepted a coffee with thanks and added two sugars before taking it over to her mother.

'Here *Maman*,' she said softly, 'the sugar will do you good.'

Laure added sugar to two more and gave them to Isabelle and her father.

'Martin's will go cold,' Laure whispered to Robert, and then just as she spoke, they heard his voice. Martin appeared from the corridor with another young doctor in a white coat.

The Bariols leapt to their feet and stood rigid, with their backs to the wall, their coffee cups still in their hands. They said nothing but kept their eyes fixed on the new doctor.

He wasn't much older than Martin, Laure thought. This surely couldn't be the surgeon? He came forward with a smile and shook hands with Isabelle's parents before he turned to Robert, who was still carrying the remaining coffees.

'Is one of those for me?' he asked. 'Or could it be, do you think? It already seems a long time since lunch.'

Robert smiled and handed over a coffee, and Laure gave hers to Martin. Martin drank it in one and then launched into speech.

'This is my friend, Guy,' he told them. 'He's not one of the doctors working on Laurent, but he has been able to find out a bit more about what has been happening, and he's allowed to give you some information.'

The young doctor nodded. 'That's right. The surgeon himself will come to talk to you when he's free, but for now, he's still in the theatre and it may be some time before your son is brought out. I'm sorry you've been left like this. Your son had lost a lot of blood when he arrived here, and they rushed him into theatre in quite a hurry.'

'He... he's alive?' Madame Bariol asked, her voice strangled.

'Yes, yes, Madame, your son is doing fine. But you'll realise that his left leg was badly injured, and the surgical team have been working to pin it together.'

'He won't lose his leg?'

It was Isabelle who spoke, her voice beyond tense, and Laure realised that she had been thinking the same as Robert, keeping her fears suppressed.

'No.' The young doctor spoke with conviction. 'I'm able to tell you that much, which is why Martin wanted me to come and speak to you. We've got an amazing team here and your brother won't lose his leg. More than that I can't say, and when you see the surgeon he'll be able to tell you what sort of recovery we can expect.'

He turned to Isabelle's father and mother, still standing completely motionless by the bench. Laure thought that their faces had relaxed slightly and Madame Bariol was no longer clenching the folds of her skirt, but a slight tremble had taken hold of her chin, and she looked as though tears might not be too far away. It was an inevitable reaction as the worst of their fears subsided.

Young doctor Guy gave them his most professional, white toothed smile. 'You'll want to stay at the hospital I know until the surgeon has finished and can see you, but we can find a more agreeable place for you to wait than here,' he gestured to the bleak space around them. There's a family room not far away, so would you like to follow me, and we'll get you installed there? It may still be quite a long wait, I'm afraid.'

'We'll be able to see Laurent?' Isabelle asked.

'Hopefully later, yes, if he isn't too groggy when he comes round.'

Martin moved closer to Isabelle and took her arm protectively. 'I'll stay with you. I want to hear what the surgeon has to tell us.'

He looked across at her father as he spoke, but Monsieur Bariol was nodding. They weren't going to let Martin go now. He was their passport to the medical world and had already brought them immeasurable relief. This might do him some serious good with Monsieur Bariol, Laure thought.

'And you?' Martin was asking Robert. 'If you go now, you can still make your evening train. There's not a lot of point in you hanging around.'

'No, it's not a lawyer you need today,' Robert agreed. 'But my train leaves from Perpignan anyway, so if you'll allow, I'll pass by here again in a couple of hours to see if you have any more information. Will you come with me, Laure?'

She hesitated. 'You won't need a car here?'

'Honestly no, Laure,' Isabelle rushed to assure her. 'Georges the driver is definitely coming back here, and there will be other people from Paulilles as well, for sure. And we could be here for such a long time. You've been so good, and we're so grateful to you both, *n'est-ce pas* Papa?'

Monsieur Bariol stood forward and held out his hand. 'You serve a good cup of coffee, Monsieur.'

Robert smiled. 'I've never met your son, Monsieur Bariol, but he's lucky in his family.' He shook hands.

Monsieur Bariol raised a slightly ragged smile in return. 'Thank you. But if it comes to that,' he said, with a nod in the direction of Martin, 'I have to say that your own family does you credit too.'

CHAPTER 34

Laure sat on the wall on Vermeilla's quayside that evening with her mother, Daniel and Sylvie. It was the best time of day to be outdoors, with the air cooling a little from the fierce heat of the afternoon, and a light sea breeze still lapping them from the bay. Around them, half of the village seemed to have chosen this spot to meet up this evening, and the village children ran everywhere along the quayside and down on the beach, their bare brown legs flashing.

Daniel had come home from Paulilles very grave. There had been no major panic at Paulilles that morning, since the accident wasn't a cross-factory emergency and there had been no risk of explosion or escalation to other personnel, but the workforce had been shocked to the core. Two of their men had been rushed to hospital, one with a suspected heart attack and the other with a shattered leg. In a close community such as Paulilles, the effect was devastating.

The arguments over who was responsible had already begun. The unions had responded quickly, saying that this was a classic case of an employee having a heart attack on a Monday morning, after suffering the common withdrawal symptoms from the nitro-glycerine through the weekend. It made it a compensation incident, they said. The management was saying nothing and had instituted an enquiry to find out if anyone was guilty of misconduct that morning. Negligence at work was the greatest crime at Paulilles, where the work was so sensitive, and someone would pay if the management could find any evidence of laxness. Meanwhile, Daniel said the workforce had completed the day's work in muted speculation, with two colleagues not among them.

Here on the quayside, they were waiting for Martin to come home with more news. Laure and Robert had visited the hospital one last time before she dropped him at his night train, and by then Laurent was in a hospital bed and sleeping. His family were waiting just to see him when he awoke and, of course, Martin had stayed on with them.

'How's the leg?' Robert had asked him in a private moment in the corridor, away from the Bariol family, and Martin had shaken his head.

'Don't quote me,' he'd said, 'but Laurent will never bend that knee again, or his ankle.'

'He'll have a permanent limp?'

'Oh yes, and probably a brace. There will be lifelong problems with that leg, and lots of pain management and mobility issues. I hear that it was touch and go whether it would have been better to amputate, and who knows if it was the right decision not to.' Martin looked quickly behind him as he spoke. 'His family know that he's got a long road ahead of him, and have been warned that he'll have a long time on crutches, and they're beginning to ask the tough questions. But for now, they just want to speak to him and hear his voice. He's alive and they can see he looks quite normal, which is enough for now. Amputation would have been a far greater psychological shock.'

Back in Vermeilla Laure had given her family only a watered down version of Martin's words, but it was enough to keep *Maman*, Daniel and Sylvie very sober as they watched the sun setting behind the hills on the other side of the bay. Along the quayside, little Julien played astride his little truck that he propelled with pushes of his fat little legs. Two village girls accompanied him, pulling the truck along with a cord, arguing over whose turn it was to lead him.

Philippe and Colette appeared just then, walking leisurely along the quay arm in arm. They would often go for a stroll in the evening, when the main business of the café was over, but this evening they were making very deliberately for the group on the wall. As they approached, Daniel detached himself and moved forward, and Colette took him into her arms. At no point had Daniel been in danger today, and he didn't work with the heavy mixers, but his mother wanted him close nevertheless.

'Martin has just called us from the hospital,' Philippe told them. 'They're making their way home now with the Paulilles driver, and they'll drop Martin off here on the way.'

'And Laurent?'

'He came to for long enough to speak to them, and gave his mother the smile she'd been waiting for, but then they put him under again. I gather he'll spend most of the next few days sleeping, just to give his body time to recover from the trauma.'

He sat in Daniel's place on the wall, adjusting his long legs to make a space for Colette next to him.

'How did the family seem to be taking things when you saw them at the hospital?' he asked Laure.

'They were just terrified.' Laure was indignant. 'It's all very well us having Martin among us, who can intercede for people at the hospital and at least get some information and humane treatment for the family, but what if he hadn't been there? They'd just been left in a corner, and not a single person had come to see them. But Martin's colleague there did explain that Laurent had lost a lot of blood when he arrived, and needed emergency care, so that was the priority, of course. And once he knew the family were there, he put them into a more comfortable room.'

'I guess the first concern has to be the patient,' Philippe said mildly. 'And then afterwards you were able to get your sweetheart to the train?'

Laure's mother looked up sharply at this, and Laure cursed Philippe under her breath.

'He means Robert, *Maman*,' she said, blushing furiously. 'I would have mentioned it, but you've been so busy, and he and I are really only just getting to know each other.'

Philippe cocked a teasing eye. 'You mean no one mentioned to you in the shop that your daughter has a new boyfriend, Pascale, when it's all over the village?' he asked Laure's mother, deliberately stirring the coals. Laure looked daggers at him, but Sylvie leapt in to save her.

'Don't worry, *Maman*, she didn't tell me anything either. You and I don't get out enough, it seems! But he's coming back in a couple of weeks, didn't you say, Laure?

And he's a good catch, *Maman*, a lawyer working for some international outfit up in Paris. We'll invite him to lunch next time he's here and give him a good family grilling.'

Daniel abandoned his mother and went over to put an arm around his mother-in-law. 'I can vouch for Robert Garriga,' he said to her. 'He's the best of fellows.'

Maman looked questioningly at Colette. 'Is he the young man who is Madeleine's brother? The family who come to stay with you sometimes?'

'That's him,' Colette nodded. 'They were a Vermeilla family, many years ago, but the war took them away and Robert was educated in England.'

'He's English?' Laure's mother was bewildered.

Laure laughed. 'Would that it was so simple! No, *Maman*, he has far more complicated origins than that! He's half Spanish, a quarter French and a quarter English.'

'That's just the usual hotchpotch of antecedents of most people around here,' Daniel said, his arm still around Laure's mother. 'Except that Robert's got a lot more money and fantastic prospects. A pretty good prospective son-in-law, I'd say! He beats me hands down!'

'Except that I've known him for a few weeks, and you're all getting far ahead of yourselves!' Laure protested, still laughing. '*Maman* forgive me but there really wasn't anything to tell you yet. I have studies to finish and an overseas trip to plan, and I will no doubt see Robert in Paris, and we'll see how we get on once he's back in his wealthy social scene.'

Maman cast her a shrewd look. 'You've been up to something all summer, if you ask me! But you'll no doubt go your own way as always.'

'There's not much you need to worry about with Laure,' Philippe cut in quickly. 'She's sound as a bell.'

Laure's mother smiled at him. 'I know Philippe and I don't worry about her. I gave that up a long time ago. But you'll take care with your father, Laure, especially if you're introducing him to someone who is potentially going to keep you away from home. I know you've got a life in Paris, and even further afield, and you're not going to come back here to work, but your father lives in his own world, and he hasn't quite got used to the fact that you're no longer his little girl.'

'Oh, but I am!' Laure protested.

'Oh yes? With your Paris fashions and your spiky personality?'

But *Maman* was smiling, and Laure went over and kissed her on the forehead. 'I always had a spiky personality,' she said. 'Even as a child. Papa might even be pleased to meet someone who can manage me!'

'Your father gave up trying to manage any of his women years ago,' Daniel joked.

There was general laughter, but his words struck a chord with Laure. It was true. Jacques Forestier had a wife with a business brain and a purposeful character, and he had two daughters who had both run rings around him in their own way, and over the years he had become conditioned to not getting his own way.

Was that the difference between him and Isabelle's father? They both had the same traditional instincts, and both liked to play the heavy husband and father at times, but underneath it all, Papa just let life go on, whereas Monsieur Bariol, with his coterie of sons and macho working environment, had never even started to let go.

In her head, she reviewed the earlier scene at the hospital when Monsieur Bariol had paid grudging tribute to Martin. For him ever to let his daughter go, it would need to be into a man's hands, she thought. But not only did he have a wife with health problems now, but also a son who would be a serious invalid for a long time to come. He would want Isabelle around even more than ever.

He had better not learn any more about Laure's own lifestyle or plans, for she wasn't in any way the role model he would choose for his own daughter. She wasn't exactly the model that her own Papa would have chosen for a daughter either, Laure thought ruefully. Sister Sylvie fitted that bill much better. But then, as she thought about her father, she had a little internal smile. When the time came for Papa to meet Robert, he would appreciate his old-fashioned courtesy. But then he would take him to play *pétanque* and beat him soundly, and the formality would be broken down. Her father and Robert would get on fine.

She gave her mother another kiss and then sat back down on the wall, tucking one hand through *Maman*'s arm and another through Colette's, as they sat together to wait for Martin to return.

CHAPTER 35

The first few days saw little change in Laurent's condition. Isabelle returned to work when her other brother came home and gave them daily reports.

Laurent was awake but groggy because of the painkillers he needed, and the only people visiting him regularly were his parents and Martin. Laurent would lie immobile in his hospital bed for some weeks yet, with any rehabilitation still a long way away. For now, no one was telling him how bad the damage was, but his family was beginning to understand.

Martin continued his night shifts at the hospital and volunteered for even more, so that he always had Laurent under his wing, but there wasn't really much he could do. Only time and the specialists could begin the work of giving Laurent back some mobility.

Martin's birthday came and went, which he pretty much ignored. Isabelle was busy every evening after work, and Martin grew a set look that Laure had never seen in him before. He seemed to be putting up a barrier to anything that smacked of idle pleasure and wouldn't even come swimming, excusing himself on the grounds of fatigue. Laure wondered if he was deliberately exhausting himself so as not to think too hard about going back alone to Montpellier. It seemed so alien – pessimism didn't come naturally to Martin.

Isabelle told her that the sunniest person as the days passed was Laurent. Now that was he spending more time awake, he could receive his brothers and his friends and kept them laughing with commentaries on hospital life, a string of very bad jokes he had gleaned from the nurses, and some more than colourful comments about hospital food.

Daniel went to see him with some work colleagues and came back reassured by the colour in Laurent's cheeks and the smile on his face. He also visited the other colleague who'd had the heart attack, and it seemed he too was better and would soon be home. Gradually, the people of Paulilles began to recover from the jolt the accident had caused, and the Paulilles accident began to fade in most people's memory, as more recent events took precedence.

At home in the Forestier household and in the bakery, all the talk was about Sylvie's baby, which was due any day. Laure helped her mother and took little Julien out to let Sylvie rest. She found herself waiting increasingly for Robert's calls, which came almost daily. He called directly to the bakery now, without pretence, and *Maman* would pass the calls upstairs with a brief smile to herself and no word to Papa.

He was coming down again, just two weeks after his last visit. He told Laure that he had unfinished business with his sister, and that he wanted to see Martin. And then he admitted that above all he wanted to see her. Laure protested that she would be in Paris within a couple of weeks, but she didn't protest too hard. They'd had a very brief weekend together and both wanted more.

It was on the Thursday before Robert arrived, just ten days after Laurent's accident, that Isabelle spoke to Laure at the café. Laure and Martin and Isabelle were sitting at the bar drinking the inevitable coffee, when Isabelle asked her question.

'Laure,' she said, 'Martin tells me that Robert is coming this weekend. Well, I happened to mention it to my father, and he asked if I meant the lawyer fellow from Paris he'd met at the hospital. And when I said yes, he asked if he could meet him.'

Laure looked at her, puzzled and Isabelle hastened to explain. 'Papa's got something on his mind, and I don't know what it is, but it's to do with Laurent. He's had lots of meetings with the union representative and comes home each day with the same bleak face. I think he wants some legal advice.'

Laure felt a good deal of misgiving. 'You do know,' she answered after a moment's hesitation, 'that Robert is a corporate lawyer working in business, and not a personal lawyer? He doesn't practice here in France and couldn't if he wanted to.'

'I know, but my father only wants advice, I'm sure, or at least an opinion from someone with a legal brain. Someone outside the whole Paulilles set up.' Isabelle looked anxiously at Laure, as if willing her to understand. 'I think maybe he just needs someone to talk to. *Maman* has her friends and the church, and she's seen a lot of our local priest, but

Papa hasn't talked at all since the accident. He won't tell us anything about what's going on at work, but if Robert would meet him, then I'm sure he would open up.'

The union which the Paulilles workers' subscribed to must have legal advisers who would know the factory's business better than Robert did, Laure was sure. But she was equally sure that if Monsieur Bariol wanted to see him, then Robert would agree to meet him, if only out of simple humanity.

She smiled at Isabelle. 'You know you really don't have to ask,' she told her. 'Martin would tell you the same. Robert will be happy to meet your father if that's what he wants. Would you like Robert to come to Paulilles?'

'No, not at all.' Isabelle was vehement. 'The children would be around, and in any case, Papa wouldn't want Robert to waste time from his weekend. My parents will be going to the hospital in Perpignan on both Saturday and Sunday afternoons, taking the train. They could easily make a halt at Vermeilla on the way back and meet Robert here.' She waved at the café behind them.

Martin had been silent, but now he looked towards the quiet rear of the café and nodded. 'That could work,' he agreed. 'If they come in the early evening we won't yet be busy with meals, and it will be easy to keep a table where Robert and your father can talk in private. Shall we say Saturday? You're working then aren't you, so it may make them feel more comfortable that you're here.'

Isabelle made a face. 'You don't think, do you, that Papa will want me anywhere near his discussions?' she asked, with a touch of bitterness in her voice, which they hadn't heard before. 'However, *Maman* will be very happy if I am here, and Papa will at least allow me to serve him a coffee. He seems to think I'm good at that!'

Saturday morning brought Robert, fresh from the night train. He paused only to shower at Colette's apartment before making his way to the bakery. As chance, or perhaps mischance, would have it, Sylvie and little Julien were visiting the shop, along with two elderly women, including old Francine, who were lingering over buying bread in order to chat about the forthcoming baby.

The conversation broke off at the sight of a man entering the shop, and the two old ladies stepped back to allow him to be served. It took Sylvie a second or two to realise who had walked in, and when she did, she gave a huge smile and moved forward to kiss him on both cheeks.

'Why Robert!' she exclaimed. 'Laure didn't tell us you were coming back so soon! How are you?'

He returned her embrace, holding her shoulders and looking down at the huge bump. 'I'm well thank you Sylvie, but more importantly, how are you?'

Sylvie grinned. 'Impatient, if the truth be known. I've just been explaining to these ladies here that I feel as though I'm carrying a baby elephant, but the midwife tells me I haven't long to go, and within a few days it should all be over.'

'So soon?' Robert showed some masculine alarm.

'Not soon enough, believe me! And what brings you back to see us? Not that we're not delighted, of course!'

Sylvie turned a wicked glance on Laure and on *Maman* behind the counter. What was her sister going to say now,

Laure wondered? Not in front of Francine, she wanted to yell at her! Some discretion now would save her from a tide of village speculation. But *Maman* was more than a match for Sylvie.

'You'll be here to visit your sister, I'm sure,' she said, stretching her hand over the counter for Robert to shake. 'Has she sent you here to collect some more paintings from Laure?'

Robert took the hand and held it for a moment. 'Why yes,' he answered. 'Laure's paintings are selling very well in Céret. How are you, Madame Forestier?'

'I'm well, thank you, Robert. It's good to see you again. Laure, my dear, take Robert upstairs and show him what you have been working on, and perhaps when you are ready, you can bring down a coffee for your father and me?'

Laure gave her mother a grateful smile. She'd told *Maman* that Robert was coming and it seemed that *Maman* was opening the way for an easy introduction to Papa. She shot a baleful look at her amused sister and led Robert upstairs.

Robert had brought the outside world with him to Vermeilla. They'd been so immersed here in domestic matters that it was easy to forget that Russia had just invaded Czechoslovakia, so the amazing, inspiring Prague spring was over. Or that over 100,000 civilians had died in Vietnam in the last six months. Robert was magic because he had the brains to understand and the heart to care.

'I'll get you on a march yet, you wait and see!' Laure told him, as they sat on the sofa together perusing the newspapers he'd brought with him.

The newspapers included *The Guardian* from London and *The New York Times*, which he challenged her to read in English. And he'd brought music with English lyrics too, records by Bob Dylan, Joan Baez and Donovan.

'We're going to get you prepared for your New York trip!' he told her. 'We'll listen to these records and translate them. Not only will you improve your English, but I've specially chosen the most current protest songs, so that you'll have all the vocabulary you need to talk to the most bohemian protestors in America.'

'It'll serve you right if I come back speaking like an American,' she told him.

'*Chérie*,' he said, taking her head in his hands, 'I've heard you speaking English already, remember? You're going to delight me for as long as I know you with that ridiculous French accent of yours!'

After what was probably much longer than they'd planned, they brought coffee down to the bakery. *Maman* was by herself in the shop, but as they placed the coffees on the counter, Papa emerged from his den at the rear, carrying a big tray of baguettes to restock the shelves. He smelled the coffee and gave an appreciative sigh, dumping the tray behind the counter. As he stood up, he looked at Laure and Robert, and his humorous, slightly ironical expression told Laure that *Maman* had already done her work for her.

'Papa,' she said, 'this is Robert.'

'So I hear,' he said, confirming what she'd thought. He reached out a hand to Robert and they shook.

'You're staying with Philippe and Colette, I gather,' Papa said.

'Yes, for the weekend. But when I come down, I usually stay with my sister in Céret,' Robert answered.

Papa nodded. 'And you live in Paris?'

'For my sins,' Robert agreed. 'I'm a lawyer up there, although I met your daughter down here.'

Papa picked up his coffee cup and *Maman* reached a small tray of *Rousquilles* biscuits from the display cabinet and offered one to him and Robert. Robert accepted and gave a deep 'Mmm' as he bit into the aniseed icing that coated the biscuit.

'These are divine,' he said, as though he meant it. 'I miss *Rousquilles* when I'm away from here, and I've even made my sister send me a parcel of them sometimes, but I've rarely had any so good. You make these yourself, Monsieur Forestier?'

Papa harrumphed but looked pleased. 'I do, and we've won prizes with them over the years.'

'You've got a great bakery here.' Robert gestured around him at the cornucopia of colours and sniffed appreciatively at the sheer smell of the place, the smell Laure had grown up with.

She smiled at Robert over her coffee. You're doing just fine, she wanted to say to him. But it was Papa who answered, with his habitual dryness.

'It's a good business, but it's not one which interests my daughter much. She's more interested in Paris.'

He cocked a slightly challenging eye at Robert, who answered quickly. 'Laure has outstanding talent, as you know. Paris is where you build your career, and I think she has every chance of building herself something quite

314

exceptional. But I think that ultimately, like me, her heart really belongs on Catalan soil and that one day she'll find her way back here.'

Papa looked surprised. 'You're a Catalan?' he asked.

'Half and half,' Robert answered. 'My roots are Catalan and, of course, my sister has made her life here, so I get drawn back all the time.'

Papa looked vaguely reassured and gave Robert a small grin as he put his coffee cup back on its saucer.

'Well, if you can keep my daughter coming back then we'll all be happy. Good luck with her, young man! She's quite a handful.'

'Papa!' Laure protested, but Robert was faster than her.

'Would you think me impertinent, Monsieur, if I said I wouldn't want her any other way?'

Papa gave another grin. 'Well, if she was any different I suppose we wouldn't recognise her,' he said simply. He cocked a playful eye at Laure.

'As daughters go, I guess you're not too bad, *ma puce*, and I'll say this for you, you seem to have bagged yourself a good one here!'

CHAPTER 36

Robert, Laure and Martin waited for the Bariols in the early evening of that Saturday on the terrace of the Café de Catalogne, where they had passed so much of this summer. Robert had ordered some light food to be served when they arrived; anchovies, a plate of charcuterie, little cod balls with a garlic mayonnaise, and some of the bakery's finest bread, which Colette ordered every day. The Bariols would be on their way back to Paulilles after a long afternoon and would appreciate a proper aperitif before they caught their train home.

By silent accord, no one discussed the meeting Monsieur Bariol had asked for. It seemed important to respect his reserve, even in his absence. Instead, they talked about Paris and the University, and the new term that was about to start. It was the last day of August today and the exam session, which had been postponed in June, was due to begin in two weeks' time. Laure could still hardly believe that she was heading back up to Paris like any other student to sit those exams, with her future at the *École des Beaux-Arts* secure. But so it was, and within a week or so she would be following Robert to Paris by train.

It was an exciting thought and Laure thought that she and Robert, with their private plans and private smiles, must be difficult company for Martin at the moment. He was always generous, but his own return to University in Montpellier was something he wasn't discussing. This would be a serious year for Martin, starting his full-time hospital internship; but for now, his thoughts were all here in Vermeilla.

Isabelle was outside when her parents arrived and she went forward to greet them. Robert, Laure and Martin all stood up, and amidst the exchange of greetings, Robert gestured towards his chair and invited Madame Bariol to sit down.

'I believe your husband wishes to have a word with me,' he said to her, in his most charming Parisian voice. 'Won't you sit here with Laure and Martin for a moment while he and I find a quiet corner?'

Isabelle concurred. '*Oui Maman, assieds-toi,* and I'll bring you something to drink – a *citron pressé* perhaps. Robert has ordered some food too, and I'll bring it soon so that when Robert and Papa have finished their talk, you can eat something before we go home.' She settled her mother, who had hardly said a word, and they all watched as Robert led Monsieur Bariol into the café.

A silence fell. 'Goodness knows what Henri wants to see that young man for!' Madame Bariol said eventually. 'He's been like a man bedevilled ever since Laurent's accident!'

Laure looked at her curiously. Isabelle's mother remained a relatively unknown character to them. She was a woman who was entirely subsumed by her family, and who lived in her husband's shadow. In Laure's mind, she featured as a victim – hit tragically by an undeserved life-changing illness and the appalling accident to her son. But for all her mildness, Madame Bariol did not seem like a casualty this evening. She shook her head over her husband's caprices, but she didn't seem to have been overly unsettled by them, and she had a ready smile for the two young people opposite her as they waited for their drinks to arrive.

'Laurent tells me that you have been taking very good care of him at the hospital, Martin,' she said, with a smile that warmed her eyes. 'We are so grateful.'

Martin demurred. 'I haven't really been able to do anything, Madame Bariol. I just like to see him regularly and know that he's all right.'

'Oh, he's all right,' she said surprisingly. 'Laurent will do well enough. You know, I could have lost my son at Paulilles, but instead he has injured his leg. Don't misunderstand me. I know how serious his injuries are, and I know it will always affect him, and I also know how much pain he is in right now, even though he doesn't show it. But he's not going to be in a wheelchair, which is what I feared, and he hasn't lost his leg. He'll live a good life and marry, and give me grandchildren, I hope, and he has the character to make the most of his life. My husband, though, is in turmoil and I wish I could make him see that things could have been so much worse.'

Laure remembered what Isabelle had said about her mother having a support network through the church and her friends. They certainly seemed to have helped her, but

Laure also thought that Madame Bariol's character was more resourceful than she had suspected, and that it could show this evening because her husband wasn't present.

'And how have you been yourself, Madame Bariol?' Martin was asking. 'Have you been having any problems with your angina?'

There was that same comfortable smile, as Madame Bariol shook her head. 'Why no, do you know, not much at all. I'm learning how much I can do, and I've been training the boys to do more around the house. I keep telling Henri that he should stop worrying about me too. He has been ridiculous! I think that men just hate having their lives upset in any way, don't you my dear?' This was said to Laure, with a very womanly, conspiratorial smile.

Laure returned her smile. 'It's wonderful to see you so well, Madame,' she said.

'It's in large part thanks to our young doctor here. If Martin hadn't been so sharp in his diagnosis, I might have ended up having a heart attack.' Madame Bariol looked across to where Isabelle was emerging from the café with their drinks on a tray. 'I think I've said it before, but at the risk of repeating myself, my daughter is a lucky girl.'

Isabelle came over and put two beers and the lemon drink on the table. 'I've served Papa and Robert and they have their heads close together,' she reported. 'Papa is talking nineteen to the dozen. I don't think I've ever seen him talk so much.'

She placed a dish of olives in front of them. '*Et moi*, I've finished work now, so I'll come and sit with you. But first

I'll bring the food, since it's all laid out in the kitchen. You must be hungry, *Maman*.'

'I'll come and help you,' Laure volunteered and went with her into the café. There in its most private corner, she could see Robert and Isabelle's father. Robert was talking now, while Monsieur Bariol was leaning back listening. Laure burned with curiosity, but she passed by quickly towards the kitchen.

When she and Isabelle came back out the two men were shaking hands. Robert got to his feet and looked over at Laure. He winked.

Laure nearly dropped the plates she was carrying. She glanced at Isabelle and saw that she too had caught that wink. They sped through the café, and as they reached the table outside, Laure blurted nervously to Martin, 'Robert's done something! He just winked at us. Quickly Isabelle, sit down, they're on their way out.'

Martin looked at them blankly, incomprehension knotting his brow, but Laure didn't bother to explain any further. She and Isabelle hastily sorted the plates and then sat down, assuming seemingly relaxed positions.

'Do you think they'll tell us what they've been talking about?' Isabelle asked breathlessly.

'Oh God, I hope so!' Laure muttered, tracking the two men out of the corner of her eye as they emerged from the café and came towards them. Madame Bariol looked placidly at her husband, and as he came to a halt at the table, she patted the chair beside her, inviting him to sit down.

'Well, Henri, has young Monsieur Garriga been able to help you?' she asked.

Monsieur Bariol looked at his wife briefly, but didn't answer and didn't sit down. Instead, he looked his daughter squarely in the eye and spoke directly to her, as though he had something he needed to say before anything else.

'Monsieur Garriga and I have talked about your education, Isabelle. You want to be a lawyer? Well, I think you should go off to your cousins in Montpellier and study to become one. It's time the little people stood up for themselves, and I don't want any more of my family to depend on Nobel for a living.'

Every face was now fixed on his. He had totally silenced the table. Twenty-five years of unfailing loyalty to the Nobel Company had just been thrown aside in one sentence. What must he have been going through in the two weeks since Laurent's accident, Laure wondered, to make him speak like this? She drew her eyes away from him and looked up at Robert, who had come to stand beside her. He placed a hand on her shoulder and she reached up her hand to cover his.

'Monsieur Bariol has had some difficult meetings with the factory management in the last few days,' he said, speaking to them all. 'It seems that they do not want to accept any responsibility for an accident that happened in their workplace, caused by a piece of equipment which people have been saying for years is dangerous to move.'

Monsieur Bariol nodded in agreement, adding bitterly, 'Not only that but they've told me Laurent was lucky to have a job at all at a time when many people have been laid off, and they have already shown more than generous loyalty to our family. They'll give him a desk job eventually, they say, if we are suitably grateful, and stay quiet and accept their terms. But they'll fight any claim for compensation on the grounds that he must have contributed to the accident by his own carelessness.'

He sighed heavily and shook his head. 'In the old days we worked like dogs at Paulilles, but we were a team and the bosses were ordinary working people like us, men who had real experience and had moved up the ranks, who understood about the most tricky equipment and what it could do to you. But now they've brought in a bunch of accountants in suits to rule over us and things have changed. They treat us like minions and I don't want my daughter to become just another lackey, or even worse, to become like them. Go to Montpellier, *ma fille*, and get yourself a qualification that the whole world will respect, and then, hopefully, no one will talk to you in your life the way those bastards have spoken to me these last few days.'

Isabelle hadn't moved and her eyes were still fixed on her father's, her expression stunned. But at this, her face crumpled, and she rose from her chair and put her arms around his neck.

'Oh, my poor Papa,' was all she said, and her father wrapped his own arms around her, burying his head in her hair.

Chapter 37

Laurent probably would get some compensation, Robert told Laure later. The union was swinging into action to defend him, but the way things were happening was new to Monsieur Bariol. The factory management was clearly acting under orders to admit nothing, and commit to nothing. It was normal corporate behaviour, but it was completely alien to Monsieur Bariol. He had believed that the 'good employer' he had known and always believed in would act with old-fashioned benevolence, and it was the personal brush-off he'd received which had so shocked him.

Things would be even more complicated, Robert suggested, because the accident had apparently been caused by a heart attack. The management was stating very clearly that there had been no sign of heart problems previously in the employee. Otherwise, they would have moved him from his physical role in the factory. And, of course, they would deny forever that his heart attack had any link to the chemicals he had absorbed at work.

Meanwhile, it was Madame Bariol who had taught them all a lesson in acceptance this evening, taking her husband by the hand and talking to him soothingly as they ate their food before heading home for Paulilles. Laurent would come home and he could spend as long as he needed to recovering, with all his family around him. Life would go on and Monsieur Bariol would continue to earn a decent wage at the factory, in a safe role with no health threats, and the family would, therefore, keep their home. And Isabelle would go to University.

That momentous revelation sank in slowly on all of them through the evening, as the Bariols lingered and relaxed, and Isabelle persuaded her father to take a rare beer, and her mother an even rarer glass of wine. As the evening mellowed, Philippe and Colette came to join them and it was only Madame Bariol's concern to check on her children that eventually drove them home.

It was Martin who drove them, in Philippe's car, following a suggestion by Philippe himself. Martin was saying very little this evening, watchful of Monsieur Bariol even in this new atmosphere. Nobody said anything about him being with Isabelle in Montpellier. All the talk was about the cousins she might be staying with, and her father would be taking her to visit them, staying in control. But the tight look had gone from Martin's face, and when he looked at Isabelle there was an eager glow about him he couldn't disguise. Laure could almost see his mind beginning to make plans.

Laure and Robert were too restless to finish their evening early, and Robert chafed at having no vehicle.

'I'd so love to take you dancing,' he told Laure.

'At the nightclub in Collioure? Well, I'm not really dressed for it and what's more, I can't see my father lending me the bakery van at this time of night! We can go dancing in Paris and I'll see how you move those lawyer's feet of yours, *mon chéri*.'

He grinned and took her hand, as they went walking down to the shore. There they found the Hotel Bon Repos still serving in the late evening, so they took a table right on the quayside looking over the bay, ordering, absurdly, champagne and ice cream sundaes. The moon was just a sliver and the bay was inky black, but on the horizon the sky was a fluorescent purple, and above them, stars were coming out, Jupiter and Venus and their companions, making the sky infinite yet close.

They still held hands like new lovers and it felt almost strange to remember that's what they were. Robert had been part of her world before she even knew it, Laure thought. He was Martin's brother and one of Philippe's adopted young, like her. He had stayed out of her orbit long enough for them to grow up and meet as adults, and the moment now felt right. In Paris, they would meet as independent, mature people and a frisson of excitement ran through her at the thought.

A noise behind them announced the arrival of Madame Curelée, the formidable matron who had held sway at the Hotel Bon Port since before Laure could remember. She smiled at their glasses of champagne.

'Are you celebrating already?' she asked Laure. 'I knew your sister had gone into labour, but surely the baby hasn't been born yet?'

Laure spluttered into her glass. In labour? She'd had no idea that Sylvie was in labour! Madame Curelée noted her astonishment with a satisfied smile.

'You didn't know? Oh, I just happened to be passing by in front of Sylvie's place an hour ago and saw your mother coming out just as the midwife went in. So I dared to ask if everything was all right, and your mother told me everything was fine and the baby was on its way, and would be born at home because it was coming far too quickly for Sylvie to go to the hospital. Your mother was just on her way to collect some extra linen from home. She looked mightily pleased with the way things were going.'

Phew! The news hadn't filtered to the Café de Catalogne, where they'd been sitting all evening. If it had been old Francine who had gleaned this news instead, the whole village would know by now, but Madame Curelée had a business to run and had simply brought the news home. But she was pleased enough to tell it to Laure now.

Laure made to get up, but then stopped. 'What should I do?' she asked Robert, half in panic, half in excitement. 'Should I go along and see what's happening?'

Robert raised a questioning eye at Madame Curelée. 'Are you going to close soon or can you serve us more champagne, Madame?'

'With pleasure, Monsieur,' she answered. 'I'll take away these dishes and the kitchen is now closed, but we still have guests out here on the terrace, as you can see, so it's no problem to bring you more champagne.'

'Then I think we should have some, don't you, Laure? Your sister's apartment will be pretty crowded right now, what with the midwife, your mother and Daniel. If you go to check too soon, you'll be in the way. Your mother sounded quite calm and in command, by the sounds of it. Stay with me and we'll watch the stars a bit longer. I want to drink to Martin and Isabelle, and to us. And then in a little while, we'll go along together to your sister's apartment and see what we can hear from the bottom of the stairs!'

Laure grinned. She had no real desire to find herself in the midst of a birth scene. It was a place more for her mother than for her. Hopefully, little Julien was sleeping, and her father too, since his bakery would still have to open tomorrow, new grandchild or no new grandchild. In a while, she and Robert could take some champagne along there with them and persuade *Maman* and Daniel to join them in a toast. Meanwhile, the night was already perfect and she had no desire to move.

She sighed in contentment and leaned back against Robert. He brought up his hand to circle her shoulder.

'I'll have time to paint the baby before I leave,' Laure murmured. 'Then I can give the new parents the most recent painting I've done of Julien, plus one of his brother or sister.'

'You could even paint them together, perhaps,' Robert suggested.

'And persuade Julien to keep still beside a newborn baby? I don't think so!'

It didn't matter much though, and she closed her eyes for a moment to listen to the slow swell of the water in the bay. It always sounded deeper at night, fuller somehow, as though waters from outside had come into the bay to shelter for the night. It was calm and rich and soothing, and mindful of the dramas that were taking place a few streets away, Laure took her moment, at this end of summer, to breathe in this moment of peace.

AUTHOR'S NOTE

Collioure and Céret are beautiful towns in Roussillon, France. The neighbouring village of Vermeilla, however, is as imaginary as all the people who live there.

The Nobel factory at Paulilles operated until 1984. Only in 1981 did the company recognise the existence of nitro-glycerine related illnesses, and begin to pay compensation to the many victims. The factory has since largely been demolished, apart from some buildings saved as part of the Paulilles museum. The bay of Paulilles is now protected as a site of outstanding natural beauty.

The descriptions of events in Paris in May 1968 are based on detailed witness accounts from the time. The specific part played by my characters is of course fictional. So many people helped me with their memories of this time, and I thank them all.

Keep in touch with Jane at
http://www.janemackenzie.co.uk,
and on her Facebook page,
Jane MacKenzie Author